THE CAPE COD MYSTERY

PHOEBE ATWOOD TAYLOR (1909-1976) was one of the most beloved and most successful mystery authors of the 1930s and 1940s, writing under her own name and two pseudonyms, Freeman Dana and Alice Tilton. The Asey Mayo character, first introduced in *The Cape Cod Mystery*, went on to star in 24 novels in a series informed by the author's generations-long family history in Cape Cod.

OTTO PENZLER, the creator of American Mystery Classics, is also the founder of the Mysterious Press (1975), a literary crime imprint; MysteriousPress.com (2011), an electronic-book publishing company; Penzler Publishers (2018); and New York City's Mysterious Bookshop (1979). He has won a Raven, the Ellery Queen Award, two Edgars (for the *Encyclopedia of Mystery and Detection*, 1977, and *The Lineup*, 2010), and lifetime achievement awards from NoirCon and *The Strand Magazine*. He has edited more than 70 anthologies and written extensively about mystery fiction

T0025672

THE CAPE COD MYSTERY

PHOEBE ATWOOD TAYLOR

Introduction by
OTTO PENZLER

AMERICAN MYSTERY CLASSICS

Penzler Publishers
New York

Published in 2022 by Penzler Publishers
58 Warren Street, New York, NY 10007
penzlerpublishers.com

Distributed by W. W. Norton

Cover image: Andy Ross
Cover design: Mauricio Diaz

Paperback ISBN 978-1-61316-323-8
Hardcover ISBN 978-1-61316-324-5

Library of Congress Control Number: 2021952740

Printed in the United States of America

9 8 7 6 5 4 3 2

INTRODUCTION

No ONE wrote more mysteries, nor more popular ones, nor better ones, set on Cape Cod than Phoebe Atwood Taylor (1909-1976), best-known for her series of twenty-four novels featuring Asey Mayo, the amateur detective known locally and to readers as "the Codfish Sherlock."

Mayo's first appearance was in *The Cape Cod Mystery* (1931), which sold out its first printing of 5,000 copies, an exceptionally strong sale for a first novel during the Great Depression (and not too bad in the present day).

In the words of the English novelist Nicholas Blake (the pseudonym of C. Day Lewis), Mayo is "an eccentric individual" who Taylor describes as "a typical New Englander . . . the kind of man everybody expects to find on Cape Cod and never does."

A former sailor who made his first voyage on one of the last clipper ships, Mayo lives on Wellfleet, where he is the handyman/chauffeur for the local tycoon but still finds time to solve an inordinate number of murders.

He is tall but unimpressive in appearance as he walks with his long, lean frame hunched over. Variously described as "wily, ornery, and homespun," he relies on his profound, albeit practical, knowledge of human nature for his success as a sleuth. "Common sense" has been the tobacco-chewing Mayo's hallmark since his first episode.

His speech is "impossible for a student of phonetics to record on paper," writes Taylor. "It resembled no other dialect in the world. Let it suffice to say that he never sounded a final *g* or *t*. His *r* was the *ah* of New England. His *a* was so flat...you couldn't get under it with a crowbar."

Mayo uses his speech to share his homely wisdom, such as "they ain't many *whys* without *becauses*." Other characters in Taylor's books are also convincingly Yankee, particularly such aptly named figures as Tabitha Sparrow, Phineas Banbury, and Aunt Nettie Hobbs.

Taylor was born in Boston, descended from the *Mayflower* Pilgrims, and received a B.A. from New York City's Barnard College before returning to live and write in Massachusetts. She uses her intimate knowledge of New England for the settings of her novels, notably such Cape Cod communities as Wellfleet, Quonomet, and Weeset. While these and other nearby towns are recognized as summer resorts, most of the books deal with the people who live ordinary lives there after the tourists have gone home.

Humor plays an important role in the Asey Mayo series, as it does in the eight books she wrote under the Alice Tilton pen name, all of which featured Leonidas Witherall, known to his friends as "Bill" because of his uncanny resemblance to portraits of William Shakespeare. A New England prep school headmaster, he supplements his modest income by writing thrillers. He also hunts for rare books for "the wealthier and lazier Boston collectors."

In his first case, *Beginning with a Bash* (1937), he attempts to prove the innocence of a former student who he encounters on a below-zero evening in Boston, running from the police in a gray flannel suit and carrying a bag of golf clubs. The novel had previously been published in *Mystery League* magazine in 1933 as *The Riddle of Volume Four* under the Taylor byline.

Anthony Boucher was a fan of Taylor's "well-ordered farces" and praised her ability to recreate such historical moments as the Great Depression and the early years of World War II, including blackouts, gasoline rationing, and wardens. The everyday life of those times and more peaceful ones gave readers a window to view Cape Cod as she knew it.

Country auctions, local politics, cake sales, teas, ladies' clubs, gardens, petty disputes among neighbors—all served as the background for Taylor's detective novels, produced with a keenly observant eye and a rich helping of amused and gentle humor.

—Otto Penzler

THE CAPE COD
MYSTERY

Chapter One
THE WEEK-END BEGINS

"'HEAT wave hits East,'" Betsey read. "'Prostration record of all time. Mercury soaring.' Well, that's gone and torn our peaceful vacation, that has. By to-night we'll have a stack of telegrams a yard high from city-sizzling friends who want to get cooled off."

I sighed a little. "I know," I said wearily. As a perennial and thoroughly experienced summer cottager on Cape Cod I sat back to await the inevitable deluge.

"You groan as though it were an earthquake or a flood instead of a few visitors, Snoodles," Betsey remarked.

Now my name is not Snoodles, but Prudence Whitsby, and for at least fifteen years I have tried to make my niece drop that absurd name she gave me in her childhood. I feel it is far from appropriate for a respectable spinster of fifty like myself. But Betsey refuses.

"No one knows better than I what nuisances record-temperature guests can be," I told her. "They simply will not be content to sit on the porch and let the cool ocean breezes blow over them. They want violent action every minute of the day and night, and by the time their sunburn has been treated and their aching muscles rubbed with liniment, I feel as though I needed a rest cure myself. And," I added, "I don't see how we can have more than two."

"We can't. And unless we ask a properly married couple, one will have to use the spare bed in my room. The only thing we overlooked in this place was the accommodation of company."

For many summers we had cast covetous eyes on the cottage we now occupied. We would still be envying the Bentleys, who had rented it from time immemorial, if they had not taken it into their heads to see Europe under the guidance of Mr. Cook. We liked our quarters principally because they neither leaked nor squeaked, two virtues which summer vacationists will recognize as paramount. The ship carpenters who had built the place in their spare time declared that Noah himself couldn't have wished for a tighter or a better substitute for the Ark.

We were entranced by the truly spacious living-room and its mammoth fireplace, guaranteed by the agent to draw perfectly. Undeniably the view was the best in town, for the cottage was perched on the flat top of a sandy, bayberry-bush-covered hill from which we could see the greater part of Cape Cod Bay. The Bentleys had bragged that on a clear day they could see Plymouth Rock and the outlines of Boston, but fruitless hours spent with binoculars compelled us to set that statement down to over-enthusiasm on their part.

The bathroom was appallingly palatial. There was an electric light system and an electric pump. To be sure, the lights would and did go out during storms, and sometimes when there was no sign of bad weather, but poking about with feebly flickering candles once in a while was much more preferable than having kerosene lamps all the time.

There was a tiny room for Olga, our cook; a garage more than ample for Betsey's car, and all the space in the world for Ginger the cat to roam about. There were no near neighbors, a fact which delighted us, for many a summer vacation had been spoiled for us by small squalling children who raced under our windows at dawn. Perhaps a hundred and fifty feet away there was the Bentley children's playhouse, now converted into a rough one-room cabin, but we knew it was too small to contain any howling youngsters. It could be seen only from the kitchen window as the agent demonstrated when we objected to it, and we accepted his word that its size and lack of improvements would make it hard to rent.

There were only two drawbacks. One was the absence of a telephone which forced us to make countless trips to town each day. The other was the lack of room Betsey had mentioned. We could have but two extra guests with any degree of comfort.

The sheaf of nine telegrams we straightway received presented us with a task.

"All the old standbys," Betsey said as she ran through them. "The Poors and Jock Ellis and his unspeakable fiancée. I say, Snoodles, here's one from John Kurth. And look. Another from Maida Waring. We haven't heard from those two since they were divorced, have we?"

"No. I had the impression that he was in Sumatra or some such place and she was in Paris."

"That may be," said Betsey, "but these are both from Boston, if the Western Union isn't being funny."

"I should like to see them again, but I understand that they've been at swords' points since they parted. The whole thing was a pity. They were two of the most amusing people we knew."

"Well, that counts them out, unless we want to ask them separately later on. How'll we choose?"

"The usual way will do as well as any"

Betsey took a handful of matches and cut them up into irregular pieces. Then thrusting an end into each telegram so that only the tip protruded, she held them out to me fanwise, like a bridge hand.

"Longer end wins every time. Draw by twos."

I drew. Betsey turned over the winning blanks.

"That's a grand combination. John and Maida, no less. Well, we'll flip a coin."

We flipped a coin, but the same two were again paired.

"I declare," said Betsey crossly, "it's a conspiracy. The fates are against us. That means we'd keep on drawing those two till Kingdom Come. And we can't possibly ask them if they're such sworn enemies."

She tossed the entire bunch into the fireplace.

"Why, Betsey!" I was surprised.

"I don't care. I'm sick of having all the waifs and strays and homeless thrust themselves on us. Let's institute a reform. Let's ask two people we really want to have down, two people who don't fly into a rage at the sight of each other. Let's let all the ex-husbands and ex-wives go hang."

I wondered vaguely why we hadn't done that very thing long before.

"Now," Betsey continued, "take Dot Cram. If the mercury is soaring the way the papers say, that settlement of hers on the East Side of Old Manhattan must be pretty uncomfortable.

But does she cry for heat relief like so many politicians crying for drought relief? She does not. So I shall ask her. You know yourself that she's one of my more normal friends, and I haven't seen her half a dozen times since we left college. What do you think?"

"If she can get away, I think it's a fine plan."

"Of course she can get away. You approve of her, don't you?"

I nodded. "I like Dot, and she does have better than average manners for this day and age. I wonder if she still burbles with adjectives."

"You mean," Betsey imitated her, "My dear, it's too simply precious and marvelous for words? That sort of lingering emphasis as though she were loath to let the next word out? I suppose she does, though it may conceivably have worn off. But I know she's still addicted to dangly earrings, and her hair is just the same."

"It always reminded me of a chrysanthemum."

Betsey laughed. "It is rather like one. At college she claimed that no one really liked her till they found out it was naturally blonde and a stranger to peroxide. Who are you going to have?"

"Whom," I corrected her, "and don't say 'No one—they.' It's a mystery to me how you ever acquired an education without gleaning a little knowledge of the English language by the wayside."

"Whom, then, teacher, do you intend to ask?"

"I've been thinking of Emma Manton. She hates the heat, and I don't think she's been away from Boston since Henry Edward died."

"I can well see how she wouldn't enjoy the heat. How much does she weigh?"

"Something over two hundred and twenty-five pounds," I answered. "The exact fraction escapes me."

"Funny, but I can't think of her as the wife, or rather the widow, of a clergyman. Not even of such an eccentric clergyman as Henry Edward. She might have been the wife of some robust Englishman out of Dickens, but not the other. She's too addicted to tweeds and jumper suits."

"She'll probably bring some fresh catnip from her garden for Ginger," I said thoughtfully.

"You old plotter! But she'll play Russian Banque with you. And she's met Dot other summers, and they get along together beautifully. And neither one of 'em will want to rip and tear and dash places all the time. Fancy Emma dashing anyway." She snickered. "I'll drive up and send 'em unrefusable telegrams."

The heat-wave head-lines had appeared in Wednesday's paper and our guests arrived Friday on the early morning train. They were promptly dragged off to the beach by Betsey.

From my steamer chair on the porch I could just see the girls on the outer raft. Despite the crowd, holiday size on a common week-day morning, Emma's large black-stockinged legs were exceedingly visible as they protruded from beneath the broad green stripes of my favorite beach umbrella.

I picked up my book, *The Lipstick Murderer*, and prepared to revel with that doughty detective, Wyncheon Woodruff, until luncheon time. But Bill Porter's voice interrupted me as I was gravely considering the value of a strand of red hair as a possible clue.

"Is it blood and thunder, Snoodles, or gin and sawdust? From the title it might be either."

Bill Porter has used my frivolous nickname as long as Betsey, and upon him as upon my niece, persuasion has no effect.

"You know perfectly well," I told him, "that I read mystery stories for the one and simple reason that they exercise my wits. I fail to get any stimulus out of these modern novels full of sordid reminiscences and biological details."

"Hooey," said Bill inelegantly. "Just as if you didn't swipe my entire stock of Old Sleuth in days gone by and force me to read Trollope or something equally wordy. You *said* you did it to make me improve my mind, but I always thought you wanted them yourself. Now I'm sure of it. Think," he sighed as though he were in great pain, "think of your reading that vulgar low-brow volume while a Dale Sanborn masterpiece sits cooling its heels by your elbow." He helped himself to an apple turnover from the plateful Olga had thoughtfully left on the porch.

"Oily," he added with his mouth full. "Very oily."

"Olga said they were particularly good to-day."

"My dear and worthy Snoodles, I am not referring to these toothsome pastries, and you know it. I refer to that Sanborn gent, who is distinctly oily. How'd he ever land in the town?"

"I've wondered at it myself. He told me he thought it would be a good place to rest in before starting another book. What's the name of the purple-covered thing on the table? *Reverence.* Well, that is his latest effort, not available to the general public till next month sometime. We were formally presented with it last night. But whatever his reason for coming, Bill, he has made up his mind to stay."

"That so? Where?"

"He's taken the cabin for the rest of the season. He moved in, bag and baggage, this morning. I should have thought the place was too rough for such a fastidious soul, but he pronounced it enchanting."

Bill made a wry face. "That may be a good two-dollar word,

but I know darn few men who'd pronounce that shack enchanting. He's a crazy sort of fellow."

"Crazy?"

"Well," Bill wound himself around a footstool. "Peculiar. He let slip the fact that he went to Harvard, but when I picked him up and asked his year, he hedged like fury. It took a good five minutes of my best Yankee pumping to find out that he was the class of '20. Just for fun I looked him up in an old register at home, but I couldn't find his name in it. Maybe he went incog., like a Student Prince. Maybe he is a Student Prince anyway. He's got all the elements. Looks a little foreign and condescending. Say, do you think he's falling for our Betsey?"

I shook my head. "I don't know for sure. Numerous young men have fallen in love with Betsey at one time and another, and he's shown some of the symptoms. Of course he didn't decide to stay here till after he met her. But the only real peculiarity I've noticed in him is his tendency to say 'Thank-you' in one syllable, as though it were a thing you played billiards with."

Bill chuckled. "I do hope he isn't after Betsey. I always had a sneaking feeling that I'd like to marry the gal myself. Would you mind awfully having the scion of the Porter millions for a nephew-in-law?"

"On the contrary, I think I should like it."

As a matter of fact I had always intended Bill to marry Betsey. Not because of the Porter money, for Betsey had enough of her own, but rather in spite of it. As Bill once remarked, it wasn't his fault that his father turned the family carriage business into a prosperous automobile company.

"But would Betsey mind, do you think? At the moment she thinks I'm a wastrel of the worst type. She even has some fantastic notion about my going to work. Why," he took another turnover, "why should I go to work?"

The question was rhetorical. There was no earthly reason why Bill Porter should work. His older brother Jimmy has carried off the business honors of the family since Porter, Senior, died, and Bill has always acknowledged his own incompetence as a business man.

"If," he went on, "I got myself a job with the Porter outfit, Jimmy would put me to work balancing ledgers or filing blotters. And there are plenty of needy individuals in this world who can balance ledgers or file blotters better than I could hope to in a million years. And now that I'm a selectman and on the school committee I find enough to do right here in the town. My taxes swell the local coffers and make for better roads and things. In the city they wouldn't even repair an aged cobblestone."

"If she wants you to go to work," I soothed him, "it's because she thinks about your future and that means she's interested, at least."

"Maybe that's so. I never thought of it in that light. I've been Billy the boy companion so long that I'm dubious of her ever thinking of me as Billy the fond husband. Besides, girls don't want to marry people they know as well as Betsey knows me. She knows how I look when I haven't had a shave and how I like my eggs cooked and everything else."

He turned and looked morosely over the bay. The brilliant July sun flashed over the tiny waves as the tide slid unobtrusively in the harbor. An occasional squawking gull made a brief white dot on the sky of the Cape's own particular blue. The gilt cupola of the house Grandfather Porter had built glittered from the left arm of the bay. Over to the right a group of town boys were diving from the dilapidated wharf that had once been the pride of the town. The oyster-shell lane that led from the cottage down the hill past the tennis courts shone like a piece of white satin ribbon. I remembered that Betsey's impractical underclothing needed new straps. Beyond the road was the sandy strip where the natives and summer people alike made splotches of bright color.

"There's Sanborn now," Bill said suddenly. "Talking with Betsey and your visitors down by the bath house. I saw Dot and Mrs. Manton at the station this morning. Dot looked tired."

"She says New York is simply a boiling steaming cauldron."

Bill laughed. "You know, the more I look at your friend Emma the more she reminds me of that mammoth bronze Buddha, the resigned one in Japan somewhere. It's fifty feet high and about double that in girth."

"You say she's like a Buddha and Betsey says she's like the wife of someone out of Dickens."

"She's a combination of both. Did you ever read any of Sanborn's books, Snoodles?"

"Not exactly. I started one of them once. That one they called *The Greatest Exposé of Married Life in America*. It was all about a man—no; about a girl who loved a man who was married to a girl—I think this is straight—who loved a man who loved the first mentioned girl. It confused me to such an extent that I left off on page forty. It was a little nasty, too. I am not convinced that his characters bear any resemblance to human beings, though I am given to understand that he takes his stories from life."

"Most authors," Bill commented, "love to call their works the creation of a fertile imagination. I had an idea that it was a

THE CAPE COD MYSTERY · 11

law of the author's union or something to disclaim any connection with real life at all."

"So did I. But he gloats over the fact that his tales are true. I haven't tackled the new one yet. I haven't had time, but I very much doubt whether I'll read it at all. I'm sure that *The Lipstick Murderer* is vastly more entertaining."

"Better not let your niece hear any such heresy. She thinks he's got Dreiser and those lads all sewed up in a sack." He grinned.

Except when he grins, no one would accuse Bill Porter of being good-looking. For one thing, his nose is far too hawk-like and his ears protrude more than is permissible for masculine beauty. He has the Porter face, too, which my father used to describe as being double-breasted in shape. There is a long scar on his forehead where an enthusiastic hockey opponent thrust several inches of skate. But when Bill grins, one forgets these details and sees only that his eyes are gray and honest and his chin is firm.

His ensemble of dungarees and a faded blue shirt were not what one expects to find the well-dressed man wearing. Dale Sanborn, I reflected, would probably not care to be seen in Bill's outfit at the proverbial dog-fight. Sanborn was always so perfectly dressed.

Bill rose from the stool as Betsey came up on the porch with Dot and Emma bringing up the rear.

"The water was too perfectly gorgeous, Miss Prudence," Dot's earrings jangled as she bobbed her head to emphasize her statement. "Wasn't it just, Mrs. Manton? Wasn't it absolutely divine? And why didn't you tell me that Dale Sanborn was here? I thought he was out on Long Island, or some other island."

"I didn't know you knew him," I said mildly. Almost any re-mark seems mild after listening to Dot flow on.

"But I do, really I do. And I think it's too utterly splendid to find him down here."

"If you have anything," Emma interrupted, "that I could read, I think I'll take it up-stairs and browse till luncheon."

She looked at the collection on the table.

"Take your choice," I said.

"Don't you have anything but murders?" she asked plaintive-ly. "Haven't you anything in a calm restful story where the hero and the heroine end up happily in each other's arms?"

"Betsey goes in for the moderns and I specialize in murder," I said. "But here's Dale Sanborn's latest. I don't know what it's about, but I feel sure it's nothing so commonplace as murder. And it's autographed."

"I'll take it." She stopped at the threshold. "Is lunch at one?"

"At two. It's dinner to-day because Olga has the afternoon and evening off instead of Thursday. It's inconvenient, but we have a pick-up supper. You can browse over Mr. Sanborn for two hours or so."

"Is it his very newest?" Dot inquired. "How too wonderful."

"Simply precious," Bill teased her. "You know, just too tru-ly splendiferous. You girls want to get the mail? If you do, I'll take you up to the post-office in Lucinda. To prove my sterling worth, I'll even take you to the grocery and let you do the family marketing for Snoodles."

"Oh!" Dot squealed. "Do you have Lucinda even now? Do you still drive it?"

"Even now," Betsey answered for him. "And he still drives the thing, though one of these fine days it's going to disinte-grate like the One Hoss Shay. Jimmy sent him a sixteen-cylinder roadster this spring. It's got a special body, silver fittings and a lalaque radiator ornament, a trick horn and Lord knows what all else. It's even got a radio tucked away somewhere. But does he use it? He does nothing of the kind."

"Why, Bill, how utterly insane of you!"

"It scares me to death," he confessed. "And the town would think I was putting on side. And Lucinda understands me like a brother."

"She ought to," Betsey returned; "you've certainly driven that wreck for ten years at least."

"Eleven," said Bill placidly. "If you're bound to malign her, give the lass her due."

"Eleven then. And do you expect us to ride with you in those awful clothes?"

Dot found a slicker in Lucinda's capacious tool chest and together they forced Bill into it.

He put his yachting cap at a forty-five degree angle, wrapped the slicker around him and struck an attitude.

"'My own convenience counts as nil,—it is my duty and I will!'" he declaimed. "Be good, Snoodles, until this here Light Brigade gets back, when and if it does."

They wedged themselves into Lucinda's worn front seat and drove off to town.

I wondered as I watched them down the hill if there were a front seat in existence into which at least four modern young people could not wedge themselves. I doubted it. Picking up my thriller, I went back to the clue of the strand of red hair.

Chapter Two
A QUIET EVENING AT HOME

It was nearly three o'clock before we left the luncheon table. The most rigorous dieter of my acquaintance, an otherwise sensible woman who makes a fetish of eating strange synthetic foods to the exclusion of everything else, has been known to succumb and to succumb very completely to Olga's cooking. And Olga, who takes delight in having company to praise her food, had fairly outdone herself. We are almost unpleasantly replete after her specialties of clam chowder and hot biscuits. Emma sighed slightly as she settled herself in the largest of our wicker chairs.

"Do you remember, Prudence, that little paragraph we were taught to say when we were children? 'I have a genteel sufficiency, thank you, more would be a superfluous redundancy'? That completely expresses my sentiments. You know, when I think of the sheer and solid pleasure I've taken in eating everything I wanted all my life, and as much as I wanted to boot, I don't begrudge one inch of my massive waist-line. Where's my knitting?"

"You left it on the table." Betsey brought it to her.

Calmly she pulled forth an afghan and began to knit.

"Isn't that a warm occupation for these days?" I asked.

"I suppose it is, but I'm always hot and I can't see that this makes much difference. And I lost millions of stitches on the train this morning."

"She simply worked at it all the way down," Dot informed us, "even at that place where we had the hot box. I don't see how she can bear it, I honestly don't." She reached for a cigarette and moaned a little. "You know I feel like that goat in the fairy story who was so full he couldn't pull another blade of grass. Only I'm so full I can't bleat as I ought to at the end. Really, if you all had eaten the countless dollar dinners that I have consumed in the last months, you would understand how perfectly heavenly real honest-to-goodness food that was actually homelike could taste."

"D'you remember college food?" Betsey asked, shuddering.

"Veal cutlet and eggplant, with maybe a little snack of some perfectly sand-strewn spinach? My dear Bets, after the thousands of veal cutlets I downed at that institution I actually feel I couldn't look a cow in the face without positively blushing like a girl."

Dale Sanborn overheard her comment as he sauntered up the steps. "Could you," he asked, "blush like a girl if you tried?"

Dot made a face at him. "Smarty."

He bowed to Emma and me. "I have a boon to ask of you. Does this perfectly well-run house possess a hammer? My hovel does not. And I have clothes which must be hung up on nails that must be driven."

"Fop," said Betsey pleasantly. "Beau Brummel. Dandy. What other words are there?"

"Dude," Dot helped her out. "Also, buck, macaroni, swell——"

"Come, come." Sanborn seated himself carefully on the lounge. "That's unworthy of you. If Wellfleet possesses no tailor, why blame a man for trying to keep himself presentable?"

"We don't." Betsey ran like a bell-boy for the required instrument.

"Dot says she knew you in New York." I made an effort at polite conversation.

"Dot did," said Sanborn indifferently.

I noticed a puzzled expression in Dot's eyes.

Emma got up. "I still feel the need of resting. I had to get up at five this morning to be at the station in time to catch that abominable train. I doubt if I ever rid myself of the cinders ground into my person, and I know I shall feel that red plush sticking into my back for hours."

As she left Betsey came back brandishing a hammer.

"*Voilà,* or is it *voici?* Anyway, take your menial tool. It has our name scrawled on the handle, so you can't abscond with it."

Sanborn took it and bowed low, sweeping the floor with an imaginary hat. He was, I thought, a little oily. I tried to make out why. It might have been the chorus-boy perfection of his too-well-cut flannels and blue coat, or possibly his highly manicured fingers. My father always warned me about men with manicured hands. Such a man, he said, was never a gentleman by birth but by accident. I decided that it was Sanborn's sleek black hair, like patent leather, that had caused Bill's comment.

"I depart to ham with the hammer," Sanborn announced. As he went down the steps Betsey called after him. "Speaking of ham, have you had your first meal at Mrs. Howe's yet?"

"Not yet, alas. I missed lunch, the meal she terms dinner, by several hours. I had to snatch a bite at the hostelry. But I shall have dinner, which she knows as supper, there tonight. I haven't yet purchased the napkin ring she demanded with my first week's board. Do you suppose I have to use one napkin all week?"

"You most assuredly do," I told him. "You get a clean one with Sunday dinner."

He wrinkled his nose. "Horrid thought. I'll have to invest in some paper ones along with the ring. Shall I see you at the movies to-night?"

"Very likely," Betsey answered. "You'll find us up front on the left-hand side, if you come late. I'm too near-sighted to see a picture unless I'm on top of it."

"Farewell, then." He flourished his hammer and walked away.

"Known him long?" Betsey asked Dot.

"Uh-huh." She was abrupt.

"Amusing, don't you think?"

"Yes. My dear, did I tell you I had seen Charlotte Waite? She's gone and got herself married to an interne from Bellevue and all she can talk of are things like low-grade morons and feeble-minded infants and degenerates of one sort or another."

"Tell me," Betsey begged rapturously. "Tell me all the news."

The two chatted in that caustically outspoken manner so characteristic of their generation. Their gossip had its humorous side, but I felt a little glad that I was not one of their absent friends. Dot had innumerable stories of their contemporaries which she recounted at length, embellishing them, I suspected, with touches from her very vivid imagination.

I picked up the paper and contentedly read the comparative temperatures of the different eastern cities. Somehow it makes me feel superior and very satisfied to learn that Boston and New

York and way-stations are melting, while I myself bask in a pleasant ocean breeze.

At half past four I went out into the kitchen.

"You're not going to get more food, I hope," Betsey said.

"Man must eat," I told her, "though I've often thought how much more simple and convenient it would be if he didn't. I have to see that Olga has left us the basis of a supper."

I found sliced bread for sandwiches covered with a damp cloth. There were fruits for a salad and a pitcher of iced tea in the electric refrigerator. That refrigerator had been another added attraction to the cottage. Until this summer we had carried our ice like the rest of the summer people from freight cars at the station whenever a load of ice happened to come in. Now we stood by and watched with an evil gleam of joy in our eyes as people raced cars home with their hunks of ice dismally dripping from a running board.

In the cake box there was a plate of sugar ginger-bread. Olga was a treasure. Sometimes she resembled a block of hard pine wood, but she was a treasure. She had remembered everything. Everything except lemons, I amended to myself, and those essential articles had probably been forgotten by the girls in their shopping trip of the morning.

I called to Betsey. "If you want your supper to be a success, you'll have to dash up to town and buy some lemons."

"Did we forget 'em, Snoodles?" She was contrite. "I'm awfully sorry, but it's all the fault of that idiot Bill. He picked out his own groceries at the store and then fussed and fumed and hurried us because we hadn't got hold of any one to wait on us. What time is it?"

"Twenty minutes to five. You have plenty of time to get there before the place closes. I know it's a nuisance, but I'd rather have an omelette without eggs than iced tea without lemons."

"Right. I'll get the car. You ask Dot if she wants to pop along."

Dot refused to budge from the porch. "It's the first time I've been cool and comfortable all in one for simply ages and ages. And I've begun your murder story. It's too enticing to leave. Really, Miss Prudence, you do have the most perfectly lovely books."

Betsey drew up by the front door in her tiny car. It is one of those bantam automobiles from which so many jokes originate and though it did very well for the two of us, it was scarcely adequate when we had guests. Betsey had been obliged to make two trips from the station to transport Emma and Dot and their luggage. Emma admitted that she had been frightened to death during the ride.

"I felt like something out of *Alice in Wonderland,*" was the way she expressed it, "only I couldn't make out whether I had drunk from the bottle that made one bigger, or whether the car had been given the shrinking dose."

"Are you coming?" Betsey called.

"No, I'm going to stay here."

We watched the little thing down the hill. As Betsey turned off on to the beach road she very narrowly escaped running into Bill Porter in Lucinda. We could hear their voices as they squabbled.

"I wonder what Bill wants," I remarked.

"He's probably coming to supper," Dot laughed. "He threatened as much this morning."

But Bill did not stop at the cottage. He waved as he went by and to my surprise when I went back into the kitchen I saw his car parked outside the cabin door.

Although I had repeatedly protested against it, Olga persists in hiding the silver. Once many years ago a case of ginger ale and three gold bowled spoons were stolen from the kitchen on her day out, and she considered herself personally responsible. I don't think she ever felt quite the same way about the town afterward. In the city she never would dream of concealing our knives and forks; indeed, there would be no necessity, for our neighborhood policeman is a countryman of hers and spends much of his spare time in our kitchen. But after that theft she has always hidden our silver at the Cape.

To-day she had surpassed herself. It was no mean task to locate the salad forks, spoons and butter knives. I found them eventually in the linen cupboard, the bottom of the bread-box and the cooking compartment of the oil stove respectively.

When I looked out of the window again, Bill's car was gone. It was not like Bill to pass us by without demanding food. Asey Mayo, his man of all work, was an excellent cook, but somehow Bill had never outgrown his stupendous adolescent appetite. I wondered absently if there had been anything the matter with Olga's turnovers of the morning and he had been too polite to say so.

Dot came out and offered to help.

I told her she could spread sandwiches. "But before you do anything else, you'd better cut a cucumber up and rub the pieces over your face. If you don't you'll have a beautiful sunburn to-morrow."

"Is it as bad as all that?" She pulled a compact out of her pocket and gazed earnestly at herself. "Why, I'm practically purple, aren't I? I mean, I'm sort of awf'ly red. I guess it's the superfluous heat or the bad coming out of me or the red plush from that nasty train. But it isn't sunburn. I don't sunburn. Ever."

She sat down and stirred mayonnaise into deviled ham. "I completely forgot to ask you, Miss Prudence, what with talking with Betsey about one thing and another, and I'm afraid you'll think I'm dumb or dull or stupid. Where's that blond cat that was so frightfully dignified?"

"Ginger? Oh, he's about somewhere. He's given up hunting on the meadow for the time being, and he plays now in the pine trees back of the cabin. It's a great relief. We find only peculiar beetles on the door-step instead of long-tailed field mice."

"He was such an uncanny beast," Dot said admiringly. "What were his favorite foods? Weren't they something bizarre like jelly rolls and doughnuts?"

"Not jelly rolls. Sugared doughnuts, vanilla ice-cream and sardines. I think he learned to like the last because of constant association. Betsey has a weakness for them."

"Don't," said Dot in a horrified tone, "don't tell me. I know. Didn't I watch her eat those edibles done in oils for four years? And Bill Porter is another addict of them, isn't he?"

I nodded.

"That boy bought a dozen tins this morning at the store, just the same casual sort of way you buy a loaf of bread or a yeast cake."

"The two of them," I observed, "have contributed materially to the welfare of Norway or Sweden or Denmark or wherever sardines come from."

"Contributed materially? Miss Prudence, I'm willing to wager they've come darned near supporting a dozen fishing villages, not to speak of making 'em so simply prosperous and flourishing as to make charity workers like me homeless and jobless."

"And why not?" Betsey came in and dumped a paper bag on the table. "Why not? We're helping humanity, that's what. And humanity is always sort of down at the heels and needing help."

"Don't be idiotic," I said, "and go and tell Emma that she can eat her supper now, if the spirit so moves her."

"There's no need. She's coming."

We heard her heavy footsteps on the stairs.

"More food? Prudence, I'm ashamed to say I'm hungry. Maybe it's the air. Or do I always say that?"

"You don't," Betsey assured her, "and you can carry in the salad."

"I forgot to ask you, Emma. How do you like Dale Sanborn's book?"

She answered New England fashion with another question. "How do you?"

"I haven't read it. None of us has. He brought it over only last night."

"I'll tell you better," she said cryptically, "when I've heard your opinions."

After supper was done and the dishes stacked for Olga's benefit, Betsey proposed the movies.

"Hmmmm," said Emma. "Do you expect to fit the four of us, including me, into that—that thing you call a car?"

"Oh, no," said Betsey. "I'll make two trips. Or Bill can take you if he drops around. Or Dale. Only I guess he's at dinner. I didn't see his car outside the house."

"Thank you, but I prefer to stay at home. I don't suppose you'd care to play some bridge?"

"With two sharks like you and Snoodles? Nothing doing.

We'd lose all our money and have to go on the dole. We'd have I.O.U.'s for years to come. We'd land in the poor-house."

"Very well," I said resignedly. "Go to your movie and we will stay here and play Russian Banque. Only bring us some pop-corn."

It has always been my impression that people went to the moving-picture theater in the town for the sole purpose of getting pop-corn from the vender in the lobby. I could see no other charm in the over-crowded room where one sat on hard chairs and watched pictures whose first flush of youth had long since passed. But the young people went religiously every night, sprawled on the uncomfortable seats, ate pop-corn noisily, and even had a type of lottery based on the number of times the machine broke down and the ornate hand-tinted "One Moment Please" notice appeared.

Emma and I sat down to our Russian Banque, and for two solid hours we played as though the fate of nations waited on the outcome.

At ten o'clock Emma pushed the cards from her. "That's enough. I refuse to lose any more to you, even at a tenth of a cent. Two more games like the last one and I'd live on stew and rice pudding for the rest of the year."

"Very well," I said mockingly. "If you're afraid——"

"I'm not afraid. I'm tired. Isn't it about time for the girls to be coming back?"

"Any minute."

"Did it ever occur to you, Prudence, that there was something between Dot and that Sanborn man?"

"Not especially. Why?"

"I don't know. Maybe it was the way she greeted him down

at the bath house this morning. She seemed terribly glad to see him, but he wasn't very demonstrative. What do you think of him?"

"I hadn't thought one way or another. Bill says he's oily and falling in love with Betsey. If I had to make up my mind I'd say I didn't like him. Case of Doctor Fell, I suppose. What's your opinion?"

She shrugged her shoulders. "I saw him for five seconds this morning and five more this afternoon. His book is rot."

"I suspected as much," I told her.

Laden with bags of pop-corn which dribbled over the floor Betsey and Dot came in.

"It was an awful picture," Betsey informed us as she doled out the pop-corn. "Reel broke four times, the pianist fell asleep, Bill wasn't there, and that wretch Dale wasn't either. And his car is in the garage and the light in the cabin is out. And you heard him say he'd see us up there."

Sanborn was keeping his car in our garage since the cabin did not possess one.

"Did you shut the kitchen door?" I asked suddenly. "I hope and pray that you haven't let the cat out."

Betsey looked inquiringly at Dot.

"Oh, my dear, I know I was the last one in, and I'm sure I didn't. D'you suppose the creature has gone and dashed out into the night?"

"Undoubtedly." I rose and tapped experimentally on an ash-tray. Ginger did not come.

"He's gone, then," said Betsey wearily. She explained to Dot. "That's his signal for food. Tapping on crockery means 'Here's your fish—come and get it.' Well, I'll take the light and reconnoiter."

"Never mind," I said. "I'll do it myself. You'll only frighten him to death and then he won't come in to-night. And there are skunks about. Olga saw one."

I found Ginger cavorting on the back step. Being let out at night was a novel experience and he was enjoying every second of it. He saw me coming toward him, heard my persuasive "Come, Ginger. Come, Ginny, Ginny."

With a flick of his tail that was the equivalent of a thumb to his nose, he turned and ran toward the pines. At the cabin he swerved and with the aid of my flash-light I saw him disappear inside.

I made winning noises and clucked my tongue sympathetically. He would not come. Warily I followed along the sandy path.

At the cabin door I rapped and called "Mr. Sanborn!" But Dale did not answer. Holding my light in front of me I stepped somewhat hesitantly into the cabin.

Ginger was half under the table, industriously lapping something from the floor. I made a quick grab at him and picked him up under my arm. He had been eating olive oil from an empty sardine tin.

I turned my flash-light around the cabin, intending an explanation to Sanborn, whom I expected to find in bed. But the bed was empty, untouched. The light rested on what seemed to be a blanket roll lying parallel to the table in the center of the room.

Still managing to retain Ginger, I bent over curiously to look at something white that stuck out from under it. It was a shoe, an immaculate white suede shoe.

Holding my breath, I knelt down and jerked the blanket aside. Dressed as we had seen him that afternoon lay Dale Sanborn, sprawled limply, face downward, on the floor. I touched him. Then, with Ginger squealing, I half ran, half stumbled back along the path to the cottage.

Dale Sanborn was dead. And men do not die and then tuck a blanket over themselves.

Dale Sanborn had been murdered.

Chapter Three
MR. SULLIVAN TAKES HOLD

"Did you get him?" Betsey asked as I entered the living-room. "Why, you're white as a sheet and you're squeezing that cat to death! What ever's the matter, Snoodles? You look as though you'd seen a corpse."

I let Ginger jump to the floor and all but fell into a chair. "I have," I told her gaspingly, "Betsey, Dale Sanborn has been killed."

"What!" Her voice rose to a shriek.

"Killed?" Emma repeated.

Dot opened her mouth to speak, but before the words could come out she gave a little shiver and slumped to the floor in a limp heap at our feet.

Emma took command of the situation. "Betsey, don't lift her head up. Leave it down. And bring some ammonia and a glass of water and a cloth. No, you ninny, spirits of ammonia."

Calmly she held an ammonia soaked cloth under Dot's nose.

"Pour some of that stuff into the glass and give it to your aunt. She looks as though she needed it. No, not any more. There, drink it, Prudence."

We found ourselves obeying like small children. I made a face, but I drank the unpleasant concoction and I must admit that though I was still trembling it made me feel better.

In a moment Dot recovered. Emma led her to the lounge in front of the fire.

"Stay put there. Now, Prudence, just what is this all about?"

Haltingly I told her of my attempt to catch Ginger and of my discovery in the cabin.

She nodded thoughtfully. Her air of resigned calm is one of the reasons why I enjoy her, but at that moment it was distinctly annoying and I told her so.

"You're exactly like the Buddha Bill was talking about," I added with irritation.

"I'm sorry, Prudence, but life with Henry Edward has dulled my natural reactions of surprise. He made a point of doing the unusual, and I suppose I am used to startling things. Of course I'm shocked by this. I was wondering what we ought to do about it."

"I'd tell you, but I don't know." And I didn't.

Betsey gave a nervous giggle. "It—it doesn't tell what to do in books of etiquette on the occasion of a murder."

"Come here." Emma spoke sharply. She took Betsey by the shoulders and shook her till her teeth fairly rattled. "This, young woman, is not the time for you to indulge in any hysterics. Have you any brandy in the house? Well, go take some and bring some to Dot."

She sat down and continued. "Now, for heaven's sakes, will you all pull yourselves together and think of what we ought to do? Isn't there a policeman up-town? I thought I saw one by the crossroads at the station."

"You mean the one who directed traffic with a rolled-up newspaper? He's only a local man stationed there to prevent collisions. I'm sure there must be a sheriff, but I don't know who he is."

"He works at the grocery store," Betsey said. "His name is Sullivan."

"And you haven't a telephone? Well, Betsey, finish that brandy and get your car. You'll have to go up and get him and the doctor."

"Right." Betsey pulled on her chamois jacket. "I'm ashamed of myself for making such a scene. I don't know about such things, but shouldn't someone go and stay till the doctor or sheriff gets here? It doesn't seem right for him—for it to be there all alone."

"We'll look after that. You get along."

"And what time is it?"

"A bit after ten-thirty. Hurry up."

"Yes. But I think the state policeman who patrols the beach ought to be around about this time. Shall I bring him if I see him?"

"Bring anyone with authority. Now, hustle!"

As she left Emma turned to me.

"I suppose there is something in her suggestion. Someone ought to be over there. I'll take the flash-light and sit outside till they get here."

"You're not going over there by yourself," I said firmly. "If you go, I go."

"Very well. Dot, will you be all right here alone?"

She looked at us through red and tear-stained eyes.

"I'll be all right."

"I hope so." I put Olga's bell by her hand. "Ring this if you think you want us. You had better lie where you are and not try any moving around."

"Thank you. Like Bets, I'm sorry I made such a nuisance of myself." She tried to smile.

"Come on," Emma commanded. She picked up a small chair and a footstool. "You hold the torch."

We planted the chair and the stool in the sand a few feet from the cabin door. There was no moon, but the sky was almost overcrowded with stars. Unconsciously I looked for the Big Dipper, then felt a little ashamed to be star-gazing while Sanborn lay dead behind in the cabin.

"Who d'you suppose did it?" Emma asked.

"I haven't the remotest idea. Why, there wasn't any one in town who knew him——"

"Except?"

"Well, except Betsey and Bill and myself, and you and Dot of course, and the house agent and Mrs. Howe who was going to give him meals, and a few shop-keepers, I suppose. And the fellow at the garage, and the hotel people."

"Practically no one." Emma commented sardonically. "I should say that Sanborn knew quite a collection of people. And if I'm any judge of small towns and this small town in particular, I'd say he was known by a still greater collection. Where did Betsey meet him?"

"On the tennis courts. The Stockton girl was to play with her, but she didn't show up. Sanborn introduced himself and asked if she would play with him."

"I see. It looks to me, Prudence, as though you would have no need to devour mystery stories for some time to come. I think that you are going to have a good material problem to work on right here which ought to keep you occupied."

"And what chance shall I have to do anything?"

"You never can tell what may turn up. I'll wager what you won from me to-night at Russian Banque—I'll double it if I lose and we'll call it quits if I win—that before tomorrow is over you'll be mixed up in this."

"Done. But I do hope you're not insinuating, Emma Manton, that I killed that man?"

"No. What I mean is that you are too like your father not to stick your nose into this pie. He was too good a criminal lawyer for you not to have inherited instincts, or whatever you call 'em, about this sort of thing."

"I can't make out whether you're insulting me."

"I'm not. Look!" She pointed to headlights rushing along the beach road. "Here they are."

Betsey was the first to draw up in front of the cabin. She trained her headlights on the door.

"I found Olga walking home so I gave her a lift. I told her all about everything."

"Perhaps she'd better go and look after Dot," I suggested. "I don't like leaving her there alone."

Olga nodded and disappeared in the direction of the cottage.

"And I found Hunter, the state cop," Betsey went on, as a figure dismounted from a motor-cycle, "and here's the doctor."

Apparently she had caught him just as he was about to retire, for I could see gaudily striped pajamas under his dressing-gown.

The inhabitants of the town resented the lanky doctor. They admitted that he was good in his profession, but they looked a little askance at his habit of mingling with the summer people. His hobby of collecting Currier and Ives prints, Victorian bric-à-brac, and almost anything that was old and full of worm holes, added to their distrust. His father, the "Old Doc," had never done anything of the kind, and they considered it "kind o' funny" on the part of the son.

"Young" Doctor Reynolds—he was called "young" although his father had been dead for years and he himself was over forty—was as likely to be found on the links or about a bridge table at the country club as in his office. He liked nothing better than to hear himself talk, he knew the life-history of everyone within twenty miles, and he was as inveterate an old gossip as ever lived.

It was charasteristic that he apologize for his costume before commenting on Sanborn.

"Just going to bed. A nasty business, very unpleasant for you at the cottage. If he really was killed there'll be no end of trouble. Hunter will stay here, so you may as well go back. I'll drop over when I'm through."

It was perhaps fifteen minutes before he came into the living-room.

"I'll wait here, if you don't mind, till Slough turns up. Hunter will stay there till morning or until we can get an undertaker."

"Who is Slough?"

"Slough Sullivan, Miss Whitsby. He's the sheriff." The doctor laughed and lighted a cigarette. "He got the job after Ben Potts died last year. Ben had been sheriff for as long as I can remember, but the flu got him at last. The town elected Sullivan because he used to be on the force in Boston and they felt they ought to keep up with the modern trends in criminology. Clerking in the grocery store is his more profitable occupation. I telephoned him from the house and he said he'd come as soon as

THE CAPE COD MYSTERY · 33

he got his uniform on. Funny, I didn't know he had a uniform. That sounds like his car now."

"Hey, Slough," he called from the porch, "come here before you go over."

I looked curiously at the man who walked into the room. I had seen him countless times at the store, but I don't suppose I had ever really taken a good look at him up till now. He wore the dark blue uniform which I knew had belonged to the Boston police of at least twenty years ago. It was complete from the high-crowned helmet to the full-skirted coat. There was even a long billy suspended from his broad leather belt.

It was very apparent that Mr. Sullivan had gained at least forty pounds since he last wore his official garb. He looked sleepy, uncomfortable, ludicrous and very dull. Nodding to us, he addressed the doctor.

"I tell you what, Doc, this seems like old times. That's what it does. Captain Kinney of the old second precinct station used to say that there was never anything in the world like a murder. He used to say that it was just like a war. It gave people a chance to talk and think, and this place ain't had a murder for a hundred years. Body's over at the cabin?"

"Yes."

"Didn't leave it all alone, did you?"

"Hunter, the state cop, is over there."

"Oh, him!" Sullivan sniffed. "Well, let's get going, Doc. Who found out about this?"

I told him that I had.

"Well, Miss Whitsby, will you come along with us? One of the other ladies can come along with you."

Betsey poked me.

"Can't they both?" I asked.

"Why, I guess so. Yes."

In Sullivan's car was a boy whom I recognized as his son.

"Now, Mike, you might as well drive the ladies over. There's plenty of room for 'em in back with your camera. Mike," Sullivan explained proudly, "wants to be a police photographer."

We were jounced over to the cabin.

The sheriff and the doctor came by the path. Hunter greeted the former genially.

"Swell job for you, Slough."

Betsey shuddered at his jovial tone, but Sullivan nodded abstractedly.

Mike lugged in his apparatus and we followed into the tiny room. The body lay as I had found it, covered by a blanket. Two kerosene lamps provided sufficient illumination for me to make a closer inspection than I had on my previous visit.

The sardine tin still lay under the table, just as Ginger had found it. From a curtained closet at the far corner of the room I could see suits and a coat hanging. A large half-unpacked bag lay on a chair; beside it was one of those expanding suitcases whose flatness showed that its contents had been removed.

The doctor had left his kit on the untouched bed. On top of the table next to the lamps were various small articles, a razor, a watch and an open platinum cigarette case full of the long brown Cuban cigarettes Sanborn affected. A tennis racquet in a press was the only object on the top of a chest of drawers.

"Everything like you saw it?" Sullivan asked me.

"As far as I can tell. I took only a brief glance."

Sullivan leaned over the body and pulled back the blanket. "That's Sanborn?"

Emma stiffened beside me, and I heard Betsey gasp. For the first time, I think, I realized what had actually happened. The kerosene lamps cast strange flickering lights on the still body and once, when the breeze came in strongly, and the lamps nearly went out, I had a queer feeling that the body had moved. I knew it was only an optical illusion, but even the doctor looked startled for a moment.

"Yes, that is Dale Sanborn," I answered at last.

"Well, Mike," Sullivan addressed his son, "you take a picture of it with the blanket and then without, and then we'll get down to business."

Young Sullivan adjusted a rickety tripod and with a great deal of difficulty succeeded in fixing his antiquated camera to his satisfaction. He poured out a liberal portion of powder on a T-shaped holder and touched it with a match. Instantly we were blinded and very nearly asphyxiated by the clouds of smoke.

"By golly!" Mike informed us ruefully as the atmosphere cleared. "If I didn't go and forget to take that slide out. Now I got to take another of that."

He took another and yet another.

"I'm all run out of powder," he said sadly.

Emma gave a relieved cough. "I trust that my face is not as grimy from those vast explosions as yours is," she whispered.

I assured her that it was.

The doctor spoke softly in my ear. "None of 'em will come out. He forgot all the slides, and he was too excited about the powder to notice. As a police photographer he'd make a whale of a bricklayer."

But neither Sullivan nor his son seemed aware that anything was wrong.

"Now," said the former, "we've identified the body and taken a picture of it for future reference. You're the medical examiner too, ain't you, Doc?"

"Yes, I am."

"What's a medical examiner?" I asked.

"Name they have for a coroner in this state. Now, Doc, what was the cause of his death?"

The doctor girded his dressing-gown more tightly about him and took the center of the floor—that is, as nearly as one could take the center of any floor perhaps twenty by twenty-five feet on which there were already six persons, odds and ends of furniture and a murdered man.

"Well," began the doctor pompously, "well, unless the autopsy indicates the presence of some natural organic trouble, and from my examination that is highly unlikely, or unless it shows the presence of poison, which may be possible, though I greatly doubt it, this man was killed by a blow struck at the base of the skull by some blunt instrument. And," he added, "whoever did it made a very good job of it, too."

"Blunt instrument?" Sullivan seemed puzzled. "Then there wasn't no weapon?"

"The blunt instrument was the weapon used," said the doctor in the tone of a second-grade teacher explaining that B follows A.

"How?"

"Well, Sullivan, the most convenient and practical agent that one can find for homicide, whether premeditated or with malice aforethought, is a blunt weapon. That is principally due to the fact that there is a great prevalence of blunt instruments"—he gave the sheriff a sidelong glance to see if his sarcasm was having any effect; it wasn't, so he went on— "and the corresponding rarity of Oriental daggers and untraceable South American poisons. At least, they're rare from Sagamore Bridge to Race Point. And in a case of what you might call extemporaneous murder a blunt instrument is pretty nearly always employed. However expert you may be in pistol shooting or fencing with a saber or smallsword, your knowledge will avail you very little when confronted with the necessity of doing murder with your choice of weapons limited, say, to a cloisonné vase of the Ming dynasty or the leg of a Louise XV escritoire."

Sullivan listened with rapt attention, though I was sure he had grasped very little of the doctor's lecture. I am sorry to say that I restrained a giggle with extreme difficulty. Somehow a nervous reaction was setting in. I knew that Emma and Betsey, too, wanted to laugh. The doctor eyed us suspiciously.

"In this case," he went on, "the murderer has not only adapted himself so well to the circumstances that the murder might have been committed with anything from a fifteenth-century war mace to a rolled-up copy of *The Saturday Evening Post*, but——"

"You mean," Sullivan interrupted, "that you don't know what he hit him with?"

"You have hit the nail right upon the head. I don't know with what instrument he or she or whoever committed the murder struck Mr. Sanborn. You see, there is nothing unique or peculiar about this style of killing a person. The blow struck sharply at the base of the skull is so simple and so deadly that it is found in nearly all types of combat between unarmed men. You know the blow in modern boxing under the name of 'Rabbit Punch.' It appears in systems of fighting as widely separated as the rough and tumble of the Irish peasants of the eleventh century and jiu-jitsu of Japan."

"Then," said Sullivan excitedly, "it might have been a Jap?"

"Or a French or Dutch or Proosian," the doctor retorted. "Or a Zulu. Such a blow, Slough, strikes the cervical plexus, and if there is any considerable force behind it, the medulla is paralyzed and death is instantaneous."

He let his terms sink in and then condescendingly explained.

"To put it in plain language, a plexus is a center or a network of nerves, and the cervical plexus supplies the medulla or lower part of the brain in just the same way that a main cable supplies a central telephone exchange that connects all the outlying stations. So that if the main cable is destroyed, the central office is useless and thus no messages can be sent out or received from any of these outlying stations. In the brain the stations controlled by the cervical plexus in turn control the functions of the body which are necessary to life, such as the respiratory organs, and so on. Consequently when the main cable or plexus is destroyed, or paralyzed, then the functions necessary to life stop, and life necessarily stops also. Do you follow me?"

"I guess so. Some one biffed him over the head and he died right off."

"Excellent, Sullivan," The doctor smiled like a leading man taking his tenth curtain call.

"But almost any one or anything might have done it?"

"Correct. In fact, it might easily have been done by the heel of a man's or a woman's hand. There is no evidence to the contrary."

"You don't think he was poisoned by eating them sardines?"

"It is possible, but I don't believe it. If you care to look closely, you will find a bruise on the very spot I've been trying to tell you about."

"Humpf," Sullivan grunted. "Well, what time do you think he was killed?"

"I can't tell you exactly, of course. All this talk about a doctor's viewing a body and saying 'The deceased has been deceased for so many hours, so many minutes and so many split seconds' is all just a lot of utter tosh. When I looked at him I judged he had been dead since, well, say a little after half past four to perhaps ten minutes or so after five. That is the best I can do for you as medical examiner, Slough, and I don't think any one could tell you much more about it than that."

The doctor thrust his hands in his pockets with an air of finality.

"Isn't there one single thing in this place," Sullivan asked pleadingly, "that might have been used to kill him with?"

"There are mighty few objects that couldn't have been used. And I doubt whether you could tell the exact weapon with a microscope or pictures or anything else used in the average case. The weapon might have been the tennis racquet yonder; it might have been a chair leg. I can't tell."

Sullivan removed his helmet. His bald head gleamed in the lamplight.

"In all my years on the force," he said plaintively, "I never saw a murder before that you couldn't tell a lot about by the weapon. And here you can't tell the weapon even, you say."

"You may find out," said Betsey encouragingly.

"You'll plain have to," said the doctor forcefully. "That's what we elected you sheriff for. We scarcely anticipated any murders at the time, but we did feel that you had enough experience with this sort of thing to be able to rise to the occasion if you had to, weapon or no weapon."

Sullivan looked at him belligerently.

"I'll find out who done this, all right, Doc. Don't you worry none about that. When I was under Captain Kinney of the old second precinct I opened the doors of eleven cells for as many killers——"

"I thought he was a policeman, not a turnkey," Emma whispered.

Sullivan glared at her. "Yes, sir, and I guess I can fix this up. Now, Miss Whitsby, you just take another look around and see if you think everything's here as ought to be here or if something's here when it hadn't ought to be."

Obediently I looked around.

"Really," I said, "I can't see anything wrong. And I'm sure I wouldn't notice it if there was."

Sullivan's face fell.

I remembered something. "Wait a minute. I do know of one thing that's missing. We lent Mr. Sanborn a hammer this afternoon. I don't seem to see that around anywhere."

"A hammer? What kind of a hammer, Miss Whitsby?"

"Just the kind of hammer you drive nails with," I answered. "A common ordinary hammer. We bought it up at the hardware store in June."

Mike and Sullivan and the doctor ransacked the cabin but they were unable to find any hammer.

"Perhaps it's outside somewhere," I suggested.

Hunter took his powerful pocket light and prowled around outside in the sand and among the beach grass and bayberry bushes.

But not one trace of it did any one find.

Chapter Four
BILL AND THE SARDINES

SULLIVAN LOOKED gleefully at the doctor. "Could a hammer have done it?"

Reynolds nodded wearily. "It could have."

The sheriff smiled. "Well, that's one thing to the good then."

"But I don't think it did, Slough. It would have crushed the skull unless whoever wielded it used the handle to strike the head."

The sheriff threw his helmet on the floor and made disgusted noises in his throat. "Cripes!" was his only audible comment.

"What about the sardine tin?" I asked. "Do you think that that had anything to do with the murder?"

Idly Sullivan picked it up and examined it. A light spread over his face. He looked like a cat who had swallowed a canary and who on the whole was finding it rather pleasant. I expected some startling revelation, but instead he asked abruptly if we had seen any one around the cabin from half past four to quarter after five.

"Why," Betsey began.

"What is it, Miss Betsey?"

"Nothing. Really nothing. I was just thinking."

And I knew what it was for I had been thinking the very same thing myself.

"Did you see any one around the cabin then?"

She looked at me appealingly. I nodded for her to continue, as the fact was bound to become known.

"It's nothing, really, only that Bill Porter was there this afternoon about that time."

"Was, was he? Anyone else see him?"

"We all did," I said.

"See any one else around there?"

"Not that I know of," I answered, "unless Olga saw some one. And that would have been long before the time of the murder." I explained that you could see the cabin only from the kitchen window.

"Any of you speak with Bill?"

"I did," Betsey said. "I met him at the foot of the hill as I was going up to town."

"Did he say anything about Sanborn then?"

"Well, yes. Yes, he did."

"What did he say?" Then, as she hesitated, "You know you got to tell me."

"He didn't say very much. Only that he was going to 'pay a formal call on that Sanborn lad.' He seemed a little upset about something. Of course it may sound ominous when I tell about it now, but I'm sure he's got nothing to do with it."

"Did he come into the cottage afterward?"

"No," I said, "he didn't."

"Strange, wasn't it? Don't he usually drop in when he's over this way?"

I admitted that he usually did.

"Now, Miss Whitsby, how long did he stay over to Sanborn's while he was paying this call?"

"I couldn't say. I didn't see him leave."

"Dot might have," Betsey suggested. "Miss Cram, who is visiting me," she explained for Sullivan's benefit. "She was out on the porch then."

"We'll send Mike over to ask her."

"Please don't," I interposed. "She's taken this thing very hard, and in all probability she's in bed by now. I can tell you that he went before five o'clock because I noticed his car was gone at that time."

"Any of you seen Bill to-night?"

"No, we haven't. He wasn't at the movies, I think you said, Betsey?"

She nodded.

"None of you seen him since?"

I was beginning to resent his questions. "Come, Mr. Sullivan," I said, "how should you expect us to know about Bill Porter's comings and goings?"

"In the name of all that's reasonable, Slough," the doctor added, "why are you so anxious to find out about Bill anyway? Surely you're not such an arrant chump as to try to pin this affair on him?"

"I guess," Sullivan drawled, "I got a right to pin this on anyone I want. Why shouldn't I suspect Bill?"

"Man alive, you're crazy. Why should Bill Porter want to do away with Sanborn?"

"Two good reasons I know of. Number one," he held up his forefinger, "number one: isn't Sanborn running around after his girl?"

"That's a lie," Betsey told him hotly. "I am not Bill Porter's girl, as you call it. And Dale Sanborn wasn't running after me."

"That so? Well, Miss Betsey Whitsby, you'd have a hard time trying to make any court think differently about it. And number two," he held up his second finger, "number two: this afternoon in the presence of a reliable witness who told my son who told me, he threatened to kill Sanborn the next time he saw him."

To say that we were startled would be an utter falsehood. We were completely overcome, downright flabbergasted. I could feel my chin droop, and every one but Sullivan and Mike had wide open mouths like so many hungry robins in a nest.

"What?" I found my voice. "I don't believe a single word of it."

"It's true," said Mike excitedly. "Lonzo Bangs told me. Sanborn run over Bill's dog and left him lying right in the middle of the road. He didn't even stop to see how badly hurt he was. And you know Bill sets a lot of store by that dog."

I knew that Bill had the same affection for Brutus, more commonly known as Boots, that I had for my cat. And Boots was no ordinary dog. He had cost a thousand odd dollars and he had as many medals as any wonder dog in the moving pictures.

"And," said Sullivan, "Bill's got the Porter temper. I guess you know that. He just probably let it loose. You can't say that the Porter temper ain't a temper. You heard how one time in town meeting he picked up a bench and threw it at that Portygee Pete Barradio who wanted to increase the taxes so as the town would tar the road that leads out to his dance hall at the Neck. And they's plenty of other times that Bill rose up and walloped people. And he knows all about that Jap way of wrestlin', too, that the doctor said might be how Sanborn got hit. I seen him do some of it myself, getting a sort of toe hold on a man who's on top. Of course, he don't stay mad long, and he's always awful sorry afterward, but you can't deny he's got a terrible temper all the samey."

None of us attempted to deny it. The Porter temper was legend.

"Yes," Sullivan went on, "he's got two good reasons. And I'll tell you something else."

He stuck his thumbs in his broad leather belt and held forth, much in the manner of the doctor. I marvelled at the effect a group of people had on the average man. I have never seen one of them who did not swell slightly when he had the opportunity to speak to more than four people who had no ostensible reason for stopping him.

"I'll tell you one thing I learned from Captain Kinney," Sullivan continued. "One murder is a lot like another murder, and one murderer is a lot like another murderer. Lie detectors and all the newfangled things they use to-day may be all very good enough in their way, but murders that happen ain't so complicated as murders you hear about. In books they's always a lot of things that point to a man's doing the killing, and then there's always someone else who did it all the time. Now, I never knew of a killer who was caught that didn't leave some track behind him. The reason they all get caught is because they do just that. There was things that pointed to 'em and the things didn't lie none."

I wondered if Sullivan was quite such a fool as I had thought. He was not as eloquent as the doctor, but he was far more earnest and every whit as logical.

"Now, you take this sardine tin." He held it up. "You see that piece of wrapper that's still on the bottom? It may be too oily for you to make anything out of it, but I can tell a lot just from looking at it. That's nothing Sanborn ever bought for himself. That's the thing in this case that the murderer left behind him." He lowered his voice impressively. "This morning a man bought a dozen tins of sardines from the store and took 'em away with him. This tin here is one of the dozen Bill Porter, the one I'm talking about, bought himself."

"What?" I ejaculated. "How can you tell?"

"For one thing, Miss Whitsby, they're Hadley's sardines and they're imported by just one house in the United States. That's S. S. Pierce's in Boston. And we're the only people on Cape Cod who carry them, and we carry them only for Bill Porter. They cost seventy-five cents a tin." For a moment his tone was that of a grocery clerk. "Seventy-five cents the seven-and-a-quarter-ounce tin."

"But see here," I said decisively, "We buy those sardines ourselves. We get ours direct from Boston, and I'm perfectly sure at least a dozen other summer people here do too."

"You can tell me a lot, Miss Whitsby, about a good many things, I'll admit. But you can't tell me much about sardines. Especially these sardines here. These have got the Pierce trademark on the bottom. See that? And the number beside it, 48, is our number. It means we're agents. And this wrapper, if you look close, is green and white. Not red and white like they used to be. I noticed it myself when I looked at the shipment that came in just yesterday."

"Well," said Emma, "suppose you did sell Bill those sardines. Suppose Bill did threaten to kill Sanborn. Suppose he came here. You can't prove that he was the murderer, can you?"

"Bill he can have a thousand stories, he can have a million if he wants, all claiming that he didn't do this," Sullivan answered. "But you can't get away from facts. This afternoon at two-thirty Sanborn ran over Bill's dog. Asey Mayo had to shoot it. Bill he found out about it a few minutes after four, because it wasn't much later than half past four that Mike told me about this threat. He said he was going to see Sanborn; you saw him come. Sanborn is found killed afterward, but the doc says he was killed during part of the time that Bill was here. We find he left his sardine tin behind him. Now, that's all straight, ain't it?"

"Yes," the doctor began, "but——"

"But nothing, begging your pardon, Doc. That's what Captain Kinney used to call a clear record of connecting facts, ain't it? Bill can lie some, but it's going to take an awful lot of lying and a couple of slick lawyers to make people think he didn't do it."

"Do you think he did it?" Betsey asked heatedly.

"It's perfectly O. K. with me if you all want to think he got struck down by a bolt shot out of the heavens that just happened to land on the base of his skull, if you want to. Or you can think it's a death ray, whatever that is, or it could be anything at all. But Captain Kinney of the old second precinct always used to say that he for one was content to think a thing out like the rest of humanity when the facts was in front of him, and leave flights of fancy-like notions to them as didn't have their duty to do. I don't know a lot about queer blunt instruments that the doc talks about, but I know a sardine tin when I see it, an' I can put two and two together with any one."

"What about the hammer?" I asked.

"Well, I guess a little searching will turn that up in the vicinity of Mister Bill Porter. It's my opinion he did this with that Jap trick. But if we find the hammer, we'll know different. The doc don't think it did the job, but I can't see but what the handle of a hammer would be as easy a way to hit a man as the head of it would. Course you don't always pick a hammer up by the head, but if Bill was in a temper as he probably was, he might just as well of done it that way. Yes, I guess that hammer had something to do with this killing. If it didn't, why ain't it here? Why? Why take it away if it ain't got anything to do with the murder?"

"Why," I asked with some asperity, "leave a sardine tin behind and take away a hammer?"

Sullivan told us why at some length. "There was a man once in Boston when I was on the force who left a body all covered over with things that pointed to him doing the murder. We arrested him. He got a shrewd lawyer who got up in court and said that the man had been the victim of a conspiracy, the one we'd arrested had, I mean. That lawyer said that no man in his right senses would leave a body all covered with clues and that it was some one who was trying to get the man we'd arrested into trouble. We all sort of agreed with him after he'd finished. But when we found another body all covered with clues that led to the same man again, we got busy. He'd done both of them murders and left things lying there on purpose so's he could say it was the work of an enemy. I told Bill Porter about it once myself."

"Why," the doctor inquired mildly, "don't you get Bill up here and ask him a few questions? No doubt he could clear the matter up."

Sullivan shrugged his shoulders. "Hunter, will you go up to the Porter house and get him and bring him here?"

Hunter grinned. "Sure. It's the big house with the gold dome, isn't it?"

We heard the chug chugging of his motor-cycle as he sped away.

"Couldn't this have been done by a tramp or someone passing by who wanted to rob him?" I asked.

"I don't think that's possible," the doctor answered. "There is his cigarette case, and his watch is still there, and here," he took a wallet from his surgical bag, "is a bill-fold with about two hundred dollars in it which I took from his inner pocket. It doesn't look that way at all."

"Will there be an inquest?" I asked.

"Oh, yes. An inquest." The doctor considered. "Well, I don't think there's the slightest chance of this being an accident. It's clearly a murder. An inquest would be more or less of a formality and we have thirty days to do it in. We can wait a few days. There's no need to hurry things right now."

The sheriff agreed. "That's right, Doc. I want to take a look about for that hammer. And I'm going to arrest Bill Porter on suspicion, and I'll take him up-county for an indictment."

"Can he do it?" I asked the doctor. "Can Bill be arrested by this man?"

"I'm afraid he not only can but that he will be."

There was a period of uncomfortable silence while we all pondered on the fate of Bill. We turned toward the door as Hunter's motor-cycle roared outside.

Hunter, chewing gum happily, entered alone.

"Where's Bill?" Sullivan demanded.

"Your bird's flew the coop," said Hunter. "There's no one there at the house at all. I banged on the door and then opened it and went in. There wasn't a soul in the house at all."

"No one, not even Asey Mayo?"

"No, sir. There's nobody there. And it looked like they'd left in a tearing big hurry, too. There were lots of things sort of strewn around."

Sullivan smiled. "You can add to that list of facts I gave you that when a man who threatens another man with murder disappears, and when the man he's threatened is found killed, you don't have to look very far to find the killer. Mike, you take the car and go up and phone to the state police to stop his car. Describe the new one and give the number of the old hack he drives around. I don't think he'd use it but he might. Then telephone the lighthouses and the harbor lightkeeper and ask 'em to keep an eye out for that shiny speed boat of his. Telephone Cousin Mike in Boston, too. He'll know what to do about looking over the harbor there. We'll get that guy even if he spends a million or two trying to get away. Have you got all that straight?"

Mike nodded.

"Go along, then, and I'll stay here and look around a little more for the hammer till you get back."

The boy rushed out. "I'll bet," the doctor commented under his breath, "that he forgets to put a nickel in the telephone slot." Aloud he said, "I suppose I might as well take the rest of his small personal belongings and get along home."

"What about the body?" Sullivan asked.

"I can't very well take it along with me, and Simpkins the undertaker has gone up to Boston with the body of the Downey woman who was drowned in the surf. He'll be back early to-morrow though. We'll leave the body here to-night, and you or Hunter will have to stay here till Simpkins can take charge of it for me. That will be all right, won't it?"

"It will have to be," said the doctor sharply. "Now, let me know what turns up." He turned to us. "I'm sorry I can't offer you ladies a lift over to the cottage, but my car isn't much larger in seating capacity than yours." He chuckled amiably at his own little joke and left.

Betsey put her car up, and Emma and I walked slowly home.

"Was Dale's car in the garage," I asked her when we caught up to her, "I mean, when you went to the movies?"

"I suppose it must have been. I thought he'd gone to supper. I'd left the bug by the side of the house, and I didn't look into the garage at all. Snoodles, isn't this perfectly awful?"

"It certainly is," I told her fervently.

In the house we found only Olga up. Dot, she informed us, had gone to bed.

"You know," Betsey remarked, "I can't just understand why that girl went to pieces this way. She was the coolest person in the dormitory when it caught on fire. And when she was on the Pearsons' yacht last year and it nearly foundered off Hatteras, they said she was the only one who kept her head at all. It's strange that a girl who's been through fire and flood, so to speak, should act like this."

I told her of Emma's suggestion that there might have been some attachment between her and Sanborn. "And," I said, "she didn't give you much information when you asked her this afternoon how long she'd known him."

"Yes, I noticed at the time that she was unusually reticent. But things do look bad for old Bill, don't they?"

Emma stifled a yawn. "They won't look any worse to-morrow. Or is it to-day? It is, and well on to Saturday, too. Prudence, ordinarily yours is a most peaceful household and I enjoy it. It rests me to be with you. But I have been more heated since I left Boston this morning than if I had stayed at home and knitted on my afghan out in the sun. I am completely exhausted and I make no bones about it. I am going to bed this very instant. You two had better do the same."

She trudged heavily up the stairs, and Betsey and I followed.

I hoped that after I got to bed I might have one of those flashes of inspiration so common to would-be crime solvers. But after I had undressed and washed some of the traces of Mike Sullivan's flash-light powder from my smudged face, I fell into bed and was practically asleep the minute my head touched the pillow.

But I remember the dream I had that night. A yellow cat that looked enormously like Dot was running after a sardine that scurried on its fins like a mouse. Other cats appeared, joined in the chase. One nearly had the sardine, but just in time the silly-looking fish leaped in between the covers of a purple book.

I awoke for a second to find Ginger gleefully exercising his catnip mouse on the foot of my bed.

Chapter Five
ENTER ASEY MAYO

OLGA woke me with difficulty at seven in the morning.

"Mister Bill's Asey wants to see you."

I dressed hurriedly and went down-stairs to find Asey Mayo sitting bolt upright in a steamer chair on the porch. Asey was the kind of man everybody expects to find on Cape Cod and never does. He was by my reckoning about sixty years old, because I am fifty, and I knew he had been "voting age," as they say in the town, when I was a girl visiting my relatives. No one seeing him for the first time could tell whether he was thirty-five or seventy. His long lean face was so tanned from exposure that the lines and wrinkles did not show. His mouth was wide, with a humorous twist about the corners, and his deep-set blue eyes twinkled disconcertingly.

He usually walked with his shoulders hunched and his head thrust forward. As he moved his worn corduroy trousers and flannel shirt flopped as though anxious to catch up with the rest of his spare frame. An old broad-brimmed Stetson set at an angle on his head gave him a strangely rakish look. He almost invariably chewed tobacco, and that habit coupled with his trick of pronouncing no more syllables of a word than were absolutely necessary, made him quite unintelligible to those who didn't know him.

Although he called himself a mechanic, he had taken a turn at nearly every trade. As steward, cook or ordinary seaman he had sailed over the seven seas in every type of ship. He had made his first voyage on one of the last of the old clipper ships, and before he had settled down in the town he had been mate of a tramp steamer. Under Bill's grandfather he had built carriages; under Bill's father he had learned about automobiles. I doubt if he had ever had more than a fleeting glimpse of the inside of a school-room, but his knowledge of the world and its inhabitants was vastly superior to that of the average man.

The town cast a critical eye upon him because he belonged to no church and rarely attended any service outside of the Christmas Eve celebration, when he went and lustily sang hymns. He was neither a Mason, a Bison nor an Elk.

But the townsfolk knew that when a garageman pronounced a car fit for the junk heap, Asey Mayo could rejuvenate it. Shortly after we had come to the Cape Betsey's tiny car had stopped. The local mechanic scratched his head and said that he was dummed if he could do anything. A man brought from Boston confessed that the trouble was too deep-seated even for him. At Bill's suggestion Asey had looked the car over. Nonchalantly he prodded a wire here, a nut there. He tinkered with a wrench, tapped with a screwdriver.

"Now then," he said to Betsey, "start her up."

Betsey started her up. The car purred happily.

"What was the matter, Asey?" Bill asked.

"Matter?" said Asey. "Wan't nothin' much the matter

'cept the whangdoodle on the thingumbob wa'n't touchin' the whatchamacallit."

His speech would be impossible for a student of phonetics to record on paper. It resembled no other dialect in the world. Let it suffice to say that he never sounded a final *g* or *t*. His *r* was the ah of New England. His *a* was so flat that as Betsey said, you couldn't get under it with a crowbar.

He greeted me as though it were his custom to appear on my porch at seven every morning of his life.

"H'lo. Wake you up, did I?"

"Good morning, Asey." I noticed that the humorous twist was gone from his mouth. "Have you heard about all this? And did Bill do it? And where is he?"

"Yup. Nope. In the pillory," said he composedly.

"In the what?"

"In the pillory, and 'twas lucky 'twasn't the bilboes."

"But why?"

"Ain't no jail."

"Perhaps," I said, "you had better begin at the beginning and tell me everything."

He drew a long breath. "Well, Sanborn he run Boots down. Did it a purpose. I had t' shoot him. Bill come home an' found out an' got mad. Don't blame him. I was myself. An' he said he was goin' to kill Sanborn an' before I could get to stop him he was off. He come up here an' asked Sanborn what the hell, I mean——"

"That's all right. What did Sanborn say?"

"He said he didn't run over any dog, but if Bill said that he had he'd make rest'ution. An' he took out a ten-dollar note an' passes it to Bill. Course Bill got madder an' left. An' after he come home I picks up the glasses an' sees some one out fiddlin' with the lobster pots I'd just set out, an' so we took that speed boat o' Bill's an' went out after 'em. Bill'd been usin' the boat that afternoon an' like a fool he hadn't put any gas in her, so by the time we borrered gas from a late quohaugger comin' in from the beds, we'd lost the tide an' had t' stay out in the harbor all night in that there mahogany contraption. If we'd used a rowboat like I wanted to we'd been all right now. Anyways, we come in hour or so ago an' there was Slough Sullivan all dressed up in his reg'mentals waitin' to greet us. He up and 'rested Bill for killin' Sanborn. That was the first we got to know about it. An' then he went an' put Bill in the pillory."

"What pillory? And why?" Betsey, who never rose before half past ten, stood in the doorway, sleepy-looking but completely dressed.

"Well, Bill said he hadn't done it, an' Slough he went on about Bill's threatenin' to kill Sanborn an' something about a sardine tin, an' seems like as if he had 't all doped out that Bill he was the murderer. Bill said all right, if Slough wanted to 'rest him, he was welcome to do it, but what was he goin' to do with him after he had 'rested him. Slough says he's goin' to take him up-county an' get him indicted. An' Bill says he can't on account of it's bein' Saturday. So Slough says, I'll put you in jail then."

Asey smiled. "We ain't had no jail here for twenty-thutty years, an' Bill told him so. An' he says that the best thing Sullivan can do is take his word he won't try to go off anywheres an' run away."

He stopped short and sniffed the air. "If that's coffee I smell I think I'd kind of like to have some. You go get me a cup, Betsey, like a good girl. I won't go on till you get back."

Betsey brought out a tray and the three of us sat and drank

THE CAPE COD MYSTERY · 57

coffee as casually as though we were guests at a garden party.
Emma and Dot probably had cause to laugh as they came out
and saw us, though at the moment I didn't see anything very
funny about drinking coffee with what amounted to a hired
man at that hour of the morning. Briefly we acquainted them
with the gist of Asey's remarks.

"Well," continued Asey, "Sullivan he couldn't see that at all.
Says he, you'll be takin' that shiny new car of yours an' beatin' it
away as soon's I leave you; else you'll run off in your speed boat."

"'Humpf,' says Bill, 'how 'bout givin' me a pair of handcuffs
an' a ball an' chain? Or maybe,' says he real sarcastic-like, 'maybe you could use the pillory that they put up for the ter-ter——'
oh, that three-hundredth birthday party the town had."

We snickered.

"But Sullivan don't see anything hum'rous in that. He thinks
it's a fine idea, so he ups and does."

"You mean to say that he put Bill Porter in the pillory for every one to see and throw things at?"

"Yup," said Asey, helping himself to another biscuit. "Your
girl makes real good biscuits, Miss Prue, an' I know a lot about
biscuits. Yup. That's what Sullivan did, all right. Only I don't
guess that there'll be any throwin'. I'm sure of that. I left Joe
Bump there for to watch out."

"What good will the village idiot do?" Betsey demanded.

"Well, I give him that long whip Jimmy got out in Californy.
Joe Bump knows how to slash it so's 'twill cut paper at fifty feet.
An' I made a sign an' stuck it up sayin' that the first feller t' start
anything would get a feel of that lash. An' I gave Joe Bump five
dollars an' told him what t' do. For less'n five dollars Joe'd cut
the King of England into ribbons."

We laughed in spite of ourselves.

"What about Bill?" I asked. "How is he?"

"Real chipper, Bill seemed. Only he don't feel that way one bit. I left him settlin' how he was t' live till Monday mornin'. That's when Sullivan says he's goin' t' take him up to the court, but I kinder think he'll take Bill out sooner'n he thinks. Bill says he wants an umberill for to keep the sun off, an' I left some money at the dog-cart to see he got fed." Asey chuckled. "He was kind of worrin' 'bout sanitary arrangements when I left him, but I reckon necessity'll show him some way out."

"But isn't he terribly uncomfortable?" I asked. "The boy who stood in it for the 'Punishments' tableau at the pageant had a stiff neck for days afterward."

"Bill's taller, an' I stuck a couple boards under his feet. No, he wa'nt sufferin' none."

"But what are we going to do?"

"Well, Miss Prue, Bill told me to come to you an' tell you everything, an' he said you an' me was t' find out who done this by Monday mornin'. You see, if Sullivan gets the crazy boy indicted, an' I don't see no reason why he won't less'n we do something, there's goin' t' be an awful lot of trouble to get him out of this. Course we all don't think he did it, but I guess most every one else will judge by 'pearances. Folks most usually do. An' we just got to get the one who did it before anything more happens to Bill."

"Did you let Jimmy know?"

"Yup. Sent him a telegram on the way up."

"Asey ought to know about the sardines," Emma suggested. "Whether they were the ones that Bill bought or not."

"I'm 'fraid they are, all right. They's only 'leven tins in the pantry now, an' it says twelve on the bill. Whatever other faults Slough Sullivan's got, he gives full measure in sardines as well as everything else, flour or butter or what all. Every one's got to have some redeemin' feature about him, an' that's Slough's. He's honest even if he is kind of dull. If he says he give Bill twelve tins, he did. Bill he told Slough that when he set out t' commit a murder he didn't usually eat no sardines on the scene o' the crime, before or after, let alone carryin' the things with him an' then leavin' the can behind."

"What did Sullivan say to that?"

"Told some story about a feller in Boston who'd left things behind so as to make people think some one else had made him the goat in a murder. Said that was what Bill'd done. Said it didn't make no difference to him when 'r if 'r how 'r where Bill ate or didn't eat 'em. All he cared about was the tin bein' there."

"I wonder how they got under the table, then, if Bill didn't bring them," Betsey remarked.

"Bill swears he didn't. I guess likely it was spirits, but most likely two-legged ones. That's just one of the things Miss Prue and me has got to find out."

"But," I wanted to know, "can Sullivan do a thing like this?"

"You mean, can he put Bill in the pillory? He has. No one can't accuse him of not gettin' results. He's got him secured by the neck 'n wrists."

"Couldn't we get detectives?"

"Sure we could. I asked Bill if we hadn't better, but he said no, that they'd get here when they felt like it and then they'd take a couple of weeks to get the lay of the land and find out all about the local scandals an' by the time they got anywhere Bill'd be behind solid steel bars."

"Does he expect us to track down whoever did this? Is the boy crazy?"

"Nope, he's got sort of batty notions, but I shouldn't go so far 's to call him plumb brainless. I guess you 'n' me can dig out facts as easy as any one else. Sullivan he found what he thought was the murderer in an hour or so. We got about two whole days to start in an' find the real crim'nal. An' I'd say offhand that we'd got as good brains as he has. That reminds me. I thought of one thing a'ready. By tonight this'll be head-lines in every paper there is. It happened too late to get into the mornin' ones, but it'll be all over the place to-night. So I brought something along with me."

He went out to the side of the cottage where he had parked Bill's new car. From the rumble seat he extracted six great coils of rope, an ax and a bundle of poles that looked suspiciously as though they had started out in life by holding up beans.

"What," Emma asked, "is all that for? A mass hanging?"

"No'm. I'm goin' to string it around this cottage here, on account of what if I don't you'll be sleepin' trippers all over your front piazza. They's goin' to be plenty of people down this way before the day is over an' not all of 'em is goin' to stay down there on the beach road an' look up, even though that's where they b'long. You all better come an' help me."

We felt foolish, but we helped him string a cordon of rope about the cottage. While we worked I asked Asey why he was using the new roadster.

"Lucinda's a good car, but she's temp'rmental. I got a feelin' we're goin' to have some ridin' to do, you an' me, before we get through this here job, an' you might's well ride in style an' comfort."

"I'm glad you think we're going to get through with it," I remarked. "You seem very sure."

"Well, might's well be a little confident. Every one can't get to Corinth, but you can read the signposts, as the feller said."

"Why did Bill pick out you and me to get to the root of this matter?"

"He 'lowed as how you an' me were the only people he feels sure didn't do it."

I reflected on that and commented on Asey's foresight in the matter of the ropes.

"Well, ounce o' prevention's worth a pound o' cure. Besides, they ain't no sense in a pack of women folks bein' bothered by a lot of old men with comic remarks t' make an' women in khaki pants starin', an' a lot o' kids throwin' papers around."

"But you were clever to think of it," I said fatuously.

"Humpf. Nothin' but common sense. Common sense, Miss Prue, that's my maxim."

For the first time I realized he had been calling me by the name the family had used long ago. It had been a good twenty-five years since any one had shortened Prudence into Prue. I stopped my wandering into the past.

"What shall we do first, Asey?"

"Well, I cal'late we're goin' to find out more about this Sanborn man. Then we'll find out more about that sardine tin. Then," he lowered his voice and jerked his head toward the other three, "then we're goin' to look into matters nearer home. Don't look so amazed like. Re-fined people do murders sometimes. Only we got to learn more about Sanborn first. We'll do that this mornin', I reckon, an' that might maybe give us something to go on."

"How do you know we'll find out anything about Sanborn?"

"Easy as pie. Bill telegraphed that Harlow boy in Cambridge

yesterday mornin' before anything happened at all. He was sort of cur'us to find out about him on general principles. Yup, we got a lot to do to-day. We just got to find out everything by Monday bright an' early."

I looked at him quickly. He was perfectly serious. There was even a certain finality about the way he made that statement, as though he had no doubt whatever in his mind but what we would. I was beginning to understand why Bill depended to such an extent on this tall raw-boned man. Was it Shaw or Wells who said of New Englanders that they were "fine and bleak"? Certainly there was a fineness in Asey which I had never suspected.

"You think so?"

"Sure, Miss Prue. I seen the Porters in scrapes afore this. They always seem to get themselves out all right."

"You mean, I suppose, that you always get them out," I remarked.

Asey smiled. "Most usually I have help. Now, you an' me is goin' to start out."

"Start out where?" asked Betsey, coming up. "Can we go too?"

"Nope. Ain't no need for you to come traipsin' around today. You go up-town an' every man-jack will start pointin' an' talkin' about you, an' you might's well stay here."

Accordingly I stepped into the front seat of the gleaming low-hung roadster, and Mr. Mayo and I drove off. Emma watched us with a twinkle in her eye. I knew she was thinking of the wager we had made the night before.

"First we'll go see Bill. Then to the post-office an' then to the telegraph office, an' then we'll interview Mrs. Howe," Asey planned out loud. "Sanborn was probably there yesterday. Say, did Betsey's friend Dot or your friend Mrs. Manton ever know Sanborn?"

"Dot did, but not Emma."

"She know he was goin' to be here?"

"She said she didn't."

"Hm. Did you ask 'em down or did they wangle an invitation off you?"

"I asked them," I said indignantly. "Why?"

"Oh, I just thought that this here hot weather might give any one a real chance to ask themselves where they knew Sanborn was goin' to be if they had any idees about killin' him."

I had not thought of that. "But," I objected, "no one knew that Sanborn was going to be here. He came to town from the Chatham Bars Inn on Tuesday, intending to spend just the night, at least that was what he told Betsey on Wednesday when she met him. Then he decided he liked the place so much that he made up his mind to stay. The hot weather didn't begin till Tuesday or Wednesday. And how would any one know, besides?"

"That new proprietor of the inn has flossy notions." Asey bit off a chunk of chewing tobacco. "He puts all the names of folks who stay there into the papers. If Sanborn came on Tuesday, then it was in Wednesday's paper, and the heat-wave talk began in Wednesday's paper too. Didn't any one ask if they could come to see you for the week-end?"

"We got nine telegrams," I informed him.

"Kind of a lot, wasn't it?"

"Yes, but nothing out of the ordinary. Once last year we got sixteen."

"Who was they from?"

"I really don't remember all of them. Betsey might."

"Any one you remember as being sort of strange?"

"Why, no."

"Wasn't any from any one who you didn't know very well or didn't expect to hear from?"

"I'm getting old and doddering, Asey. Yes, there were two that we particularly noticed." I told him of our system of drawing lots and how we seemed unable to get any combination other than John Kurth and Maida Waring. I explained about their divorce and subsequent estrangement.

"May be a little far-fetched, but we'll look into the matter later. Can't never tell in things like this how important co-inc'dences are."

He turned the car on to the strip of state highway that served as the main street of Wellfleet. Both sides were lined with the typical collection of small-town emporiums. There were ice-cream parlors, the grocery where Sullivan presided, a news-stand, a bowling alley and the inevitable gasoline stations. Opposite that focal point, the post-office, was an open lot. It had been on this spot that the town had given what Asey called its three-hundredth birthday party. Here the pillory and stocks and bilboes still stood.

The street was unduly crowded and Asey gave a display of steering which would have done credit to any New York taxi driver. He drew up in front of the post-office and coaxed the car into a parking space which I should have considered inadequate even for Betsey's vehicle.

I looked over to the lot, where, surrounded by at least a hundred gaping people, Bill Porter stood with his head and wrists protruding from a wooden frame-work. I was struck by the abnormal silence. There was a thin buzz of voices, but it was a very thin buzz indeed. Joe Bump sat on a camp stool next to Bill. He gripped with both hands the long handle of an enormous whip whose length lay coiled neatly at his feet.

Asey caught a small boy by the arm.

"Anything happened, bub?"

The youngster grinned.

"Pete Barradio, he tried to throw a rotten tomato, but Joe hit him before it left his fist, and he slashed his face open like it'd been cut by a razor. I don't guess any one'll bother him or start anything more. They don't dast."

Asey's blue eyes twinkled for a second. "Let's see what Bill's got to say."

We made our way to the edge of the crowd.

Bill waved a fist at us. "Morning, Snoodles. Hi there, old-timer."

"Are you all right, Bill?"

"Doing as well as can be expected under the circumstances, Snoodles."

"I wouldn't be too chirky if I was you," Asey advised him. "Has Slough been around again?"

"Uh huh. He's convinced I'm suffering like a Christian on a rack. I put on a pained face and told him I'd prefer the third degree. He was delighted and went away satisfied I'd break down. He thinks this'll bring me into a repentant frame of mind."

"Had anything to eat?"

"Yes. Joe here fed me a hot dog and a glass of milk. I'm going to have a Western sandwich for a light lunch soon. A man in my position gets hungry. Very hungry. Have you found out anything yet?"

Asey shook his head. "Nope."

"Well, you two had better get going if you want to see this worthy young man without shackles and a stiff neck for the rest of his life. It's all up to you."

"Don't you worry now," said Asey anxiously. "We'll fix you up all right. Come along, Miss Prue."

"Hey," Bill called after us. "Who'd you suppose I saw going by here a minute ago? He wasn't looking this way, but I howled after him. I guess he didn't hear me though."

"Whom," I accented the pronoun slightly, "did you see?"

"There, there, Snoodles. Whom. Well, it was that tall dark fellow who used to be Maida Waring's husband. The one who went to school with Jimmy. What was his name?"

"Kurth, you mean?"

"Yes, Johnny Kurth."

Chapter Six
COMPLICATIONS

"What do you think about Kurth's being here?" I asked as we walked across to the post-office.

"Seems kind of funny, don't it? He didn't tell you he was comin' anyway, did he?"

"No, he didn't. And it seems strange that after asking to come down he shouldn't let us know, or at least come and call on us, don't you think?"

"Seems so. Well, we'll have to wait a bit before we go into that. Right now I don't want to go gettin' mixed up."

He twirled the dials of Bill's mail-box and drew out a letter. "Humpf. A special delivery stamp don't mean one thing in this place. We'd ought to got that delivered at the house last night."

"Is it from Paul Harlow?"

"Yup, says so on the outside, anyways. S'pose we take the car and read this down by the station. They ain't so many people down there, an' we can see if there's any word from Jimmy besides."

More than one curious glance was directed at us as we got into the car, in itself an object of attention.

I heard whispers. "Look. Miss Prudence Whitsby. There with Asey Mayo."

I thought grimly that there was more going to be discussed that day than the Sanborn affair and Bill Porter's arrest. We stopped outside the telegraph office in the station and Asey passed me the letter.

"Here, you read it out loud."

"Dear Cap'n,"—Bill had been known as the "Cap'n" throughout his college days.

"Your long winded telegram received," I read, "and as per your instructions, I have spent several weary hours tracking down the dirt on your pal Sanborn. Couldn't find anything about any bird by that name in any class from '18 to good old '22. Just as I was giving up in despair I met old man Kampfer of the eco. department and I stopped him and asked if he'd known of a Dale Sanborn who'd been around about that time.

"The old geezer blinked and said, 'Who?'

"I shouted at him. You know he's deaf in addition to his other derangements. 'Who's that,' says he, sticking out his ear trumpet. 'No, I didn't know a David Sanborn. Perhaps you mean David Schonbrun; he was a brilliant boy. One of the cleverest and most intelligent undergraduates we ever had.'

"I pricked up my ears and the old gent chattered along. Said I'd probably remember him by the name of Red Ivan, and sure enough I did. I don't think you would, because you didn't play about with that sort of thing. The 'red' came from his leanings toward socialism and anarchism and all that, and Ivan was from that song that's on the other side of the Frankie and Johnnie record. Well, Red Ivan was always making speeches about the downtrodden masses on a soap-box and getting himself arrested in places like Lowell and Lawrence for bawling about on strikes and one thing and another. They used to claim he was all tied up with Moscow, but most likely that was a lot of talk.

" 'Poor lad,' says Kampfer, 'he was killed in a strike riot not long after he got out of college. He'd just got out of a jail sentence too.'

"Well, I played a hunch. Those names were a lot alike, so I asked the old fellow out for a beer. He mopped up the stuff as fast as the boy could bring it, and I pumped him with every swallow. Now this Schonbrun sounded pretty much like your Sanborn except that yours wore snappy clothes and didn't have a mustache like this one. Kampfer says he came from New York City, was born there and went to some city high school. I made him take me around to the hovel where he hangs out and get me a photo of the man in question. He made me promise to give it back to him as is, so don't go for to lose it or light your pipe with it. This Schonbrun seemed to be a pet of the old man.

"Of course this man may not be the one you want, but on the other hand, Kampfer might be mistaken about his getting killed. Anyway you look at it, I calls it good sleuthing, and I hereby put in an expense account of ten beers at a quarter each. That is not extortion as small beer comes high these days. What's all the shooting about anyway?"

"The rest," I concluded, "is only something about coming up to the games this fall."

Asey delved into the envelope and brought out a snapshot. He looked at it closely and passed it over to me.

"What d'you think about it, now?"

I gazed at the faded picture of an earnest young man in baggy clothes who was shaking one fist in the manner of a curbstone orator. His hair was thick and bushy and on his upper lip was a truly pugnacious mustache.

"Doesn't look much like Sanborn to me," I commented.

"Maybe not. But it is."

"I'd like to know what makes you think so."

"Well, you never saw him except in swell clothes and without a mustache, and neither did I, for that. An' we didn't see him 'cept he had his hair all slicked. But it's him."

"Elucidate."

"Huh? Well, his eyes an' nose an' expression are the same. See, he's evidently makin' a speech here. Get that hand stuck up to bang something home? An' see that glarey look? An' that angle to the way his head's held? That was the way he looked yesterday when he turned around after runnin' Boots down. Kind of fanatic like."

"That may be. But even so, this man was killed in a strike riot."

"Maybe he was an' maybe he wasn't. Restaurants call fried flounder filly of sole, but it's flounder. They's more'n one man in this world who's travelin' under a different name. Maybe he was gettin' too far mixed up in his line o' work an' thought it was a nice time to have David Schonbrun die. They ain't a lot o' difference in them names, like Harlow says. But we can make sure."

"How?"

"Chap in Boston used to cook along of me on the *Amanda S.* He works in the room on the *Clarion* where they keep back numbers an' things. We'll telegraph him to see if he can find out about it for us an' if it was a sure thing about his gettin' killed. It ought to of been in a paper. An' I guess I'll send a wire to another feller I know who works in City Hall somewhere, in New York. He can find out about the family of this David Schonbrun an' if there was such a feller anyway. We might as well do the thing up brown while we're at it."

He got out of the car. "Don't look so amazed-like, Miss Prue. I picked up a lot of friends in my time as 'd be glad to do me a favor. An' then I'll telegraph a man I used to work for out West who's the head or something of a Labor Fed'ration an' see if he knows anything about this Schonbrun bein' a labor agitator. That's what he sounds like to have been to me. May none of these do any good at all, but you might's well have all the strings you can to your bow."

As he entered the office he chuckled. "This here is goin' to cost Bill a good sum in the line of telegrams, I shouldn't wonder, but I cal'late if I make 'em strong enough we may get answers to-day."

At the moment I wondered why Bill had taken the trouble to add me to his staff of detectives. Asey Mayo had thought so far ahead of me that I was a little exhausted trying to keep up with him. His casual mention of friends scattered over the country surprised me. In the town Asey had no one outside of Bill Porter with whom he was intimate. He was a friendly soul, but his friendliness was impersonal and unconcerned. Yet this corps of acquaintances he unearthed in such an offhand manner was undoubtedly genuine.

When Asey came back his face wore a troubled look.

"Have you any word from Jimmy?"

"Yup. He can't come down. Says the Porter company is on the verge of mergin' with some other concern an' that he couldn't get away if Bill himself was killed. He says for me to go to work an' spend as much money as I want gettin' the thing all straightened out. Says to wire this man whose name he gave me in New York an' ask if Sanborn had any enemies in the city. So I did. Well, I guess we got to carry on by ourselves. Now let's go to the hotel an' see if they's any trace of Kurth there anywhere."

But at the hotel we found no John Kurth in the register.

I described him as well as I could and the clerk pondered. "No, there wasn't any one here who looked like that. Did he come from New York?"

"He might have," I said guardedly.

"Well, why don't you go over to that little camping place next to Bangs' house, where he has the cottages to let overnight? There was a man here yesterday that looked like the one you want who came here for a room, but we were full up and didn't have any room. I told him the Nobscusset or the Belmont up the Cape would be the best place for him to go, but he wanted to stay right here."

"Kind of car did he drive?" Asey asked.

"I couldn't tell you. I know it was a big seven-passenger touring car, black and shiny, and new looking. I think it had a New York plate. And it had red wire wheels."

"We'll go see. Say, if he does come back you needn't tell him we was lookin' for him." Asey placed a crisp five-dollar bill on the desk.

The clerk was more gracious. "Of course not, Mr. Mayo. Certainly not. If he does, I shall let you know, I suppose? Yes? Thank you, Mr. Mayo."

"All alike," Asey murmured as we left. "All alike. We'll go see Lonzo Bangs."

We found Mr. Bangs cleaning out a hen coop. The work seemed to hold his attention, and he did not take kindly to an interruption. I wondered if Asey would try to bribe him with money; I knew we wouldn't get our information for nothing, yet I also knew the effect of a tip on the average independent Cape Codder. But Asey had his own tactics.

"Mornin', Lonzo."

"Um," said Mr. Bangs.

"Know that rowboat of Bill's, that Cape Cod dory he had built last year up to Wareham?"

"Um." Mr. Bangs dusted off a glass egg.

"Wanted to buy it a month or two ago, didn't you?"

"Uh-huh."

"Didn't, though."

"Nuh-uh." Mr. Bangs shook his head.

"Price too high? Bill wanted fifteen dollars, 'f I recall rightly."

Mr. Bangs made an assenting sound.

"Shouldn't wonder if you could have it for twelve."

"Ten," said Mr. Bangs, coming to life suddenly.

"Eleven?"

"Ten," decisively.

"Highway rob'ry, that's what it is. You can have it for ten, though. F.O.B. our wharf."

Mr. Bangs looked hurt. "Won't deliver?"

"Course not," said Asey. "You're gettin' a bargain. Wouldn't sell 'f it wasn't we was gettin' a new one."

"Throw in oars an' rowlocks?"

"Yup, as long's you pay cartin'."

Abruptly Mr. Bangs laid down his broom and departed into the house. He came out with a roll of one-dollar bills secured by an elastic band; he gave it to Asey, who gravely counted twice through the notes.

"Right?"

"All right, Lonzo."

"I'll get th' boat t-morrer. Now, just what was it you was after me for, anyhows, Asey?"

"You know Miss Whitsby?"

"Shouldn't wonder." He bobbed his head in my direction.

"Well, she's lookin' for a man, a friend of her cousin, Mr. Handy, an' her cousin told her he was bein' in Wellfleet this week-end. We asked at the hotel an' the feller at the desk said he might be up to one of your cottages."

"Didn't know as you was related to the Handys," said Mr. Bangs interestedly.

"Remote connection," I told him hastily. "Fifth cousins."

Mr. Bangs considered. "What was his name?"

"That," said Asey ingeniously, "is just where the shoe pinches. Her cousin wrote her the name in a letter an' he writes so bad she can't make it out. She thinks it's Kurth."

"Nobody here of that name."

"He's tall and real dark," Asey went on, "an' he drives a black Cadillac touring car with red wire wheels."

"Packard," said Mr. Bangs.

"Then he's here?" I asked, concealing my pleasure.

"He was. Went down to Provincetown a while ago to see a feller an' wasn't comin' back, so he said. But his name wasn't what you said it was. 'Twas Brown. William K. Brown of New York City. Y'know," added Lonzo expansively, "'f I'd 'a' know he was a friend of any Handy or a rel'tive of yours, I'd 'a' given him a better cottage. The one he had ain't got such a good bed."

"I'm sure," I said, "that he enjoyed it."

"Well, 'f he comes back, I'll do better by him."

"Say," Asey remarked as we were leaving, "You didn't happen to notice the number of his car, did you?"

"No, I didn't. But m'wife might of. She's a real noticin' woman, Mariar is."

He returned to the business of hen-coop cleaning and Asey,

with a weary little sigh, knocked on the kitchen door of the Bangs house.

"If it's the fruit man," a shrill voice announced, "I don't want nothin'. The A and P has good enough without payin' all kinds of fancy prices. Why, Asey Mayo, is that you? An' Miss Whitsby? Well, now, you just come right in."

We went into the hot kitchen.

"I'm doin' my bakin', but I ain't got one thing t' offer you. I'm real ashamed not to be more forehanded." She waited expectantly.

Asey repeated the story of my mythical cousin and his equally mythical friend. Did she remember the number of Mr. Brown's car?

"'Twas a real funny number. 'Twas 11-C-11. I ast him if that *C* meant 'twas New York City, an' he said he didn't know what the letter meant, but he guessed so."

"That's real good you remembered. An' now, Miss Whitsby, didn't you want some tickets for the Temp'rance Union garden party? You're sellin' 'em ain't you, Mis' Bangs?"

She beamed. "I should say I am, an' if I haven't been havin' a time with them, what with those summer folks, the gull pond ones, takin' half of 'em, an' then returnin' all six because they decided to go somewheres else that day."

"I'll take the six," I said, reaching for my purse.

Mrs. Bangs accepted the three dollars with voluminous thanks. Asey and I departed precipitately.

"Whew," said Asey as we rolled along, "y'know, sometimes I kind of wonder myself at these here Cape Codders. Here's your three dollars, Miss Prue. Bill Porter is payin' all the incidental expenses like that."

I noticed that they were three of the dollar bills from Mr. Bangs' payment on the boat.

"Now we go to the phone office," said Asey, "an' strew a little bait for our fish, as the feller said."

He chose the booth farthest away from the operator and manipulated a nickel.

"Pretty fine inventions, tel'phone an' tel'graph. Yup. Gimme the state police headquarters. Yup."

"What are you going to do?" I demanded.

He closed one eye and opened it slowly.

"State police headquarters?" he asked in Jimmy Porter's precise clipped tones. "I should like to report a stolen car. . . . Yes. A stolen car. A Packard seven passenger touring car, New York license plate number 11-C-11. . . . Color? Black with red wire wheels. . . . No, the man will show you a license and registration in the name of John Kurth. But it's forged. . . . Who am I? This is Mr. Mayo speaking for Miss Dorothy Cram of New York City. . . . Yes, it was Miss Cram's car. Now, if any of your men sight that car, I wish you'd have them bring it to Miss Prudence Whitsby's cottage at Wellfleet. . . . Oh, yes! There's a reward."

He hung up the receiver and grinned at me.

"Asey, you down-right liar! What will happen if the state police find out you're humbugging them like this? There'll be an awful to-do."

"The reward'll take care of that. It'll save us the trouble of findin' this Mister Kurth. We ain't got the time to go gallivantin' all over the Cape for him. We got bigger an' better things to do. Ain't no use for Mahomet t' go t' the mountain if the mountain'll be made t' travel. An' them state police love pickin' people up. Relieves the monot'ny."

"How did you learn to imitate Jimmy like that? You had that Harvard-Oxford accent down pat."

"I made so much fun of him that I got to learn to do it pretty well. It's apt to get results you wouldn't get otherwise. You know, I liked Jimmy better when he talked like every one else."

We climbed into the car. "I feel like Doctor Watson," I remarked.

"That dumb feller Sherlock Holmes was always totin' around? Poof! I saw him at the movies. You ain't no Doctor Watson, Miss Prue. Four eyes is better than two any day of the week, an' I don't wear no glasses. Nope, no reason for you to be feelin' that way, just because I been doin' things you ain't no need to know about much. Before long I may be the one doin' the Watson act myself. Say, when we get to Mis' Howe's will you do the talkin'? She don't care for me on account of my not bein' a Methodist."

"Neither am I, Asey."

"No," he said laconically, "you ain't. But you're you."

Mrs. Howe met us at the gate of her tiny white house which looked like something from an Easter card. Here she had her dining-room where summer visitors too lazy to cook for themselves were fed.

"I'm real glad to see you two; I just know you're going to tell me a lot I don't know about this Sanborn business. Isn't that a pretty car? Is it Bill Porter's? I suspected as much. And isn't it a pity about poor Mr. Sanborn? Just as nice a man as you'd want to meet anywhere, though he was a moody one if you ask me."

"Moody?" I asked. It rarely took over one word to elicit a hundred and one from Mrs. Howe.

"Well, maybe I ought not to say exactly moody, now that the poor man's dead, but I'll tell you just what I mean. He came here yesterday to see what time meals was and he was late for dinner. Didn't seem to mind that much, said he'd just's soon go to the hotel as not. I told him he'd ought to bring a napkin ring, and he joked about it just as nice and friendly as you please. I explained to him that all mealers wasn't so honest, and I'd had so many napkin rings taken away that I had to have people bring their own or else have paper napkins and I never could abide the scrimpy things."

"And quite right, too," I told her. "But what was there moody about him?"

"Well, just as he was driving off he said what did he miss for dinner? And I told him what we had. We had nice clam chowder with crackers in it, and my own piccalilli that I make myself—we always have that on Fridays. Then we had flounders fried in deep fat, you know, rolled in egg and fried real brown, and green peas out of my own garden and hot biscuits. That is, baking powder biscuits, not riz ones. And he laughed and said he was real sorry to have missed all that."

"I don't blame him one iota," I said. "It's a meal any one would be sorry to miss."

She simpered at me, and Asey gave me an admiring glance.

"And," she went on, "I told him, I said, now we had a real nice sardine salad, too. And what do you suppose that man did?"

"What?" I asked. I was beginning to feel like the silent partner of a vaudeville act, the one who says who and where and why and what for the other member to make his points.

"Well, he shuddered like he was going to have a stroke, he did. It was just the way Mr. Howe was taken. And then he stared at me with the ugliest expression I ever saw and his eyes were sort of glarey."

I looked at Asey. He had used the same expression.

"And he just sort of stared. Then he let out a scream and said 'Sardines! Don't you ever give me any sardines or let me see them, either.'

"And just as I was going to ask him if he wanted a soda mint or something, he drove that car of his away from this very gate like I'd said it was a salad full of poison. Now, wouldn't you call that being moody, even if a man is dead?" she concluded triumphantly.

"I certainly should call it moody." I forced a touch of indignation into my voice. "A grown man acting like that about sardines."

"I know it," said Mrs. Howe. "I know it. I thought at the time, 'Well, Mr. Sanborn, you may be a book-writer and that may be some excuse for your being different than other people, but I don't think that there's any use or even any excuse for a writer acting that way about a few sardines.'" Abruptly she changed her tone. "Do you think Bill Porter killed him?"

"No; what time did Sanborn leave?" Asey asked shortly.

"He left here a little after two. We have dinner at twelve sharp and I know the tables was all cleared off and the dishes washed when he came. Yes, it must have been about a quarter past two."

I remembered that Sanborn had run over Boots at two-thirty; then he probably had gone to the hotel for luncheon and returned just before he came to the cottage for the hammer. It all hung together. I wondered if there were any possible connection between his anger and the sardines and the murder. But Sanborn had been care-free enough when we had last seen him. If he had been in a temper he had made a quick recovery.

Asey nodded thoughtfully. "Now, Mrs. Howe, you're real good to tell us about Mr. Sanborn. But you won't mention it to any one else, will you? I mean about the sardines and all?"

"Of course not, not if you don't think it would be right for me to do it. But now, I've been thinking. What should I do with that money he left here for his first week's board? Had I better keep it and turn it over to his heirs if they come down here, do you think?"

I smothered a laugh. "No, you keep it, Mrs. Howe. It's been paid you, and it's yours."

She smiled. "Well, now, that makes me feel better. It was the first thing I thought of when the Nobles' milk boy told me this morning, and I've had it on my mind ever since. And I'll see that no one knows anything about the way he acted over those sardines."

We both thanked her, and Asey rolled the car away just in time to offset a stream of questions.

He looked at me quizzically. "Gets cur'user an' cur'user, don't it? Sanborn acts like a crazy man when he hears the word sardines mentioned an' don't want to see the things in front of him. An' he goes away in such a dummed hurry that he runs over Boots to get off his mad streak. An' yet there's a sardine tin beside him when he's found killed. They was a strange sort of thing to find anyway, an' it was even stranger when they turned out to be Bill's sardines, or at least the tin as belonged to 'em. But now that this turns up, I calls it plumb downright a-mazin'."

"But what does it all mean, Asey? I wish we knew."

"If wishes was hosses, beggars'd ride. I wisht I knew, too, Miss Prudence-Doctor Watson-Sherlock Holmes. I wisht I could say 'twas ele-menteery, but I can't do nothin' of the kind."

He leaned over and pressed a button on the ornate dash-board. The arrogant notes of the musical horn floated out over the meadows.

"I can't do nothin' of the kind," he repeated. "But you an' me is goin' to find out by Monday mornin'."

Chapter Seven
DOT BECOMES INVOLVED

"Would you mind not sayin' anything to 'em at the cottage about what we found out?" Asey asked as we sped along the beach road.

"Why on earth shouldn't we?"

"Well, just for the princ'ple of the thing. You see, there ain't really nothin' to tell 'em anyways, an' it's kind of easier to make people tell things when they ain't got no idee why they're bein' asked."

"But you don't for a minute suppose that any one at the cottage did it, do you?"

"Can't tell. Might have. You got to admit nobody had a better location for it."

He hopped out, let down the rope barrier, drove the car through and then set it up again.

Betsey jumped on the running-board before we drew up in front of the house.

"Tell us everything. What have you found out?"

"Nothin' much. We seen Bill. He's all right. An' we sent some telegrams."

"Sea clam! Come on and tell us."

"Don't tease," I said, lying valiantly. "Asey has told you everything there is to tell. Bill is quite cheery, and he seems to be bearing up very well."

We seated ourselves on the porch.

"Now," said Asey, "I'd like to ask you some questions if you all don't mind. Miss Prue, where was you durin' the time the doc said this happened?"

I related the story of Olga and the silverware.

"Then you was out in the kitchen all the time?"

"Yes."

Asey's eyes twinkled. "I ain't askin' you because I suspect you any but just for general information. You're a sleuth same as me an' I'll exempt you from any more. Now," he turned to Betsey, "where was you from four-thirty to five-fifteen?"

"Up-town, getting lemons."

"An' you was gone all that time? Stuff an' nonsense, Betsey. It oughtn't to take you fifteen minutes even in that pin-box of yours to go up an' get a couple of lemons. What'd you do in the rest of the time?"

"Well, I didn't really start till about twenty minutes of five because I remember asking Snoodles the time. From half past four till then I was out here with Dot."

"That don't help. You still got twenty minutes or so to explain."

"Well, I spent about five minutes picking out lemons that were sufficiently succulent for Snoodles' taste. The other ten or fifteen I spent talking to Mike Sullivan about the baseball team."

"Can you remember what he said?"

"Clearly. He said the new pitcher was good but that he

'wasn't getting no s'pot.' And if you really want to check up, you can go over to the cabin and ask him. He's staying there now that Simpkins has taken the body away, seeing that no one ransacks the cabin."

"How can I tell you ain't primed him?"

Betsey grinned. "Prime Slough Sullivan's son who thinks he's greater than Philo Vance already just because he is Sullivan's son? You ought to know better, Asey. Go get him to tell you."

Asey ambled off and returned in a few minutes.

"He's willin' to swear he talked with you for anyways ten or twelve minutes. O.K., Betsey. That's so much for the time. Did they watch you when you went off?"

"Yes; they saw me meet Bill at the foot of the lane."

"An' they knew where you was before that. What about comin' home? Couldn't you have snuck over to the cabin then?"

"She couldn't have," Dot informed him. "I heard her car and she came in directly after. That's why I talked about the sardines. I always kid her about them. Remember, Miss Prudence?"

I nodded. Dot seemed still to be suffering from her shock of the previous night. She did not accent her words in her usual affected fashion, and her entire stock of adjectives was apparently forgotten. She was, all in all, unusually subdued, and her color was ghastly.

"Well, I cal'late that lets you out, Betsey. Have any particular reason for killin' him?"

"Don't be a dolt. I've known him only since Wednesday."

"No need to go bitin' my head off, Betsey. You don't need to know a person a lifetime to find out a reason for killin' him. But I'll give you a clean slate. Now, Mrs. Manton, where was you?"

"I went up-stairs a few seconds after Mr. Sanborn came, earlier in the afternoon. I stayed up in my room till I heard Betsey come back from town."

"What were you doin' all the while?"

"I was lying on my bed resting. Part of the time I read. The rest of the time I dozed."

"Didn't come down-stairs or go out all of that time?"

"Don't you think they would have heard me if I had?" She smiled wryly. "People usually hear me long before they see me coming."

We all smiled. I remembered how she had clumped down those stairs a dozen times since she had arrived.

"An' you didn't know nothin' of Sanborn before you came down here?"

"Of course I had heard of him and knew that he wrote books. I never read one of them, though, till Prudence gave me one yesterday. That was what I read while I was up in my room."

"Well, Mrs. Manton, I guess we can let you down out of the witness stand, too. Now, Dot, you was on the porch?"

"Yes."

"All the time?"

"Most of it." The usually loquacious Dot was exceedingly taciturn.

"Did you go off it, or go indoors?"

"Both."

"S'pose you tell us." Asey suggested.

"Oh, I went inside to get a cigarette and then I strolled down by the tennis courts."

"Be a little mite more exact, will you? Why'd you go down there?" Asey's tone was sharper than it had been.

"To see a boat."

"I should think you could of seen a boat better from up here on the hill."

"Well," Dot hesitated. "It had gone behind the wharf."

"When did you go inside?"

"It was a minute or so after Miss Prudence left. I had seen the boat and I wanted the glasses. While I was inside I lighted a cigarette and hunted for the binoculars."

"How long was you in there?"

"About five minutes."

"Now, Bill must have left about then, 'cause he told the sheriff he wasn't in the cabin more'n six or seven minutes. Didn't you see him go?"

"No. He must have left when I was inside."

"So you picked up the glasses and went walkin' down to the tennis courts to see a boat? An' you didn't even notice Bill's car goin' up the beach road?"

"That's right. I went down the lane. I didn't notice the car. I was too intent on looking at the boat."

"Kind of a boat was it?" Asey asked quickly.

"Why—why, it was just a fishing boat."

"Schooner? Smack? How many masts did it have? What was her name? You'd ought to seen that if you had even bird glasses."

"I don't know what kind of boat it was," Dot answered sullenly. "I'm not acquainted with such things. It might have had one mast or a dozen. And I'm sure I don't know the name."

"Dot," said Asey softly, "the first time you come down here I taught you about riggin' myself. I got you so's you could tell the dif'rence between a brig an' a brigantine an' a barque an' a barkentine. An' you got as good eyesight as any one I know of."

Dot said nothing.

"Was there any one on the tennis courts when you was down there, Dot?"

"Yes, there were some people playing tennis."

"Remember who they was or how many of 'em?"

"No. I don't know who they were or how many."

Asey considered. "Humpf. You knew Sanborn before you come here, didn't you?"

She nodded.

"How long'd you known him?"

Dot banged her fist with such force on the table that a vase of flowers bounced to the floor. "Miss Prudence, this man has absolutely no right to ask me any questions, and I'm not going to stand for any more of his probing. Just because I happen to have been the only person who can't account for those forty minutes to a split second I'm not going to have you or any one else suspect that I committed the murder." She ignored the expressions of surprise on all our faces. "And I can't see one single reason why I should tell you about Dale Sanborn. He's dead. I didn't kill him. And that's all you need to know."

She scratched a match furiously and lighted a cigarette. No one said anything. I watched her hand tremble as she held up the match to blow it out.

"Very well." Asey was calm, matter-of-fact. "Can I talk to that maid of yours, Miss Prue? If Dot wants to keep all she knows to herself there ain't no reason I can see for me makin' myself objectionable. If it don't make no difference to her that Bill Porter's arrested for a crime he never did while the one who did the murder sits twiddlin' his thumbs, it's all right with me. Nice friendly at'tude, Dot. But you ain't the first person in hist'ry to backslide. It's been done before. Popular in Bible days, 'twas, an' the custom's lingered."

During his speech Dot's face had grown whiter, but she made no attempt to speak. I don't think five people have ever been much more uncomfortable.

At last Betsey spoke nervously. "I'll go get Olga."

"No," said Dot wearily. "Don't bother. Asey has made his point." She crushed out her cigarette and lighted another. "I knew Dale Sanborn very well. As a matter of fact I was engaged to marry him though we hadn't intended to announce it till this fall."

All of us felt that Dot and Dale knew each other better than their behavior indicated, but we had scarcely anticipated this announcement.

"We'd had a sort of quarrel," Dot continued. "I had been going out with other men, and he didn't like it. I hadn't heard from him for two or three weeks before I came down. Some one said he was out on Long Island. That's why I jumped at the chance to come and visit you. I wanted to show him that I could go away and leave him and not pay any attention to what he did at all."

"You didn't know he was here?" Asey asked.

"No. But when I found he was and apparently so intimate with all of you, of course I wasn't going to be such a nitwit as to tell you anything about us. Much less after the way he acted when you remarked yesterday afternoon that you understood I knew him."

I remembered his answer to that comment of mine, a listless "Dot did," with a noticeable accent on the "did."

"So," Dot went on, "I thought I'd just sit tight and say nothing. I thought everything would come out all right. It always had before."

"You'd had fights with him before?" Asey questioned.

"Oh, yes. Lots of times. Dale wasn't the easiest man in the

world to get along with. They weren't serious quarrels ever. Just misunderstandings. They always got themselves settled."

She blew her nose violently. She seemed to be telling us the truth about her relationship with Sanborn even though her answers to Asey's previous questions were as full of holes as the proverbial Swiss cheese. I recalled how red her face had been when she came out into the kitchen. Of course she might have been overheated from her trip up and down the hill. On the other hand, she might have run over to the cabin and back, too. I was more than dubious about Dot.

"Does, I mean, did Sanborn like sardines?" Asey asked abruptly. "Did you ever see him eat any?"

She looked at him wonderingly. "No. That is, I don't think so. I'm sure of it. Once I ordered hors d'ouevres in a restaurant——" she stopped and looked inquiringly at Asey.

"Yup, I know what they are. Go on."

"And I asked the waiter what they had in particular because I'm fond of salmon paste on caviarettes. The waiter said they had anchovy paste, and he started to say something about sardines when Dale stopped him short and said I'd have fruit cup. I didn't want fruit cup and I said so. But Dale waved the waiter off and said that when he took me to dinner I'd have what he ordered. He didn't talk like that as a rule, but he acted as though he were awfully peeved about something, so I didn't press the point."

"Didn't tell you why he didn't want you to have sardines, did he?"

"No."

"Possibly," Emma suggested, putting down her knitting for the first time that day, "he didn't like sardines. Don't you think that most people have some one thing they loathe in the line of food? What I mean is, there's nothing so very mysterious about all this business, is there? I know that I grow quite ill at the sight of a prune. I hate to see people eat them. I had to eat a plate of stewed prunes every morning of my childhood till I finally rebelled at the age of ten. Your particular hatred is baked beans, isn't it, Prudence?"

"Not baked beans. Lima beans." I made a face.

"And Betsey?"

"Onions in any form. Ugh!"

"Dot?"

"Cashew-nuts. I can't stand them."

"I see what you're drivin' at, Mrs. Manton. I don't care overmuch for cavi-air myself."

We all looked at Asey, but he chose to take our astonishment for friendly interest.

"I was in Rooshia once an' a chap there he give me a big hunk o' that black bread all spread over with it. I thought it was some sort of jam. Hoped it was ras'bry." A look of disgust came over his face. "Smelled more like old T wharf than anything I ever smelt since. And taste! Say, I remember that taste yet. Bill he buys the stuff an' eats it, but when he does, I just have to get outside an' wait till the air's got freshed up. But, Dot, don't you know nothin' about his family?"

"Not a single thing, Asey."

"You was goin' to marry a man you didn't know nothing about, not even where he come from?"

"He was born in New York. He told me his family were all dead."

"These girls to-day!" Asey commented disparagingly. "Now when I was a boy a woman who married a man, she knew all about him. Knew about his family an' who they was an' how long they'd had money if they had it, an' where they got it from an' what his great-grandmother's maiden name was. I don't mean anything about you, Dot, an' you know I'm real sorry that anything happened to a feller you liked. But just the samey." He shook his head.

"He said almost nothing about his family, but I got the impression that they had all died when he was young, and had left him rather badly off. I always had the idea, though he never said as much, that he had got to the place he was in to-day more or less by his own efforts."

"I see." Asey mused. "Then you just went into the living-room an' down to the tennis courts an' back again an' then out into the kitchen? Can't add anything to that?"

"No." Dot bit her under lip till it looked as though it were going to bleed.

"An' you didn't know nothin' about all this till you heard about it from Miss Prue?"

"No. And I fainted when she told me. It was a silly thing to do and I never have before. But it was a shock."

I thought to myself that it might have been a shock or it might have been good acting. Of our household, Dot had more reason to kill Sanborn than Betsey or Emma. He was her fiancé; they had had a quarrel which she declared to be innocent enough, but it had been sufficient to make him leave her temporarily. She had found him apparently preparing to spend the rest of the summer in fairly close proximity to another undeniably attractive girl; she had at least fifteen minutes about the time Sanborn was killed for which she could not or would not produce an alibi. I scribbled on a chart I had been making of how and where we all had spent Friday afternoon.

"Now, Dot, honest Injun, I don't like to keep on askin' you

things like you was on a witness stand, but can't you remember anything at all about Sanborn that might help us any? Little things like what subjects he got int'rested in an' things like that?"

Dot thought a minute. "He was crazy about music and some of the modern painters like Tursky and Weiner and all that crowd who do those appalling portraits of Russian peasants and all such things." She pointed to the magazine section of an old Sunday paper. "That had one of Lenin in it that he was awfully keen about. And he liked that play, I can't remember the name, about prisons and capital punishment and all. And he used to get perfectly wrathy about those Italians every one seemed to get so excited about in Boston."

There was a gleam in Asey's eyes that said more plainly than words, "This sounds more like Schonbrun than Sanborn."

Aloud he said, "Did he, now? Did he ever get int'rested in ec'nomics?"

"It's funny that you should ask me that. He was. He talked on the subject as though he knew a lot about such things, though I am no judge. A man in New York heard him talking at a party one night about some strike in a coal mine down South, and he wanted Dale to write an article about it or speak at some forum. But Dale wouldn't. He refused flatly. He said he wasn't any authority on the subject and that it was just one of his hobbies."

"Did he ever wear a mustache, Dot?"

"Not since I've known him. I said once that I wished men would go in for beards and mustaches and things like that now-a-days, and I asked him why he didn't. He just laughed and said he'd worn a mustache when he was in college but it made him look like an I. W. W."

"What an insane thing to ask," Betsey remarked. "Really, Asey, you ought to ask about his enemies and evil-wishers and all that, not tonsorial details."

Asey grinned. "You can't tell from where you sit how the picture's goin' to look. I s'pose these things sound kind of crazy to you, but it ain't so crazy as you think. Kind of important, 'twas. But maybe you could remember some one who didn't like him so much, Dot."

"Oh, no one in particular that I know about. There was some one who started a silly lawsuit against him, but it was only something about his books, he told me. I can't think that that would throw any light on this. I don't know who it was, even, but I know some lawyer friend of his got it stopped. As far as I know, he didn't have any enemies at all."

Olga appeared in the doorway. "Luncheon, Miss Whitsby."

Asey rose from his chair with alacrity. "'F he didn't have no enemies, he was one lucky man. We'll 'journ for a while, Dot. It's a case of 'Down with your head an' up with your paws an' thank the good Lord for the use o' your jaws,' as the feller said."

Chapter Eight
SULLIVAN FINDS THE HAMMER

AFTER LUNCHEON Asey resumed his questioning.

"Can't you think of anything else about Sanborn that sort of stood out in your mind?"

Dot shook her head. "I'm afraid I can't, though it may sound absurd. About all I can think of is that I've lost him for good." She laughed cynically. "I suppose I ought to be used to losing things by this time. I lost my family even earlier than Betsey did, and my guardian lost all my money playing the stock-market. And I even lost my thesis the week before graduation. Remember that, Bets? I lost every bet I ever made in my life. If I called heads, it came tails. If I played red, black turned up." Dot stopped short. "I say, that does remind me of something."

"What?"

"Why, it was that time I lost, flipping a coin with Ellie Batten to see who'd stay at the settlement house one night when the matron was sick."

We waited expectantly.

"It was about a year and a half ago, in February. I lost as usual and spent the night there. About two o'clock in the morning the watchman routed me out of bed. The night cop on the beat had brought in an old woman he'd found who had collapsed just outside. They wanted to see if I could do anything before the ambulance came.

"She was pretty far gone when I saw her. Exposure and cold and just plain starvation. I did all I could, but it didn't help much. You could see that she had been perfectly stunning once, even though her clothes were nearly rags. I looked in her handbag to see if I could find out who she was. There was an address somewhere on First Avenue and a newspaper clipping. I looked at it and on one side was a picture of Dale. It's strange that you should have asked me about a mustache because I remember one had been drawn on his upper lip. Exaggerated, you know, the way a child would do it. On the other side there was a notice of a sale somewhere and I concluded that that was why she had cut the thing out, and that the picture and the mustache were just sort of accidental."

"Ever mention it to Sanborn?"

"No, I never did. One of the girls at the settlement got the D.T.'s that night and it drove the whole thing out of my mind. I don't suppose I've thought of it since. Probably it doesn't mean much. Lots of people of that class carry pictures around with them, like Lindbergh and the Prince of Wales and the president and all. It's a queer thing for me to remember, and it probably won't be of any use at all."

"You can't never tell," said Asey. "Tell me, did you ever find out what the woman's name was?"

"No. You see I went down there at night very seldom. That was an exception. I don't think I've stayed there over twice since.

I never saw the policeman again and the night watchman left for good soon after. There wasn't any way of finding out even if I'd remembered to ask."

"I see." He looked at her keenly. "Dot, did you kill Sanborn?"

Her cigarette slipped from her fingers, but her voice was perfectly steady as she looked him straight in the eye and answered, "No, I didn't."

Asey nodded as though he believed her, which was a whole lot more than I did.

"Now, can I talk to that hired girl of yours?"

Betsey summoned Olga, who came out wiping her hands on a dish towel. I have not described Olga before because there is very little to describe. She has been in the family for thirty years, and I know I could not get along without her. She is neither tall nor short, dark nor fair, ugly nor beautiful. She is as careful about her words as she is about the silver. When Betsey and Bill were children they used to have a game called "Getting Olga to Talk." It appealed to them because of their very complete lack of success. It was Bill's opinion that she fined herself for every unnecessary word. Olga was parsimonious to an extreme.

"Didn't see any one around the cabin yesterday outside of Mr. Sanborn, did you?"

"No." Her tone indicated that her job was not looking out of windows.

"What time did you leave here?"

"Three-thirty."

"Where'd you go?"

"I walk to village. Meet Inga. Buy things."

"Inga's Mrs. Stockton's girl?"

"Yah."

"When'd you come home?"

"We go to movies. Walk home. Miss Betsey bring me from part way back when she gets doctor. We have ice-cream after show."

"See any one, any stranger, when you walked up? You take a short-cut down the hill, don't you?" He waved his hand toward the left of the lane.

"Yah. I do. Yah, I meet a man."

"Kind of a man?"

"Bum."

"What'd you mean, bum? Tramp?"

"Yah."

"Speak to him?"

"No. He spoke to me."

Asey sighed. "Pullin' teeth is easier than gettin' information out of you. Now, what did he say?"

"He ask me where Mr. Sanborn live."

Asey smiled at her. "Now we're gettin' places. Did you tell him?"

"I don't like his looks, all dirty. I think he might come here to steal. He calls me sister. So I says——"

We hung on her words.

"I say, 'No spik English.'"

"Oh, m' God!" said Asey weakly, after we had managed to quell a young gale of laughter. "N'en what?"

"I go up-town."

"An' he did too?"

"He come on this way."

"What'd he look like?"

"Kind of tall, dark. Dark eyes. Dark skin. He talked fresh. He was a bum, all dirty. He looked like he walked a long ways."

John Kurth was tall and dark.

"Had you ever seen him before?" I asked.

She wrinkled her forehead. "I ask myself yesterday. I think he is like some one I know, but I am not knowing who. It is like he looks like some one I know than like I remember him."

"Come again, Olga, we folks don't get you."

"I do not think I see this man before, but some one who looks like him I have seen."

"Hm. I see. Didn't remind you of any one ever you saw visitin' Miss Prue?"

"No." She shook her head decisively.

"You seem pretty sure," Asey remarked.

"If he visits Miss Whitsby, he would give me money when he go and I remember next time I see him."

"That's fair enough," said Asey. "You didn't see him again? An' he kept right on headed this way?"

"Yah."

"And what time d'you meet him?"

"Mabye fifteen minutes after I leave here."

"That'd make it about three-forty-five, an' if he came to the cabin he probably got there about four or a little after. An' that would connect him with this mess puddin'."

"But," Betsey asked, "wouldn't we have seen him if he had come?"

"Why? Like Olga, he perhaps cut across the fields. Or he might have skirted the hill an' come up to the cabin from the pine trees in the back."

"I never thought of that. Then any number of people might have come to the cabin then, and no one would know whether they had or not?"

"That's right, Betsey. They could. Now, Olga, thank you for

answerin' those questions. You think real hard if you can't re-member who that tramp of yours looked like."

Olga nodded and went back to her dishes.

"Now, Miss Prue, I see you been jottin' down some times. Let's see your shee-dule an' see if it'll straighten things out any for us."

I passed over my paper. He read it out loud with comments.

" '2:00 Dot, Emma and I eat lunch.

3:00 We leave the table.

3:15 Dale borrows the hammer.

3:16 Emma goes up-stairs.

3:20-3:22 Dale leaves and is not seen again until I find his body in the cabin.

3:30 Olga leaves for town.

3:45 She meets her hobo.

4:00 The hobo might have been in the cabin.

4:30 I go out into the kitchen.

4:40 Betsey goes up-town for lemons.

4:41 Bill comes up the hill in Lucinda and goes into the cabin.

4:40-5:15 is the time the doctor says Sanborn was killed.

4:48 Dot says she went into the house for a cigarette and the binoculars.

4:48 Dot says she came out, walked to the tennis courts and back up to the cottage.'

"Bill wasn't in the cottage over six or seven minutes," Asey added, "so we'll put in that he left at 4:47 or so."

He read on:

" '5:00 I notice Bill's car is gone.

5:05 Dot comes out into the kitchen.

5:10 Betsey comes back. Her delay explained.

5:12 Emma comes down-stairs. We hear her come downstairs.' "

Asey omitted my note to the effect that Emma couldn't have gone over to the cabin and back in the time that Dot was out, ten or twelve minutes, without us hearing her, or without tall hustling on her part. He also did not read my comment that Dot had been on her college track team and seemed very red and breathless when she had come out into the kitchen.

" '5:12-7:00 We eat supper.

7:10 Dot and Betsey go to the movies. Betsey doesn't look into the garage where she would have found Sanborn's car, but takes it for granted that he is away at dinner.

7:00-10:00 Emma and I play cards while they are away.

10:10 The girls come home.

10:20 I find the body in the cabin.' "

"That seems to cover everything," said Asey. "We know he left Mrs. Howe's at two-fifteen an' he ran over Boots at two-thirty. Then he probably went an' got his lunch an' come home here. Them hotel lunches ain't nothing luxurious an' he could of done that easy in the time he had. An' from the time you saw him go off with the hammer till the doc says he was killed, we know Bill went there, an' maybe this bum of Olga's an' maybe a half-dozen others besides."

He put the paper carefully in the pocket of his flannel shirt.

"I'd give a cookie to know what killed him," he said. "Course it might of been the handle of the hammer that Slough is so upset over, because as he says, some one must of had some reason in takin' it away. You just don't take hammers off as a general thing. An' I don't think it's likely that any one borrowed it from him, 'cause they ain't no one around to do any borrowin' an' they'd 'a' come to you anyhows. 'Pears to me as if Slough's billy would of done this murder fine."

"Well," I said, "I'd give a pound of Huntley and Palmer's best cookies to know how that sardine tin got there and who took it and who left it and where the one who left it found it."

Asey smiled. "An' I'd just as soon know why that blanket was tucked over him, too. That's something Slough asked Bill, why'd he tuck him up so cozy after killin' him."

"The murderers I've read about," I remarked, "have not usually been so considerate."

"It occurs to me," said Emma, "that that sardine tin is the most peculiar thing. If Sanborn wouldn't let Dot have sardines, is it likely that he would let any one else eat them in his cabin? It doesn't seem that way to me. Isn't it possible that Sanborn might have been out while the eating was taking place?"

"Might be," Asey said.

"Down on the beach he mentioned something about finding an Indian arrow head around the cottage, and he said he was going arrow hunting in the afternoon. Maybe he was doing that and some one, possibly the man Olga saw, hit him over the head and then lugged him into the cabin."

"But with what motive?" I objected. "I mean, why didn't he leave him where he killed him? And why should a tramp kill him? The doctor said that there was no indication that anything had been taken. And the man came here before Bill did and Sanborn was alive then. And think of the job of carrying a man of Sanborn's size from the woods to the cabin. He's not big, but it would be a dead weight. And the body was lying just as it was struck down."

"Well, you don't know exactly what time the strange man came, even if he came at all. I was only citing a possibility."

"I wonder who the hobo was?" Betsey asked.

Asey smiled and rose. "We could sit here an' wonder till doomsday or the day after an' we wouldn't probably get any-wheres at all. Miss Prue, I guess you an' me is goin' to recon-noiter 'n wander some more. We'd ought to got some answers to our telegrams by now."

"Can't we come too?" Betsey asked.

"Nope. You an' Dot can amuse yourself by tryin' to find if the people who was playin' tennis saw Dot at the time she says she was down by the court. They keep a list of whoever all plays there an' it oughtn't to be hard to find out. But don't you go to cook up any stories. I can smell a cooked-up story as quick's I can smell fried fish. An' if you tell me any lies I'll put you both in the stocks longside of Bill."

"What about me?" Emma asked.

"Well, Mrs. Manton, we ain't goin' to take you neither, an' I hope you won't feel like you was bein' neglected. Fact is, I want some one here more'n that brass door-knob out in the kitchen. She may be a darn good cook but she ain't much of a hand at conversation. I want for you to sit here on the porch an' wait for a couple o' visitors that might come."

"Who?" demanded Betsey.

"No one in partic'lar. But if a cop an' another man should come here, you entertain 'em till we get back. Don't answer 'em no questions, an' if they ask you for any one by name, pretend you're dumb or something. Stick 'em on flypaper if you want, but keep 'em here till we get back."

"We will," said Betsey.

"No, you won't. You'll be huntin' Dot's alibi, an' I don't need to tell you that she needs one bad."

"Horatius," said Emma cheerfully, "could be no more effective than I shall be. I'll hold your guests if I have to pretend to have a fit."

"Well, you won't need to go swimmin' in no Tiber, anyhow. Ready, Miss Prue? By golly, look!"

He pointed toward our cordon of rope. Fifteen or twenty people were gazing at us curiously.

"I expected them," said Asey, "but I didn't think they'd be comin' in droves already. Betsey, you an' Dot had better go in your car. You don't want to walk through 'em. If they say anything, don't you talk to 'em or it'll be in the papers. Don't answer 'em any questions or tell 'em any lies. Run along."

They ran along. Asey and I followed more leisurely.

The onlookers were not at all reticent as Asey stopped to let down the rope. They commented freely and impartially on our appearance and wondered all too audibly whether "the gent was the lady's husband or just her shover." Asey gave no evidence of hearing these remarks, and I did my best to be as indifferent as he was. But I knew that my ears burned.

I asked him what he thought about Dot and he shook his head. "I don't think she done it, Miss Prue, but there's something funny about it. They's a nigger in the wood-pile. I guess she's not tellin' us everything she knows, not by a long shot. But if we just let her think everything's all right she may forget herself an' tell us accidental an' of her own accord. Don't pay to watch a pot an' blow on the coals to make 'em hot, as the feller said. Fishes don't bite when you sing 'em cajolin' songs. But we'll find out about Dot, though."

"And do you think the hobo was Kurth?"

"Don't know. It might be an' it mightn't. We can tell more about that when the cops bring us Kurth."

He stopped at the town landing, and called to one of the loafers by the dock. "Hey, do you know what time Nickerson's boat come in yesterday?"

The man addressed deliberated. "'Bout five o'clock."

"Thanks." Asey drove on. "Well, there was a boat, Miss Prue, comin' in about that time. She'd 'a' seen it on the hill about twenty minutes 'r a quarter to five. There's that much truth in what she says. She couldn't of seen it much before an' she wouldn't of seen it later than ten of five, 'cause it would of gone around the point then. Now, we'll go to Stocktons an' check up on your cook."

"What motive," I asked, "would Kurth have for killing Sanborn? I've been wondering."

"Couldn't say. Did you ever stop to think, Miss Prue, if all the people in this world who had enemies killed 'em off? Did you ever think how much compet'tion they'd be to kill some folks, or how many'd they be left? Not many, I guess. Don't you rec'lect the story of the feller who sent telegrams to all the 'portant men of a town once sayin', 'all is discovered; flee at once,' an' the next day every last one of 'em had beaten it? Well, they's a lot of different kinds of men in this world, each's got his own ideas about prohibition an' war an' so on, an' not every one of 'em is any Abe Lincoln or George Washin'ton. They all got reasons for killin' people, an' when one's found dead, there's usually a reason. They ain't many whys without becauses. You don't kill people 'cause you don't like the color of their hair or the cut of their weskit. Usually it's because they done you dirt. You can dig up the dirt, if you know where to dig. Reminds me, I didn't ask you if you done this, yet."

"I most certainly and assuredly did not kill Dale Sanborn," I said with dignity.

He grinned. "Hope I can bank on that. Well, I'll go an' ask this countrywoman of Olga's about yesterday, an' I sure hope she's not as ret'cent as her girl friend."

He disappeared inside the Stocktons' kitchen and came back inside of five minutes. "She says she bane met Olga at ten minutes of four, walked up the road to meet her, an' they bane together till after ten last night. Yah, she bane. That clears that up. Besides, I don't think Olga'd do any killin'. She'd be too afraid that some one would ask her questions afterward."

He started the car, then stopped.

"Won't need to call on Sullivan. Here he comes. Hi, Slough. What's news?"

Sullivan smiled broadly. "Just the man I wanted to see, Asey. Just the man. I wanted to save you a lot of time and trouble, you an' Miss Whitsby. I was on my way up to the cottage to find you.'

"What's up?" Asey asked amiably. "They made you head of the Pinkertons or something?"

"Not yet," returned Sullivan. "But they may at that. You and Miss Whitsby don't need to do any more detectin', you don't. You can go right home and save your wind to cool your coffee."

"How come, Slough?"

"You remember that hammer, the one Sanborn borrowed, the one we couldn't find, the one the doc said might of done the murder?"

"I heard tell of it," said Asey cautiously.

"Well, I found it."

"Where?" I demanded.

"In a place where it'll take a lot more explainin' than what's been done already to make it seem of no account."

He drew a cigar from his pocket and lighted it with more care than was absolutely necessary.

"Reporter's cigar?" Asey queried. "Smells like it. Well, where'd you find this here hammer? In some one's fish net out in the harbor?"

"No," said Sullivan, enjoying himself hugely, "I happened to find it in Bill Porter's car. To be real exact, in the back of the seat of that old car he drives around."

Asey and I looked at each other as Augustus might have looked when some one told him the sad news of his legions lost in Teutoberg Forest.

Chapter Nine
THE DOCTOR AND HIS NOTES

SULLIVAN ENJOYED our discomfiture.

"That's just where I found it. I was taking a look around his house a little while ago and I wandered around the garage. Saw that old car of his and just for fun I gave it the onceover. And right down behind the front seat, there was the old hammer."

"Might have been one belongin' to the car," Asey offered.

"Yes. Might of. But it's a nice spandy brand-new old hammer, and it's got written on the handle of it in pencil 'Whitsby, their hammer.' " He passed the article in question to me. "Recognize this, Miss Whitsby?"

It was undeniably the one we had given Sanborn. I remembered that after we had used it while putting up our curtains at the cottage, Betsey had sat down and scrawled that inscription on it. Betsey can not resist the lure of a freshly sharpened pencil. She ruins telephone pads by covering them with meaningless hieroglyphics while she talks on the phone, and she is always scribbling comments on the margins of her books.

I admitted that the hammer was ours.

"Well, that's that."

"Show it to Bill?" Asey asked.

"Yes. And you should hear what he said."

"What'd he say? Didn't he give any explanation?"

"Sure he gave me an explanation. Captain Kinney of the old second precinct he used to get a big kick out of the reasons people gave him when they had things there wasn't any need for them to have. That is, unless they were connected with a crime. I got a kick out of Bill's reasons too. He claims he was mad as hops when he went to see Sanborn. He says this hammer was on the table when he went into the cabin, and he just picked it up and fiddled with it the way you fiddle with a paper-knife or a pair of scissors or something like that. Then he says he got even madder when Sanborn says he didn't run over the dog, and he left the place more mad than when he went in."

Sullivan laughed uproariously. "He claims he was so hot 'n' bothered that most likely he just toted it off with him and forgot that he'd done any such thing. Now, ain't that a likely bit to give for an explanation? Seems as if I could hear already what the district attorney'd do to a thing like that. Picked it up and took it away, he says, so mad he don't know what he was doing, an' then he goes and forgets all about it. Seems to me if he could do that, he could of hit Sanborn over the head with it and forgot about it just as easy. Likely, ain't it, Asey? Real likely."

"Might be at that, Slough. Truth's stranger than fiction. You think he killed Sanborn with it?"

"Yes. And even if he didn't, it'll take more explaining than Bill Porter's done already to make it seem like anything so common as takin' away a pencil or something. Well, so long. I got to go to see some reporters. They're waiting for an interview."

"Let 'em take a picture of you with your uniform on," Asey suggested.

"They already have. Three times. Thank you just the same. And don't you think you two better save gasoline an' leave detectin' to those that make it a business?"

"Dunno," Asey drawled, "'s we will."

Sullivan shrugged his shoulders. "As you like, as you like."

"How's Bill?" I asked.

"Oh, him? He's all right. In fact, he's better. When I found that hammer, I knew I'd got all I wanted, so I took him out of the pillory." His tone was benign.

"Guess you found public opinion wasn't goin' t' stand for nothin' like that, didn't you?" Asey asked.

"Public opinion didn't have one thing to do with it," Sullivan retorted, though his face was rather more than pink. "I was only keepin' him there till he got ready to confess, anyhow. An' if he hadn't rubbed me the wrong way, he wouldn't of been here at all."

"Hmmm," said Asey, nodding. "I see. Well, what you done with him now, huh?"

Sullivan chewed the end of his cigar. "Well, there wasn't no place that was really safe for a killer like him, an' at first I didn't know what to do with him. But some one suggested a box-car we just unloaded with stuff for the store; it's got a good lock, and there's plenty air even if there ain't no light to speak of. Besides, it'll kind of give him a taste of the solitary confinement that'll be coming to him soon."

Asey and I looked at each other in consternation.

"Well, so long," Sullivan waved a hand airily, took back the hammer and, with a flourish, drove away.

"Well," I said.

"Hell, that's what you mean." Asey bit off a new hunk of tobacco. "Plain honest hell with fringes. What'd that fool boy do a thing like that for, I ask you? Whyn't he take his dummed ole sardine tin if he had to take something, 'stead of that hammer? An' why didn't he have the wit to say he didn't know nothing about it when Slough asked him? That's what I want to know. What's he got to go an' tell the truth for? Course," he added, "I raised him to tell the truth, but I thought I'd taught him how to discrim'nate about tellin' it too. They's some things it don't pay to be too truthful about, an' when you got yourself arrested for murder you ought to know it. I don't see's how a little white fib would 'a' hurt his soul mor'n this hammer's goin' to hurt him. Them Porters has got a streak of crazy blood in 'em, an' that's a fact."

"What'll we do now?"

"Do? What in time can we do? We can go on just like we was goin' on an' try to find out who done it. We can go on an' hope the sky falls an' lets down a shower o' skylarks an' rainbows an' the feller that killed Sanborn. We'll just forget all about that crazy fool boy. We'll go after our telegrams an' see if any one of them guys got anything for us."

"But what about Bill and the box-car?" I asked.

Asey shrugged his shoulders. "I guess it ain't so public as the pil'ry, but that's about all the better it is. I bet that boy thinks twice 'fore he eats another sardine, that's what I bet."

I nodded heavily. That was one way of looking at the situation.

At the station we found two messages waiting for us. "Nothin' like sendin' answers prepaid if you want to get real quick service," Asey remarked. "One's from the feller in Boston

an' the other's from that one in New York. This is what the first
one says:

"Man called David Schonbrun reported killed strike riot
1923 Lowell Mass. Riddled body found and identified by au-
thorities not confirmed as Schonbrun by friends or family. Half
a dozen others killed at same time believed foreign agitators
and never identified at all. Perfectly possible body of Schonbrun
might have been one of other workers and not man himself if
that answers your question. Can find no record of him afterward. Had been jailed Lowell two months previous contempt
of court. Description you give fits but Schonbrun had mustache.
Will send you all else available if and when found.

"Humpf. That kind of fits in with what Harlow said," Asey
mused. "There's a good chance, then, that he wasn't killed at
all. When was his first book out, do you happen to know, Miss
Prue?"

"Somewhere around 1924-25, I believe. I heard Betsey mention something about it."

"Well, that all fits together. I guess we'll take it for granted,
Miss Prue, that this Sanborn was Schonbrun. Maybe he ain't
after all, but it seems to me to be a nice beginnin' for us to make.
An' well begun's half done, as the feller said. Now, this other's
from the City Hall feller.

"Four David Schonbruns in records," he read. "One born Ba-
varia 1874 glue manufacturer no family. One born here 1899
died 1901 with parents in epidemic scarlet fever. One born
Stuttgart 1876 married Marie Stravinoff, children David born
city May 19, 1897, Abraham born Brooklyn October 2, 1899,
father killed blast in Jersey City plant 1903, mother died February, 1929, starvation——"

"Asey," I interrupted breathlessly, "remember Dot's story? Do you suppose the woman she told us about, the one in the settlement house, was Sanborn's mother?"

"Kind of looks that way." He continued reading:

"No record death David Schonbrun or brother. If last is one you want let me know as remember connection with strike last year and will send details."

"That couldn't be Dale, could it? Do you suppose that the brother is a labor agitator too?"

"Guess so. So the brother is followin' in the footsteps of David an' he's active enough to get his name known. I wonder if he had a hunch his brother wasn't dead an' was tryin' to find out by goin' after him that way?"

"Maybe. But Asey, if there was the other brother, why did the mother starve to death? She had him to look out for her."

"Maybe an' maybe not. Well, I'll send to these fellers an' tell them to send me all they know. N'en we'll have only that chap out West an' Jimmy's friend to hear from."

"Asey, do you suppose that that hobo was the brother, and not Kurth? That might account for Olga's thinking he looked like some one she had seen but not some one she actually remembered."

Asey slapped his hand on the wheel. "Them Portygees have a sayin' that woman's council may not be a lot, but the one who scorns it ain't none the wiser. By gum, Miss Prue, I never thought of that. We'll go right up this minute an' ask her."

But Mrs. Howe, standing in front of her house, called for us to stop as we drove by.

She bustled out to the car. "Well, I'm real glad you stopped this time. I waved and called when you went by before till folks thought I was crazy, but you two was so busy with each other that you didn't have no eyes for me at all. It's about those sardines."

"What about 'em?" Asey asked.

"Well, you know you told me not to mention a thing about them to any one and I didn't. But it's no use, and I might as well."

"What d'you mean?"

"Well, at dinner-time to-day a real pleasant lady stopped here in her car and asked if she could have lunch. She'd seen the sign out here about meals, I guess. And she was so nice I told her of course she could eat here, even though it was pretty late and most of my mealers had finished. She was real grateful and said if she was putting me out any, she'd be glad to pay extra. Well, while she was eating, she talked about this Sanborn business and said what an awful thing it was, which it is, and I think it's a blot on the town, just as I was saying to Addie Phillips——"

"Get back to the mutton," said Asey.

"Mutton? Oh, you mean the sardines. I said to her, I said, 'Looks to me like Bill Porter done it, though why he went and left a sardine tin behind him, I for one don't see.'

"And she looked real queer at me and said that she knew Dale Sanborn real well, and she knew it for a fact that he didn't ever eat sardines nor even want to have them around him or even mentioned."

"Hadn't she read about it in the papers?" I asked.

"That's what I told her, that it was in all the papers, and she said that she hadn't seen to-day's paper, she'd just heard of it while she was getting gasoline somewheres. Anyways, I thought

I'd let you know that there wasn't any use in keeping that about the sardines a secret, because other people seem to know about it too."

"Did she talk as though she knew him well, or did she tell you her name?" Asey demanded.

"Well, I suppose she knew him well or she wouldn't know what he liked to eat. She didn't say what her name was, but there was a little pin made out of some shiny stones that looked like diamonds on her dress and the initials as far as I could make them out were M. W. or maybe W. M."

"Maida Waring," I whispered to Asey. "Mrs. Howe, didn't you ask her name?"

"Well, I did the best's I could without seeming rude. I called her Miss Um and Mrs. Um, but she wouldn't supply her name. And I suggested she write in my visitors' book,—I always keep one because it's kind of nice to see who people are and where they hail from,—but she said she was in too much of a hurry. She said she had to see some one in Provincetown and she hadn't time."

"Mrs. Howe, you've been real helpful," Asey said. "But if that woman turns up again will you see we find out about it before she has time to leave?"

Mrs. Howe promised that she would, and we departed for home.

"This situation," I said, "begins to get itself complicated. If that was Maida Waring and she was going to see some one in Provincetown and if the mysterious William K. Brown, or Kurth, if it is Kurth, was also going to Provincetown——"

"It'd look," Asey finished for me, "like they was something afoot, bein' as how there's bees where's honey. Funny they both wanted to come an' see you, and funnier still they just came, willy-nilly. Well, things is pickin' up."

As we turned up the lane we met Betsey and Dot in the small car.

"Where you goin' now?" Asey asked.

"We finally found the people who were playing tennis on the courts yesterday. That is, we found out who they were and it seems that they're staying at the hotel, so we're going to see if we can find them there. Shall we keep on if they're not? I mean, shall we put on the bloodhound act?"

"Yup," said Asey, "if you don't have to track too far."

"And what are you two closed-mouth ones in your swell barouche going to do?"

"These bloodhounds," said Asey with a grin, "are havin' a rest period for the time bein'. All work an' no play's contrary to the constitution. Git along in your thimble, you two, an' don't let no sea-gull take you for a minnow an' carry you away."

Up at the house we found Emma, placidly counting stitches.

"Horatius has absolutely nothing to report. Your only visitors have been the paper boy and an itinerant fruit-seller who had an argument with Olga about ripe bananas. And young Mr. Sullivan has taken a leaf out of your book and put barbed wire about the cabin. People were simply milling about it. Oh, yes, and I can't find two stitches I lost yesterday. I'm going to sue that awful railroad. And, dear me, I quite forgot the most important thing."

"What's that?"

"Olga made a discovery. Not two seconds ago."

"What did she discover?"

"She found the hammer we lent Sanborn," Emma announced triumphantly. "Wasn't that clever of her?"

"What?" Asey and I looked at each other in astonishment.

"Yes, here it is." She passed over a hammer, an exact replica of the one Sullivan had showed us.

"Where in blazes did she find it?"

"Out by the garbage hole, beyond the beach grass."

There are no garbage collectors on Cape Cod and one either burns refuse and hopes that the wind may not turn, or else one buries it in a hole. We used the latter method and our hole was about a hundred feet beyond the kitchen.

I took the hammer from Asey and looked at it closely. On the handle was a smear that had been made by a hand rubbing pencil marks. The writing, if it had been writing, was quite obliterated.

"What are you two looking so puzzled about? It is the hammer, isn't it?"

"I don't know. You see, Sullivan has already found a hammer beneath the front seat of Bill's car, and I have identified it and said it was the one we gave Sanborn."

Emma opened her eyes wide. "That's interesting, interesting indeed! But couldn't this still be the one?"

"It could," I said. "It's new and the smear of pencil mark is about the same size as the other. And Betsey always uses soft pencils. I think I remember wondering this afternoon why the writing on the hammer Sullivan showed us wasn't more smudged. But I have identified it as ours and I don't suppose for one moment that it would do any good to show this to Sullivan, do you, Asey?"

"I don't cal'late 'twould. He'd just sit an' laugh an' say it was our idea to get Bill off. We can't prove this is the one you loaned him, an' you already said the other was the one anyway."

"What'll we do about it?"

"Nothin', I guess, right now. I reckon we'll ask Olga about that tramp."

He called her out from the kitchen.

"You been thinkin' about who that stranger was you met yesterday?"

She nodded.

"Remembered who he looked like yet?"

Again she nodded.

"Well, for the love of heaven," exclaimed Asey, "who in time was he like anyway?"

"He looks like Mr. Sanborn," said Olga complacently.

Asey got up and solemnly, to Olga's surprise and our astonishment, kissed her on both cheeks.

"An'," he added, "if I had a medal I'd give it to you too. But since I ain't got any, I'll give you this." He peeled five bills from his wallet. "Information like that comes to five dollars the word. It's worth more, but times is hard."

Olga looked inquiringly at me. I told her to take it.

She nodded her thanks. "I'll guess I know you again," she said coyly to Asey and went back to her work.

"I guess," Asey stood up, "that now we'll begin to investigate this bum situation in a big way. Mrs. Manton, we'll leave you to play the waitin' game for us again."

"I delight in it," she informed him. "It's the only game I ever played that took absolutely no effort whatsoever. You don't even have to sharpen pencils. But you'd better wait a minute. There's some one letting down the barrier for a car."

I looked, hoping it would be the touring car with Kurth,

but it was only the doctor. In white linen knickerbockers and a tweed coat he looked more like a banker at the nineteenth hole than a country practitioner.

"Good afternoon," he greeted us. "I've been doing my duty as medical examiner and I have some things I want to ask you about."

"You still stick to your idea of a bash on the skull?" Asey asked.

"A blow at the base of the skull," the doctor corrected. "Yes. I was sure last night and now I'm positive. There's no trace of poison and no trace of heart failure or any other natural cause." He launched into a lengthy description. "And I hear that Sullivan has found the hammer and that things look bad for Bill."

"He has found one hammer," I said, "but we have found its twin brother." I showed him what Olga had brought to light.

"Amazing," said the doctor. "Now all you need is to find another sardine tin and prove that Bill was just picking daisies and didn't go near the cottage at all. Did you see the crowd up-town?"

"Not since this morning. How is Bill getting along?—I hear he is now in a box-car."

"That's right. And people are crowding around it as though it were a six-headed calf. They've had to call in a dozen extra to handle traffic, and as each of the dozen has his own individual thoughts on the direction of traffic, it's pretty messy. But every one's quiet and peaceful. I think they're stunned more than anything else. And the place is simply running over with reporters. They were on your trail, Miss Whitsby, but I told them you were ill and under my care and not to be disturbed. I think I said I'd have them arrested if they bothered you. Possibly that will stop them from annoying you."

"You're very kind," I said.

"I hope it will work. They've taken Slough and Bill from every angle and I had to chase a couple out of my office before I came up here. They were very determined."

"You had something you wanted to ask us about," I reminded him.

"Oh, yes. Well, I went through all Sanborn's more personal belongings of course, and there were two or three things I wanted to find out about. I showed them to Sullivan, but he doesn't think that they're at all important. I'm not so sure, however. For instance, there's this note. It's postmarked Boston and written this last Wednesday. I'll read it to you. It came to him at the hotel special delivery Wednesday night."

" 'Dear Sanborn, [he read]

" 'I understand that you are staying at the Cape for a time, and I should like to see you at the earliest possible opportunity.

" 'If I can, I shall visit friends in the town this week-end, but at all events, I shall be down and I would advise you to see me. I have got pretty well into the truth of the matter and you are going to clear up the rest if I have to resort to force.' "

The doctor cleared his throat. "That's signed by a man who calls himself John Kurth. Now, Miss Whitsby, I have a bad memory for faces, but I never forget a name. Didn't you have a friend named Kurth who visited you and Betsey here once or twice when you had that cottage down by the hollow? And wasn't he a classmate of Jimmy Porter?"

I looked at Asey who nodded ever so slightly behind the doctor's back.

"Yes," I said, "I knew him, and he visited us."

"I thought so," said the doctor with some satisfaction. "I am rarely mistaken in the matter of names."

"You an' Addison Sims of Seattle," Asey murmured.

"And," the doctor went on, "then there is another note, post-marked Boston and dated Wednesday, also sent special delivery and delivered to Sanborn Wednesday evening. Its contents are so much like the other that there's no need for reading it. But this one is from a woman who wants him to clear something up, and it's signed Maida Waring. Now, as I remember, wasn't that the name of the woman Kurth married?"

I told him that it was.

The doctor beamed. "I thought so. Yes, I thought I was right. Now, do you think that there might be anything in those notes? Connected with the murder, of course."

"I dunno," Asey drawled. "They didn't come here, did they, Miss Prue?"

I took my cue. "No, they didn't. And I don't think they came down, or I should have seen them. I'm sure they would have come to call. I don't think either of them is in town." All that, I reflected, was true as far as it went.

"That's too bad," said Reynolds. "I mean, I thought that it might lead to something. Probably it's only a business note, though of course it is a coincidence. And why doesn't Kurth's wife sign herself with her full name?"

"Lucy Stone league," I extemporized.

"A lot of nonsense, too," said the doctor. "Why a woman shouldn't take her husband's name is beyond me. These new notions are the limit, if you ask me. Take the declining birth-rate."

"I know," I said hurriedly. "It's disgraceful."

"It's going to be the ruin of this country," said the doctor. "That's just what it's going to be. I'm writing an article about it now for the *Medical Journal*."

We listened to a discussion on the declining birth-rate. Asey at last had the courage to damn the flow of words.

"Something else you had to ask about, Doc?"

"Oh, yes. I'd quite forgotten," He fumbled in his pocket and brought out an engagement ring. "It's this. I happened to look inside. It says D.S. to D.C. Aren't those the initials of Betsey's friend?"

Chapter Ten
THE OTHER HAMMER IS EXPLAINED

For a minute we were silent. "Yes," I said hollowly, "they are."

"But I don't see as it means much," Asey reflected. "She said she'd known him in New York, but you know, Doc, there's probably a thousand people in that place with the same initials."

Emma opened her mouth as though to speak but Asey gave her a barely perceptible wink and she resumed her knitting.

"You don't put any stock in these notes and in the ring, then?" the doctor asked. He was a little ruffled.

"Truthfully," I told him, "I don't think that they are of much value. Now, if John and Maida had come to town, I feel sure I should have seen them. For all we know, Sanborn might have written them and told them what they wanted to know without their coming down. And as for those initials, I happen to know that Dot's middle name is Stevens and she nearly always signs herself D.S.C., because they used to tease her about it at school and call her the district street cleaner. I'm sure we would have known had she been engaged to Sanborn, and if that were her ring, there would be the other initial."

"Well, if you feel that way about it, I suppose that it's all right." Doctor Reynolds rose. "But I'd heard that you and Asey were riding around trying to find things out, and believing with you that Bill is innocent, I thought some of these might help you out. If you don't want help, you don't, I suppose."

I assured him such was not the case, served iced tea, and by the time he left he was feeling less hurt.

"Why didn't you tell him about things?" Emma asked.

"I'd like to of," Asey answered, "but the whole town, including Slough Sullivan, would have known about it in ten minutes after he left here. Then they'd have come an' dragged Dot into it an' probably they'd dish all chance of our gettin' at Kurth ourselves."

"Dot didn't tell us that the engagement had been broken," I remarked. "According to her, this was just a temporary quarrel, and they were still engaged. I wonder when she gave him back his ring. Maybe he hadn't given it to her at all."

"It was worn," Asey said. "I noticed that, so I guess he had. What I wonder is, when did she give it to him, an' if she give it to him yesterday?"

He pulled out his time schedule. "'Cordin' to this she could have gone easy over to the cabin yesterday when she wants us to believe she was lookin' at that boat. Could she have given it to him before?"

"Not when he came over here yesterday afternoon. How about down on the beach?" I asked Emma.

"She couldn't have then. I was with them and so was Betsey, the whole time they were together. I'm positive she couldn't have had a chance. And she was with one or the other of us all the rest of the time, unless it was from the time Betsey left her to go to the store till you saw her in the kitchen."

"Hm. Was that true about her middle initial?"

"It used to be. She always made a great show of it. But I noticed that her luggage was marked D.C., and when I commented on it, she said she'd got tired of the *S* and had dropped it for the time being."

"Then I guess it was her ring all right, don't you?"

"I don't think that there's any doubt of it," I said.

"Cur'user an' cur'user. Well, we'll be off again. Don't loose no more stitches 'n you can help, Mrs. Manton."

We got once more into the car. Asey headed out of town, following the King's Highway that led up the Cape.

"Where are you going?" I asked.

"I'm goin' to make a call on ole man Rider over Eastham way," he said.

"The hermit?"

"Yup. Seems to me we ought to find out about this brother. I guess it must of been him that Olga saw all right, an' if he's a bum or on the road, ole man Rider'll know all about him. They ain't many tramps on the road he don't know about. They all stop at his place for food."

"But will he let you in or talk to you? I thought he wouldn't see any one, let alone indulge in conversation."

"'S a lot of talk. He wouldn't come out if you was to bang on his door from now to the end of next week. He don't like ladies one bit. An' he don't care much for all the trippers that come an' look at his house. What if a man does want to live in a place made out o' vines an' driftwood an' papered with newspapers? It's his business, ain't it? Ole man Rider's a nice ole man, for all his ec-centric'ty. I brought in his dory once after it broke the anchor rope in a storm, an' I been clammin' an' fishin' with him lots o' times. He's real amiable if you don't go to 'noy him."

"I thought he turned that brute of a dog after every one who came near him."

"He don't. I been there an' seen him feed three or four fellers off the road at a time. I don't know why he does it, but he does. If he ain't heard of this Schonbrun, then he ain't on Cape Cod an' we're barkin' up the wrong tree. That ole feller he knows a lot more'n people give him credit for knowin'. There's some say he don't know's the Civil War's over, but I bet he knows more right now about this business than we do."

"I wonder why he doesn't like women," I said.

Asey cocked his head and looked at me. "Crossed in love, I cal'late. Or his wife run away with another man or he couldn't get the woman he loved. There's always somethin' like that back of a queer seemin' man."

"Why, Asey! I do believe you're romantic. I had an idea you didn't hold with love and things like that?"

"Ain't I had to listen to Bill Porter," Asey demanded, "moon on about that niece of yours for long's I can remember? Say, Miss Prue, they used to be a cap'n on a coastin' schooner I cooked for once. He stood six feet three an' a half in his stockin' feet an' he could lick any man in a rough an' tumble this side o' Hades. He went an' fell in love with a girl that waited on table in a dirty caffey in Galveston, Texas, 'bout as big as a pint o' cider, she was. An' she could make that man more miser'ble than you'd believe. I've seen him set down an' cry after gettin' a letter from her. He finally took to drinkin' an' the last I ever heard of him he was sittin' on a park bench in New York City tryin' to work a drink out o' passers-by. An' him that was one of the best sailors on the coast. All on account of a thus-an'-so in Galveston he could snap in two with his little finger that didn't care a rap for him. No,

Miss Prue, I ain't bein' romantic attall. That's just something I know about for sure when a man's queer-like."

He turned the auto off in to a tiny path bordered with scrub pines. "I don't dast to take this ark of a car any farther in here than this, so I'll leave you here. Bill might get mad if I scratched up his pretty paint. You could listen to the radio if you wanted to. The little round button like an acorn turns it on."

I heard the crackling of bushes as he disappeared out of sight. I hunted for the radio control and turned it on. With much effort I finally got a Boston station. A newspaper broadcaster was telling of a murder on Cape Cod.

"Millionaire son of automobile pioneer kills famous scribe in cabin. Local sheriff is using a pillory for a jail on picturesque Cape Cod."

I switched the thing off. If heaven, I thought, ever caught me reading another murder mystery, it would have a perfect right to strike me dead with a thunder-bolt. I watched the little spot of bay I could see through the trees. In spite of all that had occurred the water was just as sparkling and blue as ever, the sky was just as perfect. I reflected that the Pilgrims must have found some compensation on those bleak stormy strands after all.

Asey came back.

"Did he know about anything? Has the brother come to his hut? What did you find out?"

"Did he know anything, Miss Prue? Like I said, he knows more about this than you an' me do. He says there was a man ate dinner here yesterday noon who might have been the one we want. He didn't want to tell me much, but I finally persuaded him. It was Bill's father, you know, who give him the land he has his hut on, an' when I pointed out how bad 'twas for Bill, he told me. 'Cordin' to him, this man as might be the brother was goin' to hitchhike down to Provincetown. 'Pears to me like every one we're after is goin' down to Provincetown. I should think that the place'd be full to over-flowin'. Anyways, Rider says it's dollars to doughnuts he'll be back this way to-night."

"When? How can we get hold of him?"

"Rider's goin' to pull a Paul Revere."

"What do you mean?"

"He's goin' to hang a lantern up in that tall elm tree way back of his hut. We can see it from your hill, an' then we'll go poppin' after him an' bring him back."

"It sounds all right, but how can you get him to come? And how will you make him stay?"

"Sufficient unto the day is the deed thereof, as the feller used to say. I don't know, but I'll see to it that we do an' he does. Now, we might's well's not go back."

In the village he stopped at the dry-goods store and came out with a parcel under one arm. "It's a part of the game," he said in response to my question. "Now, we'll see if we can find out anything more from Mister Western Onion."

He emerged from the telegraph office with a look of disgust on his face. "Feller Jimmy told me to wire has gone an' went t' Yurrop an' the feller I wired out West can't be found. An' Jimmy says he was goin' to fly down here tomorrow, but can't make it. You know, Jimmy he may be a crack business man an' all that, but he sure ain't a real Porter like Bill an' his pa an' grandpa. They never would of left me with Bill like this to get him out of a scrape all by myself, an' with you. I sh'd think Jimmy might of forgotten about his dummed old automobiles for once."

I agreed with him.

"All he thinks of," Asey went on, "is makin' money an' money an' still more money. Don't see what he's goin' to do with it all after he gets it made. What's the use of him havin' any more than he's got already? When you get as much as that they ain't nothin' left in the world you can't have if you want it, an' then, poof—you don't want it. Well, I s'pose it can't be helped."

The crowd outside the rope was still larger. Asey smiled as the necks craned in our direction. "I cal'late we'll have to put up barb wire soon."

Emma and Betsey were sitting on the porch. From their expression I gathered something had gone amiss.

"What's the matter?"

"Hell to pay," said Betsey briefly. "Listen to this. We went to the hotel and found those people who had been using the courts yesterday afternoon. They came back early from South Yarmouth—they'd been playing golf. I asked them if they remembered seeing any one come down the lane at about a quarter to five yesterday. They thought a while, then said no, they didn't remember seeing a soul. And then the woman up and announced that a girl had come out the front of the house and flitted around back of the garage. Said she remembered it because it caught her eye and spoiled her service at set point. Said the girl came dashing back a little bit later and was on the porch for a few seconds before she went in. She noticed that because it was just as they were leaving. What do you think of that?"

"Not so good," said Asey. "Not so dum good at all. What did Dot say to it?"

"She flew into a tantrum and has gone up-stairs. Presumably to recover. But it would seem to shoot her story full of holes like a target, wouldn't it?"

"It certainly would," I said. "But are they sure it was Dot?"

"They said she had a white dress on. Dot was wearing white."

"So was I," said Emma.

"But," Betsey grinned, "if you'll forgive my mentioning it, I don't think they'd have called you a girl or said that you flitted. Nor would you dash. You know perfectly well you don't dash."

"You have me there."

"It must of been Dot all right," said Asey. "So she got mad, did she?"

"Mad as a hatter. What'll we do?"

Asey shrugged his shoulders. "Don't know as we can do much of anything. If she was a man I'd beat the truth out of her, but bein' as how she ain't, I can't. We'll wait until she recovers an' see what a little polite questionin'll do."

"Hey, look!" Betsey exclaimed. "Here's a car with a man in it and a state cop."

We looked down to the fringe of the crowd, where a long black touring car and a motor-cycle policeman were replacing the rope.

"No doubt the visitors you expected," said Emma.

"Don't know as they are." Asey peered at them. "The feller at the wheel is a cop too. Please don't get surprised like, you two." He spoke to Emma and Betsey.

The officers walked up on the porch. "This where Miss Whitsby lives? We got the car reported as stolen from," he consulted a note-book, "from Miss Dorothy Cram of New York City."

Emma's eyes widened and a smile played about her lips. Betsey looked at us suspiciously.

"Come right over an' set down," Asey invited hospitably.

They sat.

"Where'd you find that car, now?" he asked pleasantly.

"On the Provincetown road. About six miles out of the town. It was deserted."

"Deserted?" Asey and I spoke in unison.

"Yes. We found it by the side of the road. We blew the horn and shouted around for a long time, but no one turned up and there weren't any cottages about where any one would be visiting. So we left one bike there, and drove this over. Now, is Miss Cram here to identify her car?"

"I'm sorry," said Asey apologetically, "but she's driven up the Cape to see if there was any news of it. But I'm sure that's the car, aren't you?" he appealed.

"I think so," and I hoped I wasn't as hot as I felt.

Emma spoke with assurance. "Undeniably that is the car." She looked admiringly at the policemen. "And I think that you found it in record time."

They beamed happily.

"Now, about the reward." Asey pulled out his wallet for at least the fortieth time that day. "You'd better leave the car right here an' go back to your patrol. If anything comes up about it, you let us know. That's the car all right, an' I'll bet Miss Cram'll be pretty glad to get it back. I'll see to it that she writes your cap'n an' tells him about how quick you was in findin' it."

They accepted the bills and conferred in an undertone. "Ordinarily," said the one who had done all the talking, "we shouldn't do this, but we'll take your word for this being Miss Cram's car and I guess everything will be all right."

"Thank you so much," I smiled.

They touched their caps. "Glad to be of service to you. It was luck that we noticed it."

As they started down the steps Asey added, "If the chap that took this should turn up an' make a fuss, not knowin' that we spotted him an' found out about things so soon, will you bring him up to us before you do anything about it?"

"Sure. He'll have a lot of explaining to do all around when we get him."

They chugged down the hill on the motor-cycle and streamed away up the beach road.

"Now, you horse thieves," said Emma, "what's the meaning of all this?"

Asey enlightened them about Kurth. Emma seemed surprised. "So there might have been something in the doctor's note, the one from Kurth to Sanborn, after all? That's odd. But what good is it for you to have his car? How do you expect to get him?"

"Oh," said Asey airily, "he'll report it as stolen an' then the cops'll bring him here. It'll save us a lot of gallopin' all over the map to get it done that way."

"I'm just about ten miles behind you on all this," Betsey said. "Why don't you two break down and tell Emma and me all?"

"Might as well, I reckon, if it don't go no farther. I mean Dot." In a few words he gave them the sum total of our day's discoveries.

"How perfectly thrilling," said Betsey. "Then you have Kurth and Maida and this hobo who might be the brother all sort of nibbling at the cheese, haven't you?"

"Yup, only I can't say as I think we got this Kurth's wife anywhere near a nibble even. But I got a feelin' she may turn up of her own accord."

"Listen," said Betsey suddenly. "About the second hammer. I think I can explain that."

"How?"

"Well, you know last week I took the corner of the garage door off, backing out?"

"With your cream jug?" asked Asey disgustedly. "Betsey, you'd ought to be 'rested for cruelty to animules."

"Yes. But listen while I tell you. The agent said we'd have to pay for things like that, so I went up and got Simpkins, the undertaker's brother that's a carpenter, and got him to patch it up. Well, it's one he left behind."

"How'd you know?"

"Because the next day I met him outside of the post office and he said he'd lost a hammer and had any of us seen it. Of course I said no. I don't go delving about for unknown hammers as a general thing. And don't you remember he sent us a bill next day and how we thought it was awfully large? Well, though it didn't occur to me at the time, don't you suppose he was charging us for the hammer? He probably thought we'd swiped it."

Asey nodded emphatically. "Then that's most likely it. What kind of a hammer was it?"

"He told me it was a brand-new hammer and he'd made a mark on it. That explains the smear."

"Fair enough," said Asey. "Well, that seems to be the one thing we really found out to-day, an' I can't see as how it's a great help toward freein' Bill even though it may kind of relieve our minds a little."

It was at this point that Olga announced dinner, and for the third meal that day Asey was our guest. Dot said she didn't want anything to eat, but she made a very thorough job of the full tray Olga took up to her.

After dinner we sat on the porch, Asey with the binoculars glued in the direction of the hermit's hut across the bay.

"Have you," Emma asked, "any real feeling about who the murderer is?"

I told her that at the moment, as far as I could see, Dot was more complicated than any one else in the affair, with the exception of Bill.

"I'm sure she didn't do it," Betsey stated. "She may have gone over there and been afraid to admit it, thinking that in our zeal to get Bill off, we might pick on her. But if she had done it, she's the sort who would lie well and brazen it out. She wouldn't go in for fainting and near hysteria and lies that a two-year-old child would be ashamed to make up."

"Wait up a bit," cried Asey excitedly. "I see a light. Yup. It's Rider's lantern all right. Come on, Miss Prue, grab a coat an' hustle. You an' me is goin' after the errant brother."

He went inside and switched the living-room lights off and on as a signal to the hermit. Betsey ran for my jacket and a lap-robe for it was getting chilly outside.

Asey brought the roadster around to the front door.

"If Kurth should turn up, tell him some cock-an'-bull tale about us playin' a joke on him an' wantin' him to make sure he'd visit us. Pay the cops some more if you have to, but keep that feller here till we get back."

The long roadster sped down the hill. Asey tooted the horn. "Well, I cal'late we'll get where we want to get, maybe perhaps, after all," he announced.

Chapter Eleven
AT THE HERMIT'S HUT

WE STOPPED as before on the pine bordered path. Asey untied the bundle he had bought at the dry-goods store. To my joy it proved to be a complete policeman's outfit, child's size, which I knew had been a part of the window display for at least fifteen years.

"What on earth," I asked him, "do you expect to do with that fancy dress? You're not going to put it on, are you? It wouldn't fit on your little finger."

"Nope," he returned composedly. "I ain't aimin' to put it on, but I needed the badge as goes with it. I thought it would make too much talk if I went an' asked for that alone, so I had to buy the whole dum thing. They thought I was plumb crazy. But badges don't grow on bushes like beach plumbs, an' I couldn't very well ask Sullivan for the loan of his."

"Do you suppose that Schonbrun, if it is he, is going to be taken in by that toy?"

"Dunno. I cal'late maybe he will. This'll shine an' flash easy as anything else will, an' I don't have to let him examine it close. Rider burns candles anyhow at night an' that'll help some."

"But will he come if you just show that to him?"

"Can't never tell the fear of the law a feller's got till you flash a badge on him. I remember readin' about a man who captured a train robber once out West just by drawin' his coat back a little an' lettin' his suspender catch gleam in the sun for a second. An' besides, a badge kind o' adds dignity. I ain't got no uniform like Slough," he chuckled, "but I got a badge an' I guess I look's much like a sheriff as he does, even if I ain't got a bay window. Shouldn't wonder if there wasn't a pistol in this outfit, too."

He thrust the badge into his pocket and started off.

"If I don't get to come back in a reasn'ble time, you take that car an' go after some one."

"Do you think that there's any danger?"

"Nope. But I don't want you to come philanderin' after me."

I wrapped the robe about me and proceeded to wait. I repeated Mr. Milton's poem about those also serving who only stood and waited. I counted to four hundred and ninety-four by thirteens. As I am very dull about figures that took up time beautifully.

A rabbit scampered through the underbrush. I caught a fleeting glimpse of his tail by the vague light of the dimmers Asey had left on. I turned on the radio, but the same newspaper broadcaster I had heard before was gloating over the discovery of a hammer in the possession of William Hendricks Porter, arrested for the murder of the famous novelist, Dale Sanborn. I wondered if every newspaper broadcaster was engaged in shouting unpleasant news about Bill to the world at large. I fished in the pocket of my jacket and found an aged candy bar. I ate the cheap conglomeration of nuts and dubious chocolate. I figured out the ingredients and their cost and the average profit per dozen bars. I was inventing a new candy to be called Infant Joy after the child in the poem who had no name but was three days old, when I heard Asey coming back. In another five minutes I should have been quite insane.

I switched on the headlights and the big searchlight. Behind Asey was another figure.

"This gent'man," said Asey with a touch of pride in his voice, "is Mister Abraham Schonbrun. Mister Schonbrun, this lady is Miss Whitsby."

The gentleman grunted. "Well, what of it? What you want with me out here, huh?"

"Want just to ask you some questions," said Asey.

"Look here, brother, you get me out here with some story about hearin' something to my advantage an' you say you're the sheriff of this hick burg. Snap into it. What's to my advantage; what you want to know?"

"You got a brother named David Schonbrun?"

"What's it to you?" He met Asey's gaze. "Well, supposin' I have, and what then?"

"Nothin', 'cept he's dead."

"Jeese, I know that. Been dead a long time." Schonbrun started back along the path but Asey caught hold of his arm.

"Not so fast, feller, not so fast. I mean your brother, not the guy that was shot to pieces in Lowell."

"What are you drivin' at?" Schonbrun asked sullenly. "I tell you my brother died a long time ago."

"Come, come," said Asey pleasantly. "You don't deny that Dale Sanborn was your brother, do you?"

Schonbrun looked at him quickly. "My brother's name was just like mine. I don't know anything about any guy named Sanborn. What'd you think, my family all had different names or something? We didn't, see?"

"Look here, you be reasn'ble. You know Dale Sanborn was your brother David Schonbrun. An' he got killed yesterday. An' he left some money, too. An' if you'd stop bein' nasty, who knows but what you might get some of it? Or ain't you needin' any cash these days?"

"Sanborn was my brother, an' he got bumped off yesterday?" The surprise in Schonbrun's voice was forced.

"Yup. An' now are you goin' to answer some questions an' get somethin' out of it, or ain't you?"

"Well, if he was my brother, I guess I ought to have what's left. When was he killed, huh?"

"Yesterday afternoon. Seems kind of unlikely you wouldn't know about it, what with the whole Cape buzzin' like a beehive on the subject. Where you been since you was here yesterday afternoon?"

Schonbrun hesitated.

"Where?"

"Went down to Provincetown and then came back."

"You passed through Wellfleet, then, didn't you? Didn't you see that feller in the pillory? Didn't you hear nothin' about the murder?"

"I saw the guy in the framework all right but I was on the tail of a truck an' I didn't have any one to ask about it. I didn't know about any killin'."

"Was that goin' down or comin' back?"

"That was goin' down. There wasn't any one there when I come back."

"An' you didn't hear nothing about this in Provincetown?"

"Naw."

"Didn't even read a paper?"

"Naw, I didn't hear anything about it."

"Mr. Schonbrun," I remarked to Asey, "does not appear to be particularly upset about the fate of his brother, if it was his brother."

"Aw Jeese," said Schonbrun, "that guy was my brother, if you're so crazy to know. Only I didn't know he was till lately. I thought he was dead."

"When'd you find it out?" Asey demanded.

"Oh, I don't know."

"I cal'late it was maybe when you saw him up-town in his car yesterday, wasn't it?"

He repeated his question more sharply. "Wasn't it?"

"You hicks is muley. Yes, if you got to have it."

"Speak to him?"

"No, I didn't. I wouldn't have known it was him if he hadn't been so mad at something. He used to have a mustache, too. He had swell clothes on when I seen him yesterday. Say, do you think I can rate his money?"

"See here," said Asey as though the thought had just occurred to him. "You can come back with us an' talk this over an' tell us a few things about your brother, an' I'll see you get everything. How's that?"

Schonbrun laughed. "Yeah. An' because I said I was his brother, you'd have me pinned up in a wooden neckband in two secs. Yeah. I'd be apt to come back with you. No, mister. You ask me what you got to ask me right here, see? An' then when the things is all settled, you hand me over the money then, see?"

"Reckon not," said Asey, shaking his head. "Can't do that."

Schonbrun considered. "Well, if I come with you, you won't get me mixed up in this?"

"Don't see as how we can anyhows, less'n you was mixed up

in it to begin with. Nope, we won't put you in the stocks, if that's what you mean. You don't seem much cut up about this. Wasn't you an' him friendly?"

"Friendly? Say, that's a hot one, that is. Say, listen, brother, I don't know whether the guy you caught done this or not, but listen, I'd like to shake him by the hand if he did. Who done this job done a good turn to me."

"We'll take your word for it," said Asey. "Well, are you goin' to come along an' see if you can get what's comin' to you? He had a car an' some money an' they's probably a lot more lyin' around in banks. Then there's things like a watch an' a gold cigarette case——"

"Platinum," said Schonbrun absently.

"What do you mean, platinum?" I asked.

"Oh," he faltered, "I don't know what made me say that I just guessed, that's all."

"Lookey here," demanded Asey, "you were to the cabin where he lived yesterday, weren't you?"

"Naw, I wasn't," Schonbrun snarled. "An' I ain't goin' to stand here an' get asked any more questions, neither. See? All you two want is to get me behind bars somewhere. That's all. All this talk about moncy is just a lot of hooey, an' I'm leavin' right now."

He turned swiftly but Asey grabbed him.

"Cal'late the little pitcher done went once too often to the well. Give yourself away, din' you?"

"I didn't give myself away, see? I ain't got nothin' to give myself away about."

As Asey turned to say something to me, Schonbrun twisted from his hold and freed himself. He tripped Asey neatly, and before the latter knew what was happening, Schonbrun was on top of him. Now Asey was physically strong enough, but he was no match for Schonbrun, younger by thirty-odd years.

Remembering how I had always loathed women who sat by in the moving pictures and never bothered themselves to lift a hand while the hero and the villain fought, I looked vainly around for a weapon. The zipper catch in the car pocket chose that moment to get itself stuck. I couldn't budge it. And in spite of my frantic efforts, the front seat of the car would not be pushed out. I had some half-formed notion in my mind of grabbing a wrench and banging Schonbrun over the head with it.

Schonbrun, in the meantime, had picked up a pine branch and was laying it forcefully over Asey's head and shoulders. With a sudden rash of intelligence I remembered the toy pistol. I rummaged, gripped it firmly in my hand. Walking up behind Schonbrun I stuck it in the small of his back. In a voice I did not recognize as my own I demanded, "Lay off that man! Hands up!"

To my everlasting joy he did not turn around.

"O. K., lady. O. K. O. K. Don't jab that thing into me."

"Get up," I commanded. "If you turn around I'll shoot. And I know how to handle this thing."

I held the gun against him and turned to look at Asey who was getting up from the ground with difficulty. His face and neck were bruised and bleeding, but he managed to smile. "Ain't so good as I used to be in a thing like that. You keep him there a second more, Miss Prue, an' I'll get something to tie him with."

Unearthing some more of the rope he had used for our barrier, he bound Schonbrun's hands tightly behind him and tied his feet so that he could walk just a few inches at a time.

Asey took the pistol from me. "March," he said briefly. "Into the car with you. Nope. Right on to the front seat. Miss Prue,

I'm 'fraid you got to do the drivin'. I'll show you the tricks about shiftin' the gears."

He shoved Schonbrun unceremoniously into the front seat.

"But you're all covered with blood, Asey. And something ought to be bound around your head."

Feeling a little like a Revolutionary War heroine, the kind who were always bandaging people up with their under-things, I lifted my skirt, took a nail file from my pocketbook and with it tore the hem from my white silk petticoat. As I tied up his head I reflected that Betsey would now have no reason to scoff at my petticoats for some time to come.

I got into the driver's seat and cautiously started the car. Asey gave directions, with one eye on me and the other on our unenthusiastic guest. I had finally and with no small trouble achieved the fourth speed before Schonbrun wakened to the fact that my gun was an innocuous cap pistol and possibly the least deadly thing in existence.

"Hell," he said disgustedly, "was that the thing you poked into my back?"

Asey gave a one-sided grin. "Yup, that was it."

"Jeese," said Schonbrun, "you yokels take the cake, you do. You get your man."

"Usually we do." Asey smiled at me. "But like I always say, we have to have help."

I asked him in a whisper what we were going to do with the man now that we had him.

"Oh, we'll take him long 'v us. Bird in hand, you know. Like the lady in the Bible, whither we goest, he will go an' whither he goest, we'll be there too."

"I suppose," Schonbrun remarked bitterly, "that you ain't a cop, neither."

"Gettin' right caught up, ain't you? Yup, you supposed right. But you ought to thank your lucky stars we ain't cops. You'd be in worse than you are now. Miss Prue, you go up along the back road an' stop at the side entrance to the doctor's. I'll have to let him spread a little salve or something on these here wounds of mine. That is, if he ain't gallivantin' around tryin' to find out about them notes."

He emerged from the doctor's looking like a figure from the *Spirit of '76*. "These pill pedlers are a cur'us lot," he remarked. "Wanted to know how I got this way an' who biffed me over the head, an' whose silk petticoat I was wearin' an' I don't know what all."

"What did you tell him?"

"Told him 'twas an honor'ble wound received in the course o' action. I didn't tell him no more, an' he was awful' mad. Charged me double. I think he guesses Slough an' me had a little run-in. An' he's kind of mad we won't let him in on all we're doin'. Never saw a man so wantin' to be in the thick of things as he is."

"What's on the docket now?" Schonbrun asked. "What you goin' to do with me?"

"I'd like real well to stick you in irons but I can't do it. Besides, you got a lot to tell your captors 'bout your brother an' so on. I guess you just got to come with us. An' I wouldn't make no noise about it if I was you because it'll only go a whole lot harder for you."

We rode back to the cottage in silence. The crowd outside had dispersed to some extent and in the dusk they did not appear to notice either Asey's bandages or our prisoner.

Emma and Betsey were in the living-room, playing cards. Dot was still up in her room.

"Back again?" Emma asked. "And who's your unwilling victim? And what did Mr. Mayo bump into?"

I explained.

"Now," said Asey, pushing Schonbrun into a chair and taking a seat himself, "now suppose you just stop tellin' lies an' let us know all about everything, like when you saw your brother yesterday an' when you came to the cabin an' all the rest. An' if you don't, I'll take you up to Sullivan an' get you arrested as a suspect."

"An' if I tell you?"

"If you tell us a straight story an' prove that you didn't have nothin' to do with this, you get off with money in your pocket an' no one else the wiser."

"O. K." said Schonbrun. "I'll take a chance. Don't suppose you'd take off some of your rope decorations?"

"I'm 'fraid not," said Asey regretfully. "You see I only got one head an I'd kind of hate to have it smashed up any more. You're better off the way you be."

"Honest, brother, I'm sorry about that. I didn't mean to hurt you bad. I was just goin' to get you out of the way."

"Yup. I know, to err's human an' to forgive divine. It was just an mule spirits on your part. Get on with your story. An' no funny business, mind."

"I was goin' through town yesterday," Schonbrun began, "an' I seen a man in a car that looked like my brother. I thought he was dead, see? But when Dave got mad he had a kind of crazy look about him, an' this guy I saw was mad clean through. But somehow I had a hunch it was him. So I asks a guy an' he says his name is Sanborn, see, Dale Sanborn. So I asks where he lives an' thinks to myself I'll just mosey around an' look him over."

"Didn't you ever find out for certain whether that feller killed in Lowell was really him?"

"Naw. An' how you know about that beats me. We didn't have no money to go runnin' around to see if it was Dave. I was glad enough he was dead, anyway."

"An' where was you comin' from when you hit here?"

"Taunton. Things got hot for me in New York so I came up to this part of the country. I got jailed in Taunton an' I got out only last week, see? I was goin' down to Provincetown to see a guy used to work with me. I didn't have no money, an' I thought if that was Dave I might be able to touch him for something. So I hiked out here to see."

"Meet any one on the way?"

"Sure I met people on the way."

"I mean, did you talk with any one?"

"Naw," Schonbrun looked puzzled. "The guy told me where he lived gave me good directions. I ast a dumb Swede, but she couldn't talk English, if that's what you mean. I saw the cabin about that time anyhow."

"An' you went there?"

"Yeah. Wasn't any one there, so I sat down an' waited. He come in an' took one look at me an' picked up a hammer lyin' on the table an' said he'd push it in my face if I didn't beat it. I didn't want to get into a fuss so I beat it."

"Didn't find anything on your way to the cabin, did you?"

"Find anything? Naw."

"Sure you didn't?"

"Say, I was huntin' a guy I thought was my brother. I wasn't huntin' for anything else."

"Got any proof he was alive when you left him?"

"Naw, I didn't kill him, but I ain't got any proof."

"Well, did you see anybody around the place when you left?"

"There was a car comin' up. There was a guy in it."

"Must of been Bill," Asey reflected. "Well, that doesn't help Bill any, all this, does it?"

"No need to worry about that Porter guy," said Schonbrun. "He's got money enough to get out of this."

"How do you know about Bill Porter?"

"Know the name." Schonbrun was altogether too casual.

"But Bill was all I said. Not Bill Porter," Asey insisted.

"Listen, brother, why can't you forget about all this? I'm all the family that brother of mine had, an' say, I wouldn't make a fuss if some one chopped him up into little pieces with an ax. It would be perfectly O. K. by me. An' even if that Porter guy is arrested, he can get himself off."

"So you did know about the murder," Asey commented. "Well, what makes you think your brother pretended to be dead?"

"I'll tell you the way I figured it out. You see, he was in this strike racket an' he was in it pretty deep. He was all for gettin' out, an' he couldn't. They had him on the black list, an' everywhere he went, he got into trouble. They knew too much about him. So I suppose that when they thought that man they found was him, he thought probably it was a swell chance for him to get out without any one's bein' the wiser, see?"

"Yup. But didn't you have no suspicion he wasn't dead?"

"Yeah. That is, ma did, but I didn't. Ma she saw a picture in a paper once an' she thought it was Dave. But I never did, even though it had Dale Sanborn under it. Ma was always kind of nuts on the subject, always sayin' she had a feelin' he was alive. I let her rave on because she was so strong about it. But he's better off where he is now."

"Why do you keep sayin' that? What was the matter? Didn't he treat you right?"

"Treat me right?" Schonbrun gave a short bitter laugh. "Say, brother, you find me any one that bird ever treated right an' I'll climb right up on to your home-made jail an' like it."

"Wasn't he a nice man?"

"Nice? What do you think he was? A pretty colored paper doll? You may of known Dale Sanborn, but you never knew David Schonbrun, brother. An' you didn't know him very well even under his smooth name. Say, can I have a cigarette? They're in my pocket if you'll dig for 'em."

"Sure you can have a cigarette. I'll untie one hand an' let you smoke it, too. But just to know what your other hand's doin', I'll keep that just where it is."

He busied himself with the rope.

"What pocket's it in?"

"Coat pocket. Left."

Asey fumbled around and found it. He shook a cigarette out from the crushed paper package. But as he shook, a small pin set with brilliants tumbled out.

He held it up for us to see. The initials were M. W. or W. M.

Chapter Twelve
MR. ABE SCHONBRUN

ASEY PICKED up the pin. "Where'd you get that?"

"What? That? Oh, yes. That pin, you mean?"

"Yup," said Asey. "That pin I'm holdin' in my hand. Not two other pins in Chicago. This here pin now. Where'd you get it?"

"Why, I found that," said Schonbrun glibly.

"Did, did you? When?"

"A long time ago. Several months ago. Picked it up in the street, but there wasn't any chance of hockin' it up around here so I kept it."

"Sure you didn't find it yesterday afternoon? Right here on the Cape?"

"Now, listen, brother. This ain't no way for you to act at all, suspectin' everything you find."

"Listen yourself," returned Asey. "Are you goin' to tell me where an' when you found this an' who it belonged to, or am I goin' to trot you up to court on Monday mornin' an' let you get indicted for murder? You just think it over a little."

"Well," said Schonbrun resentfully, "this afternoon comin' back from Provincetown a lady give me a lift. When I got out I must have picked it up or else it just slipped into my pocket. It was hers."

"An' I suppose it just slid into the furthest corner of a pack of cigarettes. Yup. An' I thought you come back on the tail of a truck."

"Did I say that? That was goin' down. I drove back with this lady."

"Ever see her before?"

"Naw, but she was a peach. She picked me up off the road. Most ladies won't."

"An' a little child shall lead 'em," Asey murmured. "How could you have picked it up an' not known about it? How did it slip into your pocket? Did she give it to you, or did you steal it?"

"I never stole a thing in my life," Schonbrun declared. "Never. It just must of fell into my pocket."

"You didn't know the woman?"

"I think she said something about bein' a Mrs. Carey of Indianapolis."

Asey looked at him admiringly. "A truthful man's as rare as a white crow anyhows, but I got to hand it to you, Schonbrun. Of all the barefaced liars I ever see in my life, you take the grand prize. If you won't tell about the pin, we'll let it go for the time bein'. You was sayin' that your brother wa'n't such a good man."

"O. K.," said Schonbrun cheerfully. "Suits me fine. About Dave. Well, after pa died he worked sellin' papers an' things an' then he went to high school an' worked afternoons. In a factory. Then one day he come home an' packed up his things an' left. He took all the money ma had an' my bank too along with him. We found out later he'd gone to college or something. These guys he'd been working with at the factory had introduced him

to some other guys that sent him to college an' paid his way. He
never showed up more than three or four times after that. An'
he never paid back the money he stole. That guy was a dirty,—
well, he was a dirty scum if ever there was one. An' do you know
what? About four years ago it was that ma found this picture I
told you about in the newspaper. She thought it was him an' she
wrote a letter, but no one ever answered it at all.

"Well, we got on, she worked an' so did I. Then about a year
an' a half ago I got sick. There was something the matter with
my lungs, see, an' I had to go to a hospital. Ma didn't have a lot
of money an' of course I couldn't do anything an' then we each
of us wrote another letter askin' if this Sanborn was Dave an' to
give us some money. Ma went to see him, but he kicked her out
of his swell apartment just the way he kicked me yesterday. He
said he'd call the police if she bothered him again. So I thought
then that it wasn't Dave. I never really knew till yesterday, see?"

He lighted a cigarette with his free hand.

"An' ma lost her job about that time, an' I got sicker an' nearly died. An' what do you think I found out when I got well an'
out of the hospital? She'd run out o' money an' starved to death.
She'd been so sure that this Sanborn was Dave that she'd gone
there again, but he wouldn't have anything to do with her. A
woman she knew told me. An' she died on the streets. See?
That's the kind of guy my brother was. Say, I know twenty-five
people who'd kill him an' think they'd done a good day's work,
if they'd only known he was alive. It wasn't just Ma an' me he
double-crossed. Not much. That guy he double-crossed every
one he had anything to do with."

For the first time since we had found him Schonbrun seemed
actually to be telling the truth. There was nothing false about

the rancor he felt toward his brother. Even if he had lied like a trooper about the pin and about half a dozen other things, I felt that this at least was genuine.

"Does he like sardines? I mean, did he?" Asey asked.

"Couldn't say. I don't know." But I knew that he did. There had been the barest hesitancy in his answer, but I noticed it and I knew Asey had too.

"We'll leave that 'long of the pin, then," Asey remarked. "You just went there an' then got thrown out an' then went away again. That's your story?"

Schonbrun nodded. "That's my story an' I stick to it."

"You know," Asey said to me, "one thing that still seems funny to me is that blanket that you found tucked over him."

"Blan——" Schonbrun started to speak and then stopped. Asey crowed happily. "I sort of hoped I could get you even though I thought you'd made one good slip to-night. Now, you went back to the cabin after you left the first time, didn't you?"

Schonbrun looked at Asey admiringly. "Jeese, you ain't such a fool, are you?"

"Only on the outside. Let us in on visit number two. You got along a ways an' then you remembered the platinum case, didn't you? Or the watch? An' you said to yourself that you was kind of a chump to beat it as quick as you had? Was that it?"

"Yeah."

Emma looked at Asey in astonishment. "Elucidate, dear Sherlock. What drove you to that conclusion?"

"Well, from the way this feller has been talkin', he reminds me of a man I used to know out in Alexandria, Egypt. He lied like the ole Harry, but he was a persistent sort. Nothin' much of a hero about him, fact he was a little coward, just like this feller. An' it 'peared to me that if he was in Schonbrun's shoes he'd think 'n' act just that way. I don't think this feller has the—the," he searched for a word, "the innerds, to kill his brother. If he had, he'd 'a' done it a long time ago. But I knew he'd be the sort that'd go beggin' back again."

Schonbrun seemed to take no offense at Asey's analysis of him. "I thought like that," he said. "I thought I'd go back an' have another try. I was goin' to tell him I'd tell people who he was if he didn't come across."

"Blackmail," I said.

"Well, lady, you can call it blackmail if you like. Anyway, I went back an' before I went around to the front door I peeked in a window. He was layin' by the side of the table, but there wasn't no blanket on him when I saw him. I thinks to myself, some one's found you out, buddy boy, an' give you what you been askin' for all these years. I wanted to go in an' take that case an' see if he had any money, but I didn't. I was scared some one would spot me doin' it an' then if I tried to get rid of them there might be trouble. So I beat it again."

"What time was it when you come back?"

"I don't know exactly. I heard a clock strike five. It was that clock in town, that one on the church with the green top."

"Congregational church," said Asey. "Yup. That's the only one you can hear from this place an' it's always right, bein' as how it's electric. Did you hear it before or after you looked into the window?"

"Quite a while before. I remember because I'd just bu'sted my shoelace an' there was so little of it that wasn't bu'sted that I had a hard time gettin' to mend it any more." He stuck out his feet in their dirty worn oxfords. The laces were nothing but a series of knots. I thought of his brother's hand-made footwear.

"An' so you thought some one had killed your brother, but you weren't goin' to let any one know anything about it?"

"Not a chance. I didn't dare. See, the first thing any one would do would be to put the bracelets on me. An' I had enough of the wrong side of the bars in Taunton. I wasn't cravin' another stretch with maybe the chair at the end of it. But anyways, there wasn't no wrappin' on him when I saw him."

"See any one when you left the cottage the second time?"

"Naw. I went around by the back of the cabin. I didn't want to be seen. I went way in back of the meadows. I didn't touch the road till I come out nearly on the main street."

"Was there a path?"

"A sort of a one."

"You're tellin' the truth about that then, because that's the tracks from the cranberry bogs. But I guess you wouldn't tell if you had seen any one, would you?"

Schonbrun's pig-eyes twinkled. "Not unless you got me arrested an' I was in a hole. I told you the guy that done this was a friend of mine. He done something I never got the backbone to do."

"Hm. How much would it take to make you tell? The truth, that is. Not just another fairy story."

"A century note," said Schonbrun promptly.

Asey pulled out his wallet. "Here you be. I'll stick it in your vest pocket for you."

"Thanks. Well, it was a man I saw edging around the woods as I was comin' back the second time."

"Kind of a man? What'd he look like?"

"He was about as tall as I am. Dark an' very tanned. I noticed that. I slid down behind some bushes an' I don't think he saw me. I didn't take such a look at his face, but he had on good clothes. You could tell that. An' he wore one of them blue caps close to the head. What d'you call 'em?"

"Berries," explained Asey.

"He had one of 'em on. An' he had a sort of green shirt, I noticed that, an' his suit was gray flannel or gray something."

"I wonder," I said, "if it could have been Kurth?"

"I hope to goodness it is. Everything's sounded like him since we started in this mornin'. I declare to goodness I think every tall dark man in New England was makin' a call on Sanborn yesterday afternoon. Well, could you tell him if you saw him again?"

"Perhaps. But probably not unless he had on the same outfit I wouldn't."

"Now," said Asey cajolingly, "tell us how you got that pin."

"It's like I told you the last time. A woman picked me up comin' out of Provincetown this afternoon. It must just have slipped into my pocket. Her name wasn't what I told you. I don't know her name. But the initials on the car were an *M* an' a *W*. I noticed that as I got in. She told me she'd been down looking the place over."

"Didn't she say anything about this here murder?"

"Not a thing. Honest. She was a lousy driver—we didn't talk much of any; why she even nicked a couple of fenders goin' through the main street here, she was so punk."

I knew that Maida Waring had rarely taken her car out of the garage that she didn't do some injury to it. It was a marvel among her friends that she herself had escaped injury.

"An' you don't know if your brother liked sardines?"

Schonbrun shook his head.

"An' you didn't see any sardine tin when you was there at the cabin, either time?"

As he started to reply, Dot Cram, dressed in pajamas and dressing-gown, came down-stairs.

She took one look at Schonbrun, he stared at her, and for the second time in twenty-four hours, she fainted.

Emma and Betsey took charge of her and led her back to her room.

"Well," I remarked to Asey, "I wonder what that means?"

Asey wondered too.

"Mr. Schonbrun," I asked, "have you ever seen that girl before?"

He shook his head. "No, I never did. An' I found out it don't pay to tell you two sleuths anything but what's true. But I'll tell you something more I remembered. I thought I saw some one in a white dress in the woods when I came up to the cabin the second time. It wasn't till after I saw that man. But I might of been mistaken. It might of been clothes on a line or something. I ain't real sure of it."

"You saw the man after you found your brother dead," I reflected, "and you think you saw some one before you found him?"

"The first's right, but I'm not so sure of the other."

"What made you think of it now?" I wondered if he had seen Dot and if that had recalled it to his mind.

"I don't know. I just did."

"I wisht," Asey sighed, "that we could be sure of anything you say."

"Listen, brother. Everything I told you lately is true. You two are a little too good for me. But, say, did that girl know my brother?"

"She was engaged to marry him."

"I asked because she might of thought I was him or something. But she oughtn't to be flopping. She ought to be thankin' God she's well out of a bad bargain. He'd probably pull a fake marriage an' then ditch her."

"What makes you think so?"

"Because, lady, like I been tryin' to tell you, that guy never did a straight thing in his life. He got a girl I know of into trouble before he left home. He wouldn't stick to one woman if some one chained him to her, he wouldn't. She was his cousin, too. The daughter of one of ma's sisters. She jumped into the river after he left. Sounds like something you read about in the papers, don't it, or like a movie? Yeah. But the difference is that it's true."

Asey and I were silent. It occurred to me that possibly it was instinct and not his patent-leather hair that had made Bill Porter suspicious of Sanborn. I had almost forgotten about Bill and I said as much.

"Bill's got to learn to take care of himself," Asey replied. "I'll run around by the station on my way home an' see that Joe Bump stays there just to make sure there's no funny business to-night. He sleeps in the fields all summer, an' he won't mind parkin' on a camp stool till Monday mornin'. I don't reckon Bill'll do much sleepin', but it sure ought to teach him a lesson, all this."

"Where do I bunk?" Schonbrun asked.

"You come home along o' me an' sleep in your fetters, feller. I hope a good night's sleep'll refresh your mem'ry about sardine tins an' a lot o' other things, too. That's something we got to look forward to to-morrer, Miss Prue, findin' out about that tin an' about Kurth an' his wife. I reckon Schonbrun an' me'll be gettin' along."

"But how can you drive?" I protested. "And oughtn't some one to look after your head?"

"It'll be all right. I forgot to say I guess the doctor kind of recognized that petticoat."

"What?"

"Yup. I'm kind of 'fraid your 'scutcheon is goin' to suffer a blot or two from this day's goin's-on."

"Well," I said resignedly, "no one talks about escutcheons till there's a blot on them anyway. I shall hold Bill responsible for any damage done to my reputation."

"You could sue him," Asey grinned.

"But what do you think about this business, Asey?"

"Who do I think done this murder? Well, Dot went over there an' gave Sanborn back his ring, 'cordin' to all 'counts. Then this feller here went there twice. Then there was Bill. Far's I can see, first they was the brother, then Bill, then Dot an' then the brother again. Then there's the stranger that might of been Kurth, an' the white skirt that might of been almost any one. An' Schonbrun says the brother was alive when he left——"

"He was," Schonbrun interrupted.

"An' Bill says he was alive an' he left him that way. We don't know about Dot, an' I ain't so sure about your second visit, Mr. Schonbrun, though I don't think you got the spirit to do it. But the strange feller might o' done it, an' maybe not. I don't know. That one-syl'ble' maid might of done it 'f she'd had wings like an angel, an' so might Betsey an' so might you if I didn't think you two was too much Cape Codder by blood to do anything of the kind. An' so might Mrs. Manton, if she'd weighed anything less'n a million pounds. An' then there's the lady of the sparkly pin. I s'pose you know," he spoke to Schonbrun, "that the woman that picked you up an'

gave you a lift is the wife of the gent most likely you saw me-
anderin' around the cabin?"

"She is? Say, listen, brother. Then I can tell you something
more. I guess I got a little fresh with her or something, for she
looks at me an' laughs when I kidded her an' says nothin' doin',
that she's got a perfectly good husband of her own, an' she don't
play with strange men. I says why ain't he on the job then, an'
she sort of smiles an' says she's right on her way to see he does
now. I asks her if it's golf or another woman, an' she says it was
another man an' another woman both." He stopped and lighted
a cigarette.

"Damn your weed," said Asey with the first show of irritation he had made all day. "Get on."

"So I asks her if he's run away or she's run away, and she
says no, they'd been divorced. An' she says she's down on the
Cape huntin' him because he's found out the truth about the
other man, an' she's afraid he'll do something crazy. Say," said
Schonbrun excitedly, "it was Dave who was the man? Do you
think so?"

"I haven't a doubt of it now, if what you say is true, have you,
Asey?"

"Is it the truth, feller?"

"Gospel," said Schonbrun.

"Well," Asey grinned, "I guess that's that, an' I guess the
rest will keep till mornin'. Mister, I hope your limbs is as stiff
to-morrer as my head is sore right now. Give us your other hand.
I'm goin' to tie you up all nice an' safe."

Schonbrun submitted cheerfully. "I guess I got it comin' to
me, all right."

I assisted them to the car. "Good night," I said, "and for mer-
cy's sake, do be careful of your head, Asey. And please, Mr.

Schonbrun, see that he doesn't go rampaging around any more to-night."

They drove off down the lane. Wearily I sat down in the living-room and thought. I was reminded of Bill's stock and somewhat vulgar expression. "No matter how thin you slice it, it's still bologna." That sentence expressed my thoughts admirably. No matter how carefully I mulled over our list of suspects, they were, so to speak, still bologna.

Betsey came down-stairs. "We've finally got Dot to sleep and Emma says she's retiring before anything else turns up. Snoodles, I'm getting surer by the minute that Dot must have done this. Although the brother is sort of in the limelight, isn't he?"

"As far as I can make out," I told her, "with this feeble and sleepy and thoroughly useless brain of mine, Asey is right; practically any one at all might have done it. I'm that confused, Betsey, that I'm not sure but what you and I did it together. If I think one more thought about Dale Sanborn, who would seem to be where he very rightly belongs, I shall be seized with fits, like a cat. And that reminds me. Has Ginger been fed and looked after to-day, or hasn't he? It's the first time in years that I've neglected him."

"Come on to bed," said Betsey comfortingly. "Ginger's in his basket in your room. I'll make you a hot toddy and run you a tub and you'll feel like a new woman when you've finished with them."

Ordinarily I do dislike being coddled, but somehow it was restful being coddled that night. I sank down into bed and wondered how many gray hairs I'd added to my scalp during the day.

In the middle of the night Ginger woke me by prancing on my stomach. I tried to quiet him, but he refused to be quieted.

Now many people insist that a cat is dull in comparison with a dog, but as I always remark to the intense annoyance of all my dog-loving friends, Ginger is a remarkable cat. I do not claim that he is psychic, but it was he who discovered the burglar last winter in our home in Boston and roused me by licking my face so I was able to telephone the police in time to keep the Whitsby pearls in the family.

I turned on my flash-light and looked at him, tail five times normal size, all the hairs on his back standing on end. It occurred to me that his prancing this time might not be without reason. I snapped out my light, closed my eyes tightly and listened. Distinctly I heard some one move in the living-room. I pulled on my kimono, picked up the torch and crept down-stairs.

At the foot of the staircase I bumped into some one. I turned on the light. It was Dot.

"What is the matter?" I demanded.

"I'm sorry to disturb you, Miss Prudence. I craved a cigarette and Betsey was sleeping so peacefully that I hadn't the heart to disturb her."

"Bed is the place for you," I said severely.

"I know it is. Miss Prudence, I'm sorry for the way I've acted, all this silly fainting, I mean. But when I came downstairs to-night and saw that man, I thought it was Dale."

"You've never seen the brother before?"

"I never knew he existed." She gave a little sigh. "But he is built like Dale, and oh, I don't know. I've been pretty shot all day, I guess. I'll try to be more sensible to-morrow."

We went up-stairs together. At my door she leaned over unexpectedly and kissed me.

"Please believe in me, Miss Prudence. I didn't kill him. Please believe in me."

I patted her shoulder and told her to run along to bed, that to-morrow everything would be cleared up.

In my room Ginger blinked at me. His hair was still fluffed up on end. I pulled off my kimono and told him to get into his basket. "It wasn't a burglar," I said, "and everything's all right. You're a nice cat, but to-night you let your enthusiasm run away with you."

He looked at me, blinked again, and walked with studied carelessness to his basket. The insolent flick of his tail and the proud curl of his whiskers said as plainly as words, "All right, if you say so, I'll obey. But you're wrong."

And his very assurance about it put me into one of those nervous states where, in our house that never squeaked, I heard noises and footsteps till dawn.

Chapter Thirteen
ASEY TRACES THE SARDINES

ASEY AND Schonbrun, the latter without his confining ropes, arrived Sunday morning just as Olga was serving breakfast.

"Kidney hash," exclaimed Asey delightedly. "We had a little breakfast, Abe an' I, but if there's plenty o' that I don't know but what I could do with some."

"Abe?" I asked, as Olga set the extra places.

"Yup. Schonbrun here. We got down to first names since last night." Asey attacked the kidney hash. He looked over at Dot. "You all recovered?"

She nodded. "Yes, I am."

"Feelin' more like tellin' us what really happened?"

"Yes."

"S'pose you do it right now," Asey suggested.

"You know now that I didn't tell you the truth, I suppose. That is, about going down the hill to the courts. After Miss Prudence left me on the porch I went into the living-room and got a cigarette. I picked up the binoculars, too, so if any one asked me what I was doing I could tell them I wanted to look at that fishing boat."

"How long were you in there?" Asey asked.

"About five minutes. That part of it was true."

"Then?" Asey prompted.

"Then I skirted the top of the hill and went around to the cabin and in the back door. You see, when Dale acted the way he did on the porch Friday, I decided that things had better come to an end. I had my engagement ring on a chain around my neck and I made up my mind to give it back to him."

"Did you?" Asey reached for a popover.

"Yes."

"An' what happened? What did he say?"

"He, well, he was perfectly horrid. He took it and laughed and said that he was glad I was coming to my senses. He said he never had any intention of marrying me anyway, and, well, he said a lot of nasty, untruthful things about me."

"Didn't I tell you he was like that?" Schonbrun interrupted. "You were lucky to get out of it, miss."

Dot shuddered. "After hearing him talk yesterday, I am beginning to think I am, though I never thought so before. He made me perfectly furious. I don't think I've ever been madder in my life. I was so angry I couldn't talk. I just ran out of the cabin and tore back as fast as I could."

"How long were you over there?"

"Not long. Only a few minutes. I ran both ways. I stopped on the porch after I got back to catch my breath, then I went out into the kitchen with Miss Prue. That was at——"

Asey consulted the time schedule. "That was at five minutes after five. You came out o' the house 'cordin' to this at four-forty-eight. That gives you seventeen minutes before you saw Miss Prue. A couple minutes either way goin' an' comin', six or seven minutes there, an' four-five minutes on the porch. That makes it come out right. Did you have the binoculars in your hand all the time?"

"Yes. I held them swinging by the strap."

I knew why he had asked her that. A pair of binoculars "swinging by a strap" might well have made the blow the doctor described.

"He didn't seem at all hurt that you was breakin' the engagement?"

"On the contrary. He said if I'd had any wits at all I'd have broken it a long time ago. He thought it,—well, amusing is the only word I can think of that would fit. He even said that the next time he wrote a book he thought he could fit me in very nicely. And a lot more like that."

"He did, did he?"

"Ain't I been tellin' you?" Schonbrun put in. "Ain't I been tryin' to tell you what he was like?"

"Listen, Abe, was she the woman you saw when you come back to the cabin the second time?"

"I don't think so. I couldn't say for sure."

I did some calculating. "She couldn't have been."

"Why not?"

"Dot came out into the kitchen at five minutes after five, and if what you said is right, she must have left the cabin seven or eight minutes before to get here then. And Schonbrun says he heard the clock strike five some time before he came back to the cabin."

Dot looked at me gratefully.

"That's right." Asey considered. "She must of left a minute or so before five anyways, even a couple of minutes earlier, maybe, if she's tellin' us the truth. An' you say it was—how much longer after five you seen this flash of white, Abe?"

"Must of been six or seven minutes after. Maybe eight."

"Um." Asey pondered.

"But," I asked, "have you and Mr. Schonbrun signed enough of a peace treaty for you to be sure that he's telling the truth now?"

"We been all over everything," Asey returned, "him an' me have, an' I guess like he said the last version of his stories is true. I sure paid him enough to have it as straight as an encyclopediay. Dot, is your last story right, too?"

"Yes, Asey. I've told you the truth. The only reason I didn't yesterday was that it sounded so sort of awfully thin. You two were so set on finding out who did it that I felt sure you'd land on me. It never occurred to me that you would doubt my story about going down to the tennis courts, but I didn't figure on Asey's shooting my story to pieces so beautifully with the confounded fishing boat. Has any one found the ring?"

"The doc has. But we kind o' led him astray about it, though. He recognized them initials."

"Those initials!" Dot gritted her teeth. "Dale told me he'd been a fool to have them put on, because he'd either have to have them erased or else get engaged next time to some one with the same initials."

"Merciful heaven," Emma exclaimed. "You know I'm beginning to agree with Mr. Schonbrun here. I think that his brother might well have been done away with years ago."

"You got the idea," said Schonbrun approvingly. "That's what I said. It don't make no difference that this Porter guy is arrested. He can get a good lawyer and get himself off all right. What are you all so crazy to find out who done it for anyway?"

"Could Bill get off, do you suppose?" I asked Asey.

"Stranger things have been an' happened," he replied. "But I dunno about this. They's been about six murderers let off in the last year in these regions an' all them little tabloid newspapers'd begin to holler as how Massachusetts was lettin' rich men off 'cause they got money an' then they'd be a lot o' talk about capitalism an' how if Bill didn't have a penny he'd been 'lectrocuted the day after he done it. We could 'peal an' peal, 'cause as far's I can see, they ain't nothin' but circumstan'tal ev'dence against him, but something'd probably let slip itself somewheres, an' by the time we got a verdict one way or 'nother, Bill'd be a poor ole broken down jail-bird with gray hair an' a cane. No, I kind o' feel symp'thetic like about whoever done this,—Abe told me a lot more about that brother of his last night,—but I reckon we got to keep right on tryin' to find out who did it."

"I thought you couldn't convict any one on circumstantial evidence," Emma remarked.

"Well, that's the way the law goes. Law says a child with jam all over its face an' the jam pot empty an' indigestion next day ain't guilty of stealin' jam if no one didn't see him do it. Might of been the dog that ate the jam an' then the kid played with the dog an' got the jam all over itself that way. An' maybe the stomach-ache was on account of something else altogether. But when it's a case of murder in the courts, with the newspapers all riled up an' what they call public opinion gettin' itself all pink in the face, that's another brand of cat altogether. You start a newspaper razzin' a district 'torney an' he'd claim George Washin'ton stole cherries an' started a cannery. Nope, I don't guess we can leave much to chance in this attall."

"But he was alive when I left him," Dot said, "and when I saw him, for that matter. Wouldn't that let Bill out?"

"It might an' it might not. It would let him out only to get you put in his place. You see, far's I can make out, when there's a crime done some one has to get punished. That's just one of them idees people have got since they was civ'lized. Eye for an eye an' all that. But the law don't really care much who gets punished 'cordin' to my way of thinkin'. If they get the right one, well an' good. If they get the wrong one, the one who done the crime is the only one that knows an' he or she ain't goin' to stick their nose into any noose. But whether it's the right one or the wrong one, the effect is just the same. The papers is satisfied an' the people is satisfied an' the police gets promoted an' we all think it's a grand an' glorious country. So there you are. It'd be worse for you than it is for Bill, because as Abe says, if worse comes to worse, why Bill he's got the money to spend to get himself off. I shouldn't wonder if he couldn't ordinarily, but like I say, he's too rich to get off without trouble."

"You haven't much of an idea of justice," I remarked. "Or else you emphasize money too much."

"Not attall, Miss Prue. If a poor man c'mits a crime, he gets his, 'cause he ain't got money enough to get off by hirin' smart lawyers. If a rich man gets mixed up in a crime, he's got the money to get himself off, but the people are against him because he's got money. Far's I can see, all crimes ought t' be done by what the papers call the moneyed middle class."

"That's all very well," I said, "but I can't see that it's getting us anywhere. And although I don't like to say this, we haven't any more proof that Dot is telling the truth than we have that Schonbrun is. No more do we know who the strange man who was prowling about the cabin was, nor do we know about the woman in white, if there was a woman in white. I can't see that we're making any headway at all."

"We got two more people anyways to get worked up about,"

Asey reflected. "What I want to know is about that sardine tin. We got to do something about that right now."

"Just what are you intending to do about it?" Emma asked.

Before he could answer, Olga interrupted. "Boy to see Mr. Bill's Asey."

"Who is he?"

She shrugged her shoulders. "Town boy."

"Show him in," I said.

She brought in a freckle-faced lad whom Asey greeted pleasantly. "'Lo, Little Lon." He explained to the rest of us, "This here's Lonzo Bangs' boy. They call him that though it ain't your name, is it?"

The boy shook his head and grinned. "Nossir. It's Ebenezer Philemon Bangs, but they call me Little Lon."

I mentally reflected that they would have to.

"What can we do for you?" Asey asked.

"Nawthin' much. Pa wanted me to say as how he'd got the dory all right yest'day aft'noon, an' he wants to know will you give him a diff'rent anchor. He don't like the one's on it now. Too light, he says."

"Good godfreys mighty," Asey sighed. "If he wants another anchor, let him take another anchor. He can have the one in the tender to Bill's motor-boat. They's just alike, but he can have it. You tell him not to go thinkin' up anything else though."

"All right." Little Lon made no effort to move.

"Anything else on your mind?"

"Uh-huh. Kind of. I was up here to this end o' town Friday night."

"Was, was you?"

"Uh-huh. 'Twas about eight o'clock. Feature pitcher don't begin till eight-forty-five's a rule an' I drove up with Hi White."

"What's that got to do with the price o' beans?"

"Nawthin' much." Little Lon was a typical Cape Codder. No over-statement of facts for him, I reflected. "'Cept I saw a light in the cabin there where Mr. Sanborn lived."

"What?" The six of us spoke like a carefully trained Greek chorus. "What?"

"Uh-huh. They was a light there. I noticed it flash on while I was drivin' by, an' by the time I'd turned back, five minutes or so later, it wa'n't there."

"Why didn't your pa tell us that?"

"He didn't know. I forgot all about it till some one uptown said he'd been killed before six. I told pa last night an' he said to tell you to-day." He turned to go.

"Wait up a bit. Was there any cars goin' along the beach or parked there round the lane then?"

"Uh-huh. Lots of spooners."

"Notice a Packard tourin'?"

"You mean," said Little Lon delightedly, "that one you was askin' pa about? That Brown's that you got parked out back? Naw. I didn't notice it. Say, is he in this?"

"Don't know. That all you can tell us?"

"Guess so." He grinned and replaced his visored cap which proclaimed Nutter's varnish to be the only one worthy of any one's consideration, and left.

"Oh, m' God!" said Asey. "Oh, m' God! Who was that an' what was they doin' there? I declare to goodness I never seen a feller as got called on so much, dead or alive, as this Sanborn."

"I know," I said soothingly. "But what about the sardine tin? You were saying something about it when you were interrupted by the son of Bangs."

"Yup. Betsey, what was there in that rumble seat of Lucinda's when you all come back from the store? What groceries, I mean?"

Betsey frowned. "There were a couple of dozen ears of corn, and a bucket of clams, and a bag of potatoes, and a dozen bottles of ginger ale and all the rest of the things we got at the store. I'll get you the bill if you're really interested."

"No need. How many other bags was there?"

"Two or three, anyway."

"An' Bill got all his own things, didn't he? I noticed they was all loose."

"He waited on himself."

"An' he put the things in the seat, or did you?"

"He did."

"Well, now, I guess I can explain how that tin got where it got," Asey announced. "Y'see, Lucinda's got a sort of cavity in her back; it ain't a real rumble seat like in the new roadsters at-tall. An' it was full of groceries, see?"

"No," I told him.

"Well, that there cavity slopes. It's real deep near the center an' the middle of the car, but up along toward the back where the spare tire is, it ain't more'n a foot. An' Bill's a lazy piece. Probably he just stuck everything in the back where the cover goes down. It's a real heavy cover an' it's a job to lift it. It goes all the way down to the cover rack where the spare tire and the trunk is. It don't stop a couple of feet away like in cars to-day, see?"

I nodded.

"Then with all those things piled up, it wouldn't fit, the cover wouldn't. An' so when Bill hit a jounce, if the sardines was on top, as they probably was, they'd fall out. Lucinda's springs ain't nothin' to brag about. Them sardines wasn't in a bag, 'cause when I pulled our things out they was all sort of strewn around. Now, question is, where'd they jounce out? Would there be one place more likely than another?"

"Yes," said Betsey eagerly, "there would. You wouldn't notice it in that pullman car you've been rolling around in, but I know from driving the bug. It's the far side of the tennis courts, where the water that runs down-hill washes out a hollow by the side of the road."

"By the side?" Asey repeated.

"Yes. Just as we were coming to it on Friday morning we passed a rubberneck bus that crowded us way over. It was when I bit my tongue, do you remember, Dot?"

"And you dug your elbow into me. Yes, I remember."

"That was probably when it fell out. I don't know why I didn't have the wit to think of it before. It just never occurred to me, I suppose."

"Look here," I said excitedly, "was that tin opened by a key or by a can opener, does any one remember?"

"By a can opener. I remember because it caught my eye and I thought at the time that no one ever could open a sardine tin with the key that went with it. I'm positive it was chopped open by a can opener," Emma said.

"Then," I said triumphantly, "let's go and see if the key is still there."

"You an' me will go," Asey announced. "The rest of you can stay here an' meditate."

Before any of them could protest, we were on our way.

"I wanted a chance to talk to you real bad," Asey said, "an' I ain't had a chance since last evenin'. But I'll tell you somethin'. If Bill thought Sanborn was oily, I'd like to know what he'd think of the brother."

"Do you suspect him?"

"I don't know's I suspect much of any one a lot, but that Schonbrun! Say, him an' Ananias is just like that." Asey held up two fingers. "You know how that tin got from where ever it landed to the cabin, don't you?"

"How?"

"Old Honest Abe Schonbrun took it, that's how."

"How do you know?"

"Because last night before I went into Rider's hut, I peeked into the window to see that there wasn't anything funny waitin' for me. Rider was openin' a can of sardines, or maybe they was herrin'. He bu'sted the key." Asey stopped the car. "Come on, let's get out an' pretend to hunt. Rider cussed an' Schonbrun laughed an' pulled a key from his pocket. Rider didn't use it, though. He acted just the way every one else does, like Mrs. Manton said. He went an' got a can opener. I noticed it."

He crawled around energetically on his hands and knees.

"Kind of hate to get my Sunday trousers all dirty, but we got to give a good show. The others is probably watchin'. Anyhows, Schonbrun he put the key back in his vest pocket an' last night when him an' me was playin' in our little fight, I felt in his pocket an' got the key. I looked at it later. It's one just like those on Bill's cans. It's near two inches longer than the av'rage key, an' it's got two slits, not one."

I picked up a stick and scratched industriously among the bayberry bushes. "If that's so, what on earth are we hunting for? There's nothing for us to find."

"I know. But we're goin' to find a key."

"I don't understand."

"It's a duplicate of the one I found on little Abie, the one he don't know I got. I took it out of one of those other 'leven tins. We're goin' to find it an' bring it back."

"Why?"

"I'll tell you. When you bait a lobster pot you want to leave room for the critter to get in. This Schonbrun guy has told the truth about everything except them sardines, an' whether or not he did kill his brother. That is, he's told as near the truth as he can. Truth an' falsehood's like the sides of a penny. You don't know where one begins an' the other leaves off, only Schonbrun is kind of more welded than most pennies. He thinks we all believe him now. He flattered me all last night on how good an' bright I was till I thought pretty soon that he'd take to scratchin' my moskeeter bites for me. There's something in this sardine business he don't want known. So we're goin' to let him have his own way, but we're goin' to confuse him a little. He thinks he's got us buf'loed. But we're goin' to bring back this key an' let him see it an' maybe he'll give himself away. He's done it before."

"What about Dot?" I asked, grubbing under a stone.

"I dunno about Dot. I dunno about any of 'em. The suspected an' the guilty look a lot alike on the outside. They ain't got no glarin' dif'rences. But now you give a cheer an' clap your hands for the ben'fit of our audience an' I'll find the key an' put it into my pocket an' then we'll go back an' be foxy. Little Abe's a mite too anxious to let this business go by the boards. I want to know why."

We got into the car and drove back. "You follow my lead, won't you, Miss Prue? You an' me has agreed with every one's thoughts so far an' we're goin' to make ourselves keep right on. People talk so much more when they don't meet any op'sition. They kind of let themselves go more'n they'd intended to."

We walked up on to the porch.

"You didn't find anything, did you?" Schonbrun asked.

"Abe, you got a wrong impression of our 'bilities in this sleuth line. 'Course we found it. I reckon the wrapper must of been torn an' the key slipped out when it fell from the car. Leastways that's how it 'pears to me."

I watched Schonbrun as Asey drew the key from his pocket. He focused his eyes on it, as did the rest, but there was the slightest involuntary movement toward his vest pocket.

"Ain't you the detectives? I guess you're good," he said admiringly.

"Ain't we just, though?" Asey answered.

"Got to hand it to you. Now I guess as soon's you find the guy that took them sardines from the road there, or whoever ate 'em an' left the tin there, you'll get the guy that done it." But a deathly pallor came over his face as Asey looked at him and said gently, "Why didn't you say so before, Abe?"

Chapter Fourteen
KURTH FINDS HIS CAR

"SAY WHAT before?" Schonbrun asked belligerently. "What you talkin' about?"

"Why didn't you tell us before that this sardine tin was so all-fired important?"

"Whyn't I tell you? Ain't you been belly-achin' about it ever since I seen you?"

"Maybe we did wonder about it, but none of us said as how the person who found it did the killing. That was all your own idea. An' what I want to know is, why didn't you say something about it before?"

"I knew you was tryin' to get me mixed up," said Schonbrun angrily. "Here I do everything I can to help you, an' Jeese, you even tie me up an'——"

"An'," Asey interrupted, "with the aid of a few of Uncle Sam's strips of cur'ency with Cs in the corner of 'em, we ask you a few questions."

"Didn't I deserve 'em? Huh? Didn't you come an' take me away by force when I wasn't doin' anything but mindin' my business like a good citizen?"

"Don't let's go into all that again. We been over it so many times already that I've c'mitted it to mem'ry. Will you tell me why you think the feller that took them sardines is the one that done the murder?"

"I don't know," Schonbrun replied a little crossly. "I just thought of it."

"I s'pose it didn't occur to you that the best person to pick that tin up, that is, the one that had more chance to do it than any one else, was you? You crossed that way on your trip up to the cabin, an' it seems to me that you might of found it. Did you?"

"Naw. I told you a million times already I didn't. Wasn't it there half the day, huh? Why pick on me?"

"Look," said Betsey excitedly, "here comes one of those cops who were here yesterday."

"You get into the dining-room an' stay there," Asey commanded Schonbrun. "Is it Kurth?"

"It's Johnny all right," said Betsey.

The policeman and Kurth strode into the living-room. They looked a little grim.

"See here," said the officer, "this guy reports a car stolen from him and you say it was stolen from you, but we called up New York and it's his all right. What kind of a game is going on here, I'd like to know?"

Kurth's greeting was chilly. "I'm sure there's been some mistake. It's awfully nice to see you all again, Miss Whitsby, but I wish you'd tell me why you've been appropriating my car."

I looked pleadingly at Asey, who proceeded to rise and shine.

"Of'cer, we shouldn't of done it. But we'll see that you don't get into any trouble, an' we'll, um. We'll fix it up with you."

I resented Asey's use of the plural pronoun. All this complication was his own fault, and I knew from the beginning that no good would ever come of it. And here he was, blithely including all of us in his little joke.

"Joke, huh?" The officer eyed him truculently. "It ain't going to be so funny to explain to the captain. He doesn't like jokes like this. And I suppose you think it was a joke to have us take this man's car and leave him stranded miles from everywhere. Yeah. You folks has a nice sense of humor. Go on."

"That's right," Asey went on ruefully. "It sounds kind of punk now, but this is the way it was. We saw Mr. Kurth drivin' around in his car up-town an' he didn't notice us attall. Now," he looked at Betsey and flicked an eyelid.

"You see," Betsey drew a long breath. I thanked heaven that the girl had an imagination. I myself should not have known how to continue. "You see. Mr. Kurth had wanted to come and visit us this week-end, but unfortunately we had asked other guests. And so of course when we saw him and he didn't notice us, we thought he was angry or something." She smiled at the officer. "So we thought it would be sort of amusing to say that his car was stolen and have him arrested."

The policeman looked at her scornfully. "Yeah?"

Emma put down her knitting. "Surely, Lieutenant"—he was obviously not a lieutenant but he looked at her with more respect than he had shown any of us so far. "Surely you don't suspect us of being real criminals, do you? You see, we felt that Mr. Kurth might be angry with us, as Miss Whitsby has said, and we did want to see him because he's been away for a long time. We thought it would be rather sport to have him arrested and brought here, because we felt he wouldn't come of his own accord. And you'll have to admit it's a unique method of making people visit you."

"It's all that," said the officer. Our lengthy and elaborate explanations were having little effect on him. It was very evident that in his opinion we had been having sport at the expense of the police and he for one was not going to stand by and let us get away with it.

"Now," Asey appealed to him. "I'll warrant that Mr. Kurth here offered you a reward, didn't he?"

"No," said the officer stolidly.

"Well, that was probably just because he was too excited. Now, you just take this for all your trouble. You know yourself, Cap'n, that we couldn't tell you fellers would be so smart an' so on your job as to snatch Mr. Kurth's car out from under him, as I guess you must of. Now, isn't that all right?"

The policeman mellowed under the influence of Asey's oratory, or his wallet.

"Well, if you say that everything's all right, I guess it is, an' I'll let it go. How do you feel about it, mister?" He turned to Kurth.

"Mr. Kurth," I hurriedly interposed, "has a fine sense of humor and I am certain that he is going to be kind and forgiving to us for our horrid practical joke, aren't you, John?"

He looked blankly at us all. "I'm sorry I made such a fuss if this is true," he said lamely. "Only usually when you find your car gone, apparently dissolved into thin air, you don't deduce the fact that some one wants to see you badly enough to make the police bring you to them."

He smiled and added another bill to the donation of Asey's. "It's all right, officer. Perfectly all right. You don't need to make any charges, or even to report this if you don't want to."

"Will you ever forgive us, Johnny?" Betsey asked as the policeman left. "It was a scrimy thing to do, but it seemed awfully funny at the time. Really it did."

"Don't give it another thought," he assured us. "The only thing that hurt was that I was out visiting Terry Carpenter, and he lives miles out on some sand-bar. You know where it is, don't you? Peaked Hill, they call it. And after plowing through acres of sand to come back and find my car gone and me miles from everywhere, was depressing, to say the least. But I got a lift back to Provincetown and sent the alarm in." He laughed. "That's a new one. Think of the possibilities of reporting peoples' cars as stolen!"

"Why didn't you come to see us if you were here on the Cape?" I asked.

"I knew you'd have a house full of company and I didn't think it would be the thing after angling for an invitation myself. I haven't seen you for how long? Two years?"

"All of that," I answered. "But where were you staying?"

"Down at Provincetown," he said. Asey and I looked at each other. "I tried the local hotel here, but they were all full. Isn't it around here that the murder was done? Or is that why you have that rope outside? And I hear that Bill Porter has been arrested. Grim."

"It's more than that," I replied. "But look, you didn't know Sanborn, did you? We're having an awfully hard time finding out anything about him."

"Knew him in a business way, that's all."

"Mr. Kurth," Dot, who had been staring at him since he had been introduced, spoke up, "weren't you the one who had some lawsuit with Dale? It seems to me I remember your name. Dale told me about it."

Kurth looked at her. His face was white under his heavy coat of tan.

"Lawsuit?" He repeated unsteadily.

"Yes, about those in his book or something like that."

"Oh, yes! Yes, of course." His voice was relieved. "Those lawsuits. There was some trouble about the book. Of course. Yes. There was a lawsuit, but we managed to get it settled before we got to court." His explanation was glib. "I'd almost forgotten all about that."

I could cheerfully have murdered Dot for suggesting an answer for him. Asey looked vexed with her, too.

"You haven't been down this way for some time," I remarked.

"No, I've been out in China till very recently. Been doing newspaper work there. But tell me about this Sanborn case. Bill Porter didn't do it, did he?"

"We don't think so," I said, "but it's a curious affair all around."

"How was he killed? The papers weren't very explicit about the weapon."

"We don't know what killed him other than that it was a blunt instrument. The local sheriff clings to the idea that the weapon was a hammer wielded by Bill, one that Dale Sanborn borrowed from us. That is, he thinks it was the handle of a hammer. But no one knows for sure."

"Hasn't any attempt been made to find out?"

"The sheriff is so sure of Bill and the hammer that he hasn't tried to work along any other lines at all."

"But aren't there any foot-prints or finger-prints or things like that?"

"Foot-prints wouldn't leave any trace in the soft sand around the cabin." I wondered if it were my imagination or whether Kurth had given a sigh of relief. "And finger prints," I went on, "are too advanced for this particular corner of the world."

"No clues of any sort?"

"There are clues enough, but they're not such mammoth aids. The principal mystery at the moment is the sardine tin that belonged to Bill which was found under the table and which was spirited away from Bill's car up to the cabin and its contents devoured by some unknown person."

Kurth nodded thoughtfully. "It beats me. It all seems so simple. I don't exactly mean simple, but there's such a lack of complications."

I sniffed inwardly. If John Kurth wanted to imagine that our discoveries since the previous morning had been simple and without complications, he was privileged to do so. But I knew better.

"I forgot all about Abe," Asey remarked contritely. "Betsey, will you run and tell him he can come out?"

Schonbrun came in, took one look at Kurth and smiled cheerfully. "So you got him? That's good."

"Got who?" Asey asked.

"The guy I was tellin' you about wandering around in the woods in back of the cabin Friday afternoon."

"You mean me?" Kurth laughed easily. "My dear man, you're sadly mistaken. I was in Boston Friday afternoon."

"I ain't mistaken. You had on a gray suit an' a green shirt an' a green tie an' a blue berry. I didn't think I'd know you without them, but I remember your face, it's so dark. I know it was you."

Kurth appealed to me. "Won't you explain to me just what this is all about?"

"Mr. Schonbrun," I said slowly, "thinks he saw you here on Friday. He has been helping us, that is, Asey and me," I foundered.

Asey came to the rescue. "We've been tryin' to get Bill Porter off, an' Abe's been helpin'. He saw a man behind the cabin Friday an' thinks you was him."

"I'm sorry. That is, I'm sorry to disappoint your discoveries in this amateur detecting stunt, but I really was not the man. Do I look like the sort of person who'd wear a green shirt and a beret?"

In his white flannels, brown coat, white shirt and brown tie he resembled a collar advertisement more than anything else.

"I don't know what sort of a man you are," Schonbrun said stoutly, "but whether you wore green shirts or not, you had one on Friday afternoon."

Asey looked at him. "Maybe you're mistaken, Abe. Perhaps it was just some one who looked like Mr. Kurth. Forget about it."

Tardily I recalled Asey's instructions to follow his lead. "Yes," I said, "perhaps you'd best say no more about it."

Schonbrun looked from me to Asey and back again. "Oh, very well. O.K. by me. Can't seem to please you two at all. Give you some information an' you get worked all up over it an' ten minutes later you want me to forget about it. O.K. by me. I will."

"Have you seen anything of——" I was trying to be tactful and at the same time ask him about Maida, but it was proving difficult.

"Of Maida?" He was very unconcerned. "No, I haven't. I believe she's in Paris."

"We're having more callers," Emma said pointedly.

I looked toward the doorway, where Doctor Reynolds stood waiting expectantly.

"Good morning. Possibly you didn't hear me. How's the head, Asey? Miss Prue, how did that sea-horse get bunged up last night?"

"Head's all better," said Asey. "I told you how I hurt myself. Fell off a roof."

"You didn't tell me anything of the sort," he expostulated.

It occurred to me that very soon I should have to introduce Schonbrun and Kurth and I wondered how I could do it without having the doctor demand all the information we had about the two of them.

Asey solved the problem. "This here is Mr. Abe, Doc, an' this is Mr. Kurth."

"Of course, Mr. Kurth." The doctor shook hands. "I have a very clear recollection of that grand slam you made when you were down here last. You bid it, if you remember, and made it doubled and redoubled. I had forgotten your face, Mr. Kurth, but not your achievement or your name. That reminds me, Miss Whitsby, did you ask Mr. Kurth about that note?"

"As a matter of fact he's been here only a few minutes and I've barely had time to say how-do-you-do."

The doctor was surveying Schonbrun. "I didn't catch the name," he said.

Schonbrun looked at him resentfully but made no answer.

"Abe," said Asey hastily. "Abe. He used to have another name, but he changed it. Just Abe. Great admirer of Lincoln, he is."

"Indeed." The doctor peered at Schonbrun. "Yes, yes. Of

course. Somehow he reminds me of some one I have seen, though of course I have a wretched memory for faces."

"It is hard to remember everything, isn't it?" Emma asked sweetly. She accented the "everything" ever so slightly.

"Quite so," said the doctor. "But I don't suppose you'd object if I were to ask Mr. Kurth a question or two? I'm connected with this case, after all."

"Go right ahead," Asey told him. "If Mr. Kurth don't have no objections."

"Well, Mr. Kurth," the doctor began, "in my examination of Mrs. Sanborn I found a note signed by you and although I brought it over here and showed it to Miss Whitsby, to ask her opinion on it, she said she was sure it had nothing to do with the case. For that matter, she said you were not in this country at all."

Kurth flashed a look at Asey and me. "I'm beginning to understand a lot of things," he said knowingly. "Miss Whitsby knew nothing of my whereabouts, Doctor. She was telling you the truth. Have you the note with you?"

The doctor passed it over, and Kurth read it through thoughtfully. "Yes, I remember that. I had just been telling these people here that I knew Dale Sanborn slightly in New York, and at one time I had had a lawsuit brought against him which was later satisfactorily cleared up, all but one or two points. Sanborn had used means to obtain information about the affair which I didn't consider strictly honorable. I found out about it only a week ago, and this is what the letter refers to. I'll admit that it seems a bit formidable after what has happened, but that is all there is to the matter."

"Did you hear from him?" The doctor asked.

"No, I didn't. I thought of course that my letter had missed him, and you'll find another just like this, more or less, at his New York apartment. I decided that my information about his being down here was wrong. I'd read about it in the paper."

Asey and I looked at each other.

"I came down here," Kurth continued, "to see Terry Carpenter. You know him, don't you?"

"The artist who lives on the dunes? I've heard of him though I don't know him personally." The doctor's tone implied that nomadic artists who lived on sand-dunes were scarcely numbered among his acquaintances.

"Well, I was coming down to see Terry, and I thought it would be a good plan to clear up loose ends with Sanborn at the same time."

"I see."

John Kurth's story was perfectly honest and straightforward as he told it; that is, it would have been if Asey and I had not known that he spent Friday night at one of Lonzo Bangs' cottages under an assumed name and if Schonbrun had not declared him to be the strange man of the green shirt.

"I see," the doctor repeated. It was evident that the doctor would not dream of questioning the word of a man who had bid and made a grand slam, doubled and redoubled.

"I'm glad." Kurth smiled. "That letter is more than ordinarily ominous. And it would have been unpleasant for me if it had fallen into the hands of some one who didn't know me. I can't imagine what I must have been thinking about."

"I see," said the doctor for the third time, "but what about that letter from your wife?"

"From my wife?" Kurth was genuinely puzzled. "But I haven't a wife. That is, Maida and I are divorced."

The doctor looked reprovingly at me. "And you with all your Lucy Stone talk. You know, Miss Whitsby, I don't like to be unpleasant, but the more I think of it the more it seems to me that you must have been deceiving me. In fact, it seems definitely suspicious to me."

"Don't be an utter idiot," I said with dignity.

"I'm sorry if I've hurt your feelings, but really, it is suspicious when any one has misled me the way you have. And Asey too." The doctor thumped his fist emphatically on the table. I was sure he hurt it. "Now, Mr. Kurth, you say you and your wife are divorced?"

"Yes," said Kurth shortly.

"Can you explain this letter?" He passed over Maida's note.

Kurth read it eagerly. "I'm afraid I can't," he said regretfully. "You see, it sounds as bad as mine does when you know none of the circumstances which surround the case. I don't happen to know what Maida's doing, but very likely she's in business and this is simply something connected with it. That's all the explanation I can give. Of course, it is a coincidence."

"Do you know if she's down here or whom she might be visiting?"

"My dear Doctor," said Kurth gently, "I believe she and I know people who summer in every town on the Cape. I'm sure of it. She might be anywhere from here to Plymouth or down to Provincetown. I couldn't tell."

"Hm." The doctor put the notes back in his breast pocket. "You don't seem to be much more of a help in the matter of these letters than Asey or Miss Whitsby. But I believe that

they're important. Your wife's, if not yours, Mr. Kurth. I'm going to find out more about them even if you say they're bridge
scores or invitations to a golf tournament. I think there's something behind them. I'm going to find out."

He stamped down the steps and drove away.

"Peppery sort, isn't he?" Kurth remarked. "I do hope you find
out who the guilty one is, but in spite of those rather incrim-
inating letters, I assure you that I am not the murderer, and I
don't believe Maida is either."

"The doc's just mad because he don't know more," Asey assured him. "He can't live happy till he knows all about everything. He's that sort."

Kurth rose. "I'm afraid I shall have to bid you all good-by.
Terry is all worked up about my car, and I shall have to run over
and let him know that everything has turned out all right. I'll
come back and see you again and I hope you won't have to steal
my car to make me."

Asey was making little motions with his forefinger.

"But you won't go right now, will you?" I protested, watching
the finger and trying to glean directions from it, "won't you have
a glass of ginger ale or something before you go? Betsey will
look after it, won't you?"

Kurth hesitated. "That's very kind of you."

But it was Asey who leaped from his seat and got but to the
kitchen before Betsey could move. "I'll get it" he said as he left.

It was some time before he came back bearing a tray and
glasses. I noticed that his hands were grimy, grease-smeared,
and that the nail of his right thumb was torn.

Kurth drained his glass. "Fine. Now I must be going."

We all followed him out to where his car stood by the garage.

In his absence Asey had done more than to open a few bottles of ginger ale. He had apparently turned burglar in a large way. The trunk on the back of the touring car had been rifled and an open suitcase lay on the running-board.

Over the radiator the irrepressible Asey had laid out a gray suit, green shirt, green necktie, and on top of all of them was the "berry."

Chapter Fifteen
ASEY GETS MYSTERIOUS

"WHAT DID I tell you?" Schonbrun chortled. "Was I right or was I right?"

"You put them there yourself." Kurth tried to bluff it out.

"Look at the name in the coat," Asey suggested. "Maybe I put John Kurth there, too? Mr. Kurth, I don't aim to be nasty, but if people won't tell me things, I got to find out for myself, ain't I?" He looked sadly at his torn nail. "See that? I got that an' a busted head this far in this 'vestigation all on account of what people won't tell me nice in'cent little things that most likely they could explain without any trouble attall if they was a mind to an' if they wasn't so scared some one'd arrest them. Are you mad, Mr. Kurth?"

"I'm not mad at all, Asey. I have been acting like a fool. I can explain everything, and there's no need of my being so childish. Only I don't see how you forced that lock. It's burglar proof."

"Used to chum around with a first-class second-story man from St. Looey," Asey informed him. "Real good cook he was, too. I learned a lot off him, one way and 'nother. Now shall this here meetin' 'journ inside an' get this matter all kind of straightened out now?"

We trooped back into the living-room.

"Now, Mr. Kurth, I want to find some things out, if you don't mind. Seems to me I asked more questions in the last day'n a half than I ever asked before'n my life. I'm goin' to 'ply for a job on the deestrict 'torney's squad after this is all done an' finished with. Now, you was to see Sanborn, wasn't you?"

"Yes."

"Time?"

"It was about a quarter or twenty minutes after five on Friday afternoon."

"You didn't drive up the road here. How'd you come?"

"I left my car stuck into the little blind lane about half a mile up the road. I came by foot the rest of the way and walked up the other side of the hill."

"Been there before ever?"

"No."

"How did you know so well how to get there, then?"

"Truth is," said Kurth haltingly, "I drove out along here earlier in the day. In the morning. I looked over the lay of the land then. I didn't want to be seen by the people here, because, well, because I didn't want to be seen."

"So you went the back way. See any one?"

"No, I thought I heard some one. Probably it was your friend here who was so sure he'd seen me. But those woods crackle underfoot and I didn't think much of the noise I heard."

"Go on. What'd you find in the cabin?"

"I looked in the window. Sanborn was lying on the floor."

"Didn't you go in?"

"No, I didn't. I've seen dead men before, Asey, and I knew he was dead. He wasn't in a faint or anything like that. I was in a fix. To begin with, if I went back and reported it to some one, they'd begin asking me questions. Then they'd ask Miss Whitsby about me and learn that I'd asked to come down. There would be the suspicious fact that when I'd come to see Sanborn I'd left my car and walked up here. I thought that a small-town sheriff would scent a plan and promptly put me in jail."

"Did a lot of thinkin'," Asey commented.

"One does, in a situation like that. Then I recalled the note I'd written Sanborn. It was two to one that that was lying around somewhere and that would be against me. You know," he reddened, "I read detective stories and it always seems that the person who finds the body is immediately suspected. I've told you that I'd had dealings with Sanborn, and that I had cause to think that he was not one of the more honorable men. In fact, *de mortuis* and all that, but he really didn't have too savory a reputation."

"We already deducted that," Asey said.

"So that my concern was not so much that he had finally been overtaken by fate as that my own position would be difficult to explain, that is, with any degree of lucidity. If I said I was coming to make a business call on him, then the business would be investigated and some one might think that there was sufficient personal animosity for me to have killed him. So like a villain in the movies, I slunk away the way I'd come. That's really all. I might add that the reason I didn't want to be seen was that I thought Miss Whitsby might be annoyed at my turning up after I hadn't heard from her and think she ought to do something about it."

"Did he have a blanket over him?"

"Who? Sanborn?" Kurth looked blankly at Asey. "No, he didn't. Did he have one on when he was found?"

"Yup. He did. That's the way Miss Whitsby found him."

"But he was just lying there when I saw him. There was nothing over him at all."

"Where were you Friday night?"

"Provincetown." John spoke assuredly, but more as though he were trying to convince himself than us.

"Why did you say you were in Boston Friday?"

"It was a lie. I wanted to see if I could get out of any complicity in this."

"Sure you weren't in town?"

"I was in Provincetown. Ask them at the Red Inn."

Asey smiled. "Don't suppose you ever heard of a man named Brown in New York City."

"There are any number of Browns in the city. The name is nearly as common as Smith."

"Feller I mean is William K. Brown. He drives a shiny new black Packard with red wire wheels. Number is 11-C-11. Sure you never met up with him?"

Kurth grinned. "Don't shoot. I'll come down. I admit it. Every bit of it. How did you know?"

"Do you expect to spend a night in a town that's got about nine hundred in it, most of 'em gossipy summer folks an' the rest gossipy natives without bein' spotted by some one? It can't be done, as the feller said when he tried to chew his elbow. No, sir. We knew all about you on yesterday mornin'. It was that an' not the green shirt or the note that got you took up by them police."

"I see." Kurth did not appear to be troubled.

"Look here, Mr. Kurth, don't you really know nothin' more about that note your wife sent?"

"Not a thing, Asey. I honestly didn't know she was on this side of the Atlantic. I haven't even the remotest idea of where she is now."

"Humpf." Asey considered. "Now, Mr. Kurth, will you be agreeable an' stick around here for a day or so, right where we can see you? I ain't got no 'thority to keep you, but I kind of think 'twould be the better part of valor if you was to stay."

"What do you mean?"

"Well, it wouldn't do you no good if we was to tell the doc an' the sheriff about you, would it now?"

"It certainly wouldn't."

"Well, I don't like to threaten any one, but I guess we'll have to tell 'em about everything 'less you kind of stay around till we get this matter threshed out. See?"

"I see, I'll stick."

"Can I depend on that?"

"I give you my word. I'll stay here and if there's anything I can do to help you get Bill off, I'll do it."

"Fair enough. Now, Miss Prue, I want you to come up to town with me. I want to see if we got any more telegrams. Bein' as how it's Sunday 'n Zenas at the office rings the bell in the Meth'dist church, I don't know how we're goin' to get 'em, but we'll manage. Abe, are you goin' to stay put too?"

"Yeah."

"Well, Mr. Kurth, I'll make you responsible for Abe anyhow. You see he don't go dashin' off somewheres. An' Abe, I think it would be just as good if you didn't do a lot of talkin'. You just sit an' watch. Pretend you're one of them monkeys as can't see nor hear nor talk no evil. Get me?"

Schonbrun nodded.

"All right then. Come along, Miss Prue. If that doctor comes wanderin' around, humor him but don't tell him nothin'."

We made our way through the curious-minded group that still hung about the rope along the beach road.

"Well," said Asey, "what d'you think?"

"Think? I've stopped thinking. I haven't had a constructive thought since Friday night."

"You know this Kurth better than I do. Do you think he's lyin'?"

"I don't know. I am far from satisfied with that 'book' idea Dot gave him. I don't think that's true. And I don't think it was why he came to see Schonbrun or Sanborn, whichever we ought to call the man. But I think the rest of what he has told us is true. I'm certain that what he said about his fear of being incriminated is so. Besides, if John Kurth had done this, he'd have been back to China by this time. He wouldn't have left any green shirts behind him. He's not a dull man."

"Might of been just a clever thought to get himself incrim'nated a little, if he knew he couldn't get out of it altogether."

"True enough. But I'm sure he doesn't know anything about Maida. I'll admit I thought there was some kind of plot between him and her, but he looked honestly worried when that doctor showed him the note of hers. And that doctor is annoying me. I wish he'd keep out of this."

"He's a dumb nuisance," Asey agreed. "Puts me in mind of a

bald man who pretends to have hair. He's just that set up about himself. What about Dot?"

"I think she's told us the truth at last, just as you predicted. But at the same time, Sanborn was alive when Bill left, if we are to believe Bill, and alive when she went to see him. And he wasn't alive later, if we are to believe Kurth and Schonbrun. You know, Asey, our trouble lies in the fact that we're dealing with ordinary people."

"How do you mean?"

"Every one has acted more or less as they would have acted. Both Dot and Kurth lied at first. It was the natural thing for them to do. But when they saw they couldn't get out of it entirely they told us the whole story. Both are incriminated, but both have loopholes to crawl out of. Schonbrun hasn't told us everything yet, I don't think, and as I said, I think Kurth is holding something back. But what I mean is, there are no masterminds at work to lead us astray. No one has been laying false trails or anything like that. The real murderer hasn't tried to cover anything up. I'm even inclined to agree with what Kurth said, that this was simple, or at least without complications."

"Maybe that's so." Asey sighed as he drew up in front of the telegraph office. "Now let's see how we can get holt of our telegrams."

He conferred with the baggage man.

"He says the best plan is to phone Hyannis an' see if there's anything there. Did anything happen at your place last night after we left? I clean forgot to ask you if any reporters had been botherin' you."

"I thought I heard some one down-stairs in the middle of the night, but it was only Dot getting a cigarette."

"Wouldn't it be hard on people," Asey said with a grin, "if

they didn't have cigarettes or books or pieces of candy to go trai-
lin' about after. So Dot was wanderin' about, was she? How'd
you happen to hear her?"

I told him about Ginger. "He seemed to think that there was
more to it than just Dot. I had the hardest time trying to get
him quiet. But I think he was just hearing things. Perhaps it
was some reporters or something prowling around."

"You mean he kept on actin' funny even after you an' Dot
came up-stairs?"

"Yes. But you don't think it was anything else, do you?"

"Don't know. I'll go in an' call Hyannis an' see what we got."

He came back. "Jimmy's wired me a thousand dollars f'r
expenses, an' I hear from that feller in Boston that Kurth an'
Maida had a suit for libel brought against Sanborn an' it was two
months ago. Now, what do you think about their bein' together
in this? I don't like to shake your opinions none, but p'raps Mr.
Kurth an' his wife is together in this thing after all. But the suit
got quashed. An' the feller in New York says only what we know
about Schonbrun bein' an agitator of sorts. He got run out of
the city. When was it Kurth said he come back from China?"

"He didn't say exactly. Just that he'd come back very lately, or
something like that. But the two of them, and a libel suit. That's
strange."

"Sure is. I guess maybe the ole doc was right. Maybe they
was more to them notes than we thought. Do you mind takin' a
little drive?"

"Of course not, but what for?"

"I want to think," said Asey plaintively, "an' I think better
when I'm movin'."

For perhaps two hours we roamed over back roads and small
woody lanes. His forehead was puckered. If he had worn oth-

er clothes and nose glasses I would have felt that he was a bank president pondering on a billion-dollar loan.

"You know," he said finally, "I think they's more to what Dot told us. I'm kind of sure that there's more in this Kurth an' his wife business than we know about, an' I'm sure Schonbrun's holdin' out on them sardines. But I don't think any of 'em did it, nor I don't think Bill did either."

"You exasperate me," I said. "Why?"

"Most folks, Miss Prue, is like other folks. I don't mean that they're all alike in everything, because they ain't. But from all the people I seen one place an' another, it seems to me that every one's got some little trick or other that's the same as some one else. Don't some of your friends remind you of other people?"

"I suppose they do," I admitted. "But what does that lead to?"

"I been thinkin' about the people as is connected with this. I been tryin' to remember who they was like an' what the quirks the other people they was like had. You take Dot. She might of been mad enough to strike Sanborn. I wouldn't think much of her if she hadn't. But she'd of slapped him in the face. She ain't the kind who'd killed him careful like he was killed. 'Cordin' to Slough, the doc said that most offhand murders was done by a blunt instrument. That's all right. But he said it was like a rabbit punch, too. Most women don't know nothin' about rabbit punches. If Dot had swung them binoculars at him, she'd of caught him in the face with 'em. She wouldn't have hit him when he wasn't lookin'. Bill might of socked him on the jaw, but he wouldn't of used the handle of a measly old hammer. Nor jiu-jitsu neither. Them two ain't that kind of person. Now Kurth would of shot him. They was a gun in that suitcase, but it was loaded an' a box of cartridges beside it was full too, an' the gun hadn't been used in a dog's age."

"But couldn't he have used it as a blunt instrument?"

"He could of. An' that's something I didn't think of. But just the samey, he'd of used the gun the way God meant for guns to be used. An' the brother would of used a knife. He carries one, I found out. That was what cut me up last night, not that stick he used. I got the knife away from him, but I didn't have the strength to do any more than throw it far's I could. He's just like that feller I said he was like. But Sanborn wasn't killed by a knife, an' I honestly don't think, Miss Prue, that he's got the innerds to kill, that Abe. He fought me more because he was skeared than because he wanted to hurt me. He's too frightened of cops to do a thing that would get him stuck into jail for good. No, I don't think any of 'em done it."

"Then who did?"

"Well, let's go over that mob that visited him. First the brother, then Bill, then Dot, then the brother again, then some one who visited the cabin at night. Now 'cordin' to my opinion, there was some one who slipped in right after Dot an' after doin' the job, left just as quick before Schonbrun got there. Did you ever see a pack of gulls after a fish?" He asked abruptly, stopping the car.

"Of course," I said impatiently.

"Look over there." He pointed to the bay. "Watch them birds. They's half a dozen there, circlin' an' swoopin'. See, every last one of 'em's made a try at that fish an' none of 'em's got it. But see that one comin' up?"

Far beyond the noisy gulls a streak of white sped across the sky.

"Watch him. Look!"

The bird flew high over the little flock. Suddenly like a landing aeroplane it zoomed down through them, snatched the fish in its vermilion beak and sped away before the others were fairly conscious of what had happened.

"That there's what I mean," said Asey thoughtfully. "You see? It was quick, like that, but it was careful too. I don't think it was any one who'd planned to do it before-hand, but they did it quick, and thorough like. If it'd been a plan, we'd 'a' found more traces of it, because when a spider makes a web, you find it. Don't no animal attall set out to do anything that it don't leave some traces of it. That's the trouble here, Miss Prue, not so much that we're dealin' with common people. You can't find no traces of any plan attall. If any one had thought it out before-hand, most likely they'd of done it at night anyway, so that by the time that it got found out, he or she could of been num'rous miles away. You know, the Cape ain't the best place in the world to do murder. If you try to get away by sea, you got to know an awful lot about the coast; if you go by land, they's only two directions you can go. If you go to Provincetown, you're bottled up. They's nowhere left to go. An' unless some one got away quick, they'd get caught comin' up the Cape, like tryin' to crawl out the neck of the bottle."

"I thought of that on Friday night," I said.

"So I don't think much of this was planned beforehand. An' if that's the case, the person who done it is still around, because most likely it's some one who can't get away now without askin' for trouble."

"But who?"

"Only other people connected with this as far as we know are you an' Betsey an' Mrs. Manton an' Olga. Olga an' Betsey is all alibied."

"Possibly," I said with some frigidity, "you think that she and I did it together."

"I didn't say any such thing. Only you an' her has only got say-so alibis, though I got to admit I believe both of you. Well, we'll get along home. Maybe we can dig up the rest of the stories from these folks. Right now I feel like a kid as has been playin' hide-an'-seek. I've sort of looked in all the places where people'd hide in that I could think of, but some one's gone an' found a new spot. We got to know more yet before we can get to find the one that ain't got home to the goal."

"I certainly hope you won't make me, and Emma Manton too, the ones who are 'it,'" I said disdainfully. "Really, I didn't kill Sanborn, and I should sooner think of a checker player in a Rogers group making a move than of Emma being guilty."

"There, there," said Asey soothingly. "You keep cool. Else I'll think you got a guilty conscience. Don't go for to get mad at me."

At the cottage we found every one amiably settled on the porch.

"Mr. Schonbrun has been teaching us how to shoot craps," Emma informed us tranquilly. "I haven't had such fun since I played tiddley-winks when I was a girl."

"Emma Manton! Do you mean to tell me that you, you of all people, have been shooting craps, and of a Sunday morning?" I sighed in mock horror but Schonbrun thought I meant it.

"You don't need to worry none about this lady here, you don't. She's lifted my roll off me an' she's cleaned out the rest."

"Beginner's luck," said Emma modestly.

"Not only that," Kurth added, "but she's beaten each and every one of us, individually and collectively, at every game we've played to while away the hours."

"My luck comes in streaks," Emma remarked. "They're very few and very far in between streaks, too. Speaking of whiling

away the hours, Prudence, and not meaning to be rude or anything like that, but do I smell dinner cooking or do I not? My
luck is always accompanied by an equally phenomenal appetite."

"I'm sorry. I'd forgotten all about my duties as a hostess. I'll
go out and tell Olga to hurry."

Asey got up from his chair. "Don't you bother, Miss Prue.
You didn't know you was feedin' this whole regiment today. I'll
go out an' help the girl; it's more kind of like my line of work."

As he disappeared into the kitchen I wondered what new
idea he had, for something certainly was in his mind. It was
perfectly possible that he wanted to help Olga, on the other
hand after his discovery of Kurth's clothes while supposedly being a kitchen helper, I couldn't help being curious. I made some
attempt at conversation, then excused myself on the pretext of
looking at the roast.

I came into the kitchen just in time to see Olga stuffing a
small wad of bills into her pocket. Asey was garbed in a blue
checked apron, apparently engrossed with a succulent-looking
gravy.

He looked at me and grinned. "Now, we don't need you one
bit, Miss Prue. Olga an' me is gettin' along famous. You run
right back to your comp'ny, an' we'll get dinner done before you
could say Jack Robinson."

"I don't want to say Jack Robinson. And I'm not going to be
ordered out of my own kitchen."

"Course you ain't. But you'd be real foolish to stay here an'
get all hot when you didn't have to."

I reflected that Asey Mayo could make people feel very ri-
diculous. I went back to the porch, but in a few minutes I heard
Olga go up-stairs. I listened as well as I could with the conversation of the rest buzzing at full speed.

Olga was going into my room.

"Did you find out any more?" Betsey asked.

"Not a thing," I replied absently. Now Olga was moving into Emma's room. I thought I heard a drawer squeak. What was Asey up to?

"See Bill in his box-car?"

"We didn't go around that way."

"Did you meet the sheriff or Doctor Reynolds?"

"No," I said irritatedly, "we didn't see any one at all." Olga had moved on into the girls' room. I heard a closet door bang.

"Snoodles, darling, don't be mad. Remember, we haven't been barging all over creation the way you have. We haven't been away from here for ages and we're naturally curious."

"I know." I pulled myself together. "How did you like China?" I asked Kurth desperately.

Kurth told us about China, and I thanked heaven that his voice was low and that the others had stopped talking to listen. I hoped that no one would take advantage of his monologue to wind a watch as is usually the case when one strains one's ears to hear something. Putting on an interested face and looking as though I were taking in every syllable, I listened as I had never listened before for Olga's footsteps.

She was back in my room.

What in the world had Asey sent her for, and what was she hunting in my room? Whom in the household did he suspect? And why had he not told me?

Chapter Sixteen
MAIDA PAYS A CALL

WHEN OLGA came down I made another excuse and followed her out into the kitchen. Asey was tucking some small object away in his pocket.

He smiled as he saw me. "You seem to be real uneasylike about this dinner. But it's all done an' ready an' you call your folks out of the porch to eat this instant minute."

I told Olga to call them. As she went I turned to Asey. "What is all this about? What have you been sending her for? Whom are you suspecting now?"

Asey grinned. "You really want to know what she give me?"

"I most certainly do. What was it?"

He lowered his voice. "I busted a button an' I needed a safety-pin. She just went up to find me one as was big enough."

"Don't tell me whoppers like that and expect me to believe them. What was it really?"

"Honest an' truly, it was only a safety-pin." He peeled off his apron. "Now you run along into the dinin'-room an' let me repair my damage."

After dinner Betsey proposed a swim. "After all, I don't see why we shouldn't go down to the beach. There's not much of a crowd and I don't think any one would bother us. May we?"

"You might as well. Or do you think, Asey, that some of those roving reporters might pounce on them?"

"They might's well. If they collect a mob they can always run back home. Sure, go along."

Betsey went to the hook where the bath-house key was kept. "We'll have to take turns getting ready. I say, Snoodles, where's the key?"

"Just where you left it."

"But it isn't. And it was here this morning, because I noticed it not an hour ago."

"Maybe it's fallen off the hook," Emma suggested.

Betsey knelt down and searched the floor. "It hasn't. Now what do you suppose can have happened to it? This is silly. Did any one pick it up the way Bill picked up the hammer?"

"I'm sure I don't know. Has any one seen it?"

No one had.

"This is absurd," said Betsey crossly. "Now, how can we go swimming at all? All the suits are in the bathhouse."

"Break in," Dot offered.

"You simply can not do any such thing," I said sternly. "The last time we had to break in I told the carpenter to arrange it so that we couldn't break in again. This is the fourth key that's been lost this summer, and I'm sick and tired of paying bills for repairs to that lock. You can wait till tomorrow and have some one file the lock off or make you a new key."

"Haven't you a spare key?" Emma asked.

"Betsey lost that a week ago."

"How about getting the carpenter now?"

"Can't," Asey said. "He's chief umpire for the baseball league an' to-day he's up to Dennis."

"Aren't there any extra suits in the house?" Dot asked.

"Olga has hers," I said, "if you don't mind orange stripes, and there's mine. Betsey, you have an old one somewhere, haven't you?"

"That'll fix up the girls," Emma remarked, "and probably Mr. Kurth has a suit with him. Mr. Schonbrun and I can sit and watch. I refuse to appear in orange stripes. They can get dressed up here."

After much bustling about they finally crowded into Kurth's car and drove down to the beach.

"Now, Asey," I said, "will you tell me why you had Olga take that bath-house key?"

"How long's a bath-house key been a safety-pin?" he drawled.

"You must have that key. I'm sure that it is what Olga gave you. Why do you want it?"

"Poof," he returned. "Dot might have taken it last night absent-minded when she was huntin' for her cigarette. Or it might of got brushed up when Olga was sweepin'."

"But Betsey said she saw it this morning."

"Just because she's so used to seein' it there she took it for granted. Probably it wasn't there attall."

"Look here, Asey," I was indignant, "you have some idea and you're keeping it from me. Why? And what is it?"

Asey looked as though an ice cube wouldn't melt in his mouth. "Miss Prue, you've got so used to suspectin' people that you just can't get yourself out of the habit."

"Your innocence doesn't fool me one bit. I should say that

it was you who were used to suspecting people and I'm afraid you're suspecting me."

"Honest injun," he said aggrievedly, "it ain't that attall. Now what I want to know is, what about that there libel suit? Don't that seem kind o' funny to you?"

"If you won't tell, I suppose it couldn't be dragged from you by wild horses. I don't know any more about Kurth and his old libel suit than you do. As a rule," I added acidly, "people have a good and sufficient reason for the things they do."

"Yup. They do. Hey, here's the old doc again."

Reynolds came up the steps wearing a triumphant smile on his face. "I hope," he said complacently, "that I'm not interrupting you two ferrets, but I have a little something I should like to tell you."

He sat down, lighted a cigar and crossed his long legs.

"Fire away," said Asey in a tired tone.

"I intend to. I have just called up a friend of mine in New York. A member of the card club I belong to. He collects Sheraton, but that's beside the point. Kurth belonged to that club too, if you recall."

"I didn't," I said politely.

"I asked him if he knew anything about Kurth and Sanborn. He did. Kurth lied when he said that his lawsuit against Sanborn was a matter 'about a book.' It was a libel suit."

"We found that out too," Asey murmured.

"Why didn't you say so then? Really, Mayo, I can't see that you and Miss Whitsby have been very fair or very intelligent in keeping all your information sealed up as though it were in a Federal Reserve vault. Why don't you do something about it?"

"If you held on to a jack long enough in this bridge or whist or whatever 'tis you fancy so much, didn't it usually take a trick?" Asey asked.

"What's that got to do with the matter?"

"Nothin' 'cept we're holdin' on to all the jacks in the pack. That's just the way we like to play games."

The doctor snorted. "Furthermore, Kurth's wife is mixed up in this too. And Kurth and Sanborn are open enemies and have been for the last four or five years. On one occasion a few months ago, Kurth publicly insulted Sanborn and knocked him down."

"Did Sanborn fight back?" Asey asked interestedly.

"I'm sure I don't know. As a matter of fact, my friend said that he didn't. But can't you two get it into your heads that there's something in all this?"

"Nope," said Asey.

The doctor clamped his teeth down on his cigar.

"Very well. If you won't accept or act upon my suggestions, you may take the consequences. I'll take the whole matter to Sullivan and lay it before him. He couldn't be much stupider about this than you are. It's my opinion that you're shielding Kurth, or," he threw out a Parthian shot as he descended the steps, "else you did it yourselves."

"Hm." Asey looked after him thoughtfully. "Did you ever notice, Miss Prue, what curious people doctors was? They want to know everything, even though they pretend it's all just for p'fessional purposes, an' they git mad if they ain't told. But I don't see for what he's wanderin' around so much tryin' to get some one else mixed up for. It really ain't none of his business attall. If he comes around much more I'm goin' to suspect him."

"Why don't you?" I suggested. "He and the sheriff are the only two you've overlooked."

"You got me all wrong, Miss Prue. I'm tryin' to use what experience I got and what common sense I think I got. I can't do no more. If I was one of those fellers that makes up a list of words an' then get people to listen to 'em an' say the first thing that comes into their heads, I'd do it. What you call that way?"

"Word association?"

"Yup. Well, if I was a feller as understood that, I'd use it. If I understood about finger-prints an' microscopes an' things like that, I'd use 'em up too. But I don't. Like the kid in the piece he wrote about two apples an' a piece of pie,—I ain't 'temptin' any flights of fancy but just's the things that's in me. A handful of common sense an' a little imagination is worth all them notions anyways. I told you I got an idea, that some one flipped in after Dot an' done it. It may of been her, or Kurth, or his wife. Or others. But I think I got it all straightened out my way, an' I kind of think my way's right."

"I didn't mean to cast any aspersions on your efforts, Asey. I only wanted you to tell me what you were sending Olga after."

He smiled. "They always said your father was like a snappin' turtle in court, Miss Prue. That two thunderstorms an' God A'mighty couldn't stop him when he made his mind up to get something out of a witness. You're like him. Now, s'pose you just trust me an' let it go at that. I know it seems funny for me to go sneakin' a bath-house key——"

"Then it was that?"

"Yup. But I got a reason. Now——"

"But why didn't you ask me for it? I should have given it to you."

"I know. Only I kind of wanted it to seem like it was lost. I still do. An' I don't want you to say nothin' about it to any one."

"Very well."

"Don't say a word even to the cat. Promise?"

"I shan't mention it to a soul. But I do think it's a little foolish."

"Even ole Sherlock Holmes, Miss Prue, had to do somethin' funny every so often so's folks would keep on bein' 'mazed by him. He had to let 'em know he was thinkin' about fifteen miles ahead of 'em, so's they could say wasn't he wonderful when he broke down an' explained it all. Maybe I ain't so trans-trans-something——"

"Transcendant?"

"Yup. That. Maybe I ain't as much that as I ought to be, but I believe in givin' the public a show for its money. An' it's just possible that I caught sight of the gull that got the fish. Here's something comin', Miss Prue. It's reporters, or else——"

I turned and looked.

"It is, Asey, it's Maida!"

She was thinner and harder-looking than when I had seen her last, but she was every whit as charming and as well-dressed.

"Miss Prudence!" She kissed me effusively. "I shouldn't be running in on you like this, but I read about that dreadful Sanborn affair in the papers and about your finding him and all, and I simply couldn't resist coming in to see you. That barrier is such a clever idea. What a darling cottage and a wonderful view!"

I answered as millions have answered before to such comments. "We like it."

"I should think you would. But haven't you been bothered to death by reporters and people?"

"The doctor has kept off the newspapermen, and the rope has kept off the rest. You know Asey Mayo?"

She smiled at him. "No, but I've heard of him from Jimmy. Tell me, what have you done to get Bill out of this?"

"Lots of things," Asey replied. "Did you pick up a man on the Provincetown road yesterday an' give him a lift to Wellfleet?"

She seemed surprised. "You mean in the afternoon? Yes. How did you know?"

"Ever seen him before?"

"Not that I remember. Why do you ask?"

"It's been a sort of habit with me lately. I can't get myself out of it. Please don't think I'm rude or anything, but are you sure you never seen him?"

"I'm sure, though I remember thinking he reminded me of some one. I don't remember who, though."

"Could it have been Dale Sanborn?"

Maida rose from her chair. "What do you mean?"

"Don't get excited, now. If he didn't that's all right. Have you found the little pin you lost, the one with your initials on it yet?"

Maida looked from Asey to me and back again. "I don't understand you. Have you second sight or something like that?"

Asey pulled the trinket from his pocket and passed it to her. "Where did you find it? How did you know it was mine?"

I explained that Asey and I had been doing some detecting on our own account.

She fastened the pin on her dress. "I still don't understand."

"Do you mind if I ask you more?" Asey wanted to know.

"Not if you've found anything else that belongs to me. I lost an adorable beaded bag a week ago and nothing would please me more than to have you drag that out of your pocket in a rabbit's mouth or wrapped in an American flag."

" 'Fraid it isn't anything as pleasant as all that. Tell me what you were doing about or in Sanborn's cabin on Friday night."

Her toe tapped against the floor. "But I wasn't there."

"But we know you was, Mrs. Kurth."

"Please don't call me that."

"All right. Miss Waring, then. You were there, weren't you?"

"I certainly was not."

"Well, where were you?"

"I was staying with friends in Hyannis." She turned to me. "You know the Cutlers, don't you?"

"Yes," I said. "But they left last week for California. I'm sorry, Maida, but they did."

She was silent.

"Hadn't you better tell us right now, Miss Waring?" Asey suggested. "It's goin' to be kind of unpleasant like if you don't. Now, you was at the cabin Friday night?"

"Yes, I went there."

"And you found Sanborn?"

"Yes. He was dead."

"And what did you do?"

"I had a flash-light. I looked at him, saw he was dead and left."

"Humpf. What'd you go to see him about?"

"On business."

"Miss Waring," said Asey listlessly, "will you stop lyin'? Miss Prue an' I have been over this business since yesterday mornin'. We know a lot. We know about your letter. Don't try to hedge like the rest. I used to think that the human race told the truth once in a while anyways, but I'm changin' my mind. This ain't just ord'nary lyin'. This is gettin' to be plag'rism. Now, you tell us why you went there an' what you wanted to see him for."

"It was all a matter of business," said Maida firmly.

Asey sat up very straight in his chair. "I am gettin' tired of people that think I'm dull b'cause I don't use big words. I'm tireder of havin' people tell me fish stories. I'm tireder yet of havin' to drag things out of people. In fact, I'm gettin' downright plum honest-to-goodness mad. It's been comin' on for a long time. There ain't nothin' like havin' patience. I was always taught t' admire Job. But twenty Jobs an' sixty Griseldas wouldn't be able to stand this. Miss Waring, I'm givin' you one more chance. You tell me why your husband an' you started that libel suit against Sanborn. Tell me why you went to see him. Tell me why you didn't let people know he was dead. Tell me why you put that blanket over him. An' hurry."

I looked at Asey. His lips were pressed tightly together. His eyes blazed. For the first time since I had known him he seemed thoroughly angry. His pose of nonchalant indifference had melted away like a snow-storm in April. Maida looked at him and decided to answer.

"I didn't tell because I lost my head when I saw him lying there. I was utterly frightened to death. I touched him and every bit of common sense just went from me. I put the blanket over him because I felt I ought to do something, and it didn't seem right just to leave him lying there. That's the truth."

"I hope it is. It's funny to me that all the people who saw him an' knew he was dead just edged away into space again. How'd they know he was killed? He might of had heart failure or a dozen different things, yet every one was skeared to tell. It ain't like he'd been shot or stabbed."

"Any one who knew Dale Sanborn," Maida blazed out, "would know in an instant he didn't just die. He wasn't the sort of man who just dies. They say some people were born to be hanged. Dale Sanborn was born to be murdered. No one who knew him would stay around if they found him dead; no one would ever tell of it. Because every one who knew him had a good reason for killing him."

"We know that," said Asey abruptly. "Why did you seem surprised when Mrs. Howe told you that there was a sardine tin next to him? Didn't you see it?"

"No. I went all to pieces when I found him. I didn't notice the tin at all. I didn't know about it till she told me."

"You haven't told us yet why you went to see him."

She repeated that she had gone there on business.

"Please tell us your real purpose," I urged. "We have reason to think that if you do it will clear Bill and get him out of that wretched box-car. Won't you?"

"It was business."

"Well," said Asey decisively, "if you won't tell us there's only one way left for me. Here comes the rest. That's fine. We'll do the whole matter up brown right now. Hurry up, you. I want to talk to you."

Kurth gave one look at Maida. "What are you doing here?" He rushed to her and took her in his arms.

"Just like a movie," said Asey. "A bad third-rate movie. Mr. Kurth, will you wait up a minute? I've got something I want to say."

Kurth paid no attention to him. "You found out too? How did you find out? Were you coming to see him?" he murmured.

"Will you listen to me?" Asey spoke in a quarter-deck voice.

He waited till John and Maida turned to him. "Now, if all of you is listenin', I've got something to say. I'm tired of fussin' around an' bein' credulous an' kind an' nice. If I had my way I'd belt the truth out of you with a piece of hose. You listen to me,

Kurth, an' you too, Miss Waring, an' Schonbrun, an' all of you. I'm goin' to march you up to the sheriff this instant. I'm goin' to tell him everything I know an' a lot I suspect. Shut up!" This to Schonbrun who started to remonstrate. "Keep quiet! All of you three is keepin' something back, even if what you told me is true, which I ain't so sure of. I'm goin' to give you ten seconds to make up your minds. Kurth, are you an' your wife going to tell me about this lawsuit, an' those notes, an' how well you knew Sanborn an' what you had against him an' what you come to see him for? Or are you goin' to tell it to the judge to-morrer mornin'? Well?"

Kurth looked at Maida. She nodded. "Yes."

"Glad you got a little sense. Now, Schonbrun, what about you? You comin' clean about the sardines or not? Yes or no?"

"You said——"

"I know I did. But it's an old custom to change your mind an' break your promise when folks don't hold to their part of a bargain. I said I wouldn't get you into no trouble 's long's you told me everything. You ain't. What about it?"

"O. K.," said Schonbrun sulkily.

"Fine. Get seated, every one. Get set." Asey pulled a jackknife out of his pocket and pulled out the long gleaming blade. Carefully he balanced it on his knee. "May not seem much of a weapon, but I can slice a pin head with that at a right good distance. I could hit any one that gets in a hurry to beat it a whole lot easier. Get goin', Kurth. Break down. Spill the beans. Come clean. What's all this about?"

Chapter Seventeen
GETTING DOWN TO BUSINESS

"Where shall I begin?" Kurth asked quietly.

"Where do you usually begin? Begin at the beginnin' for a change. It's about time for some one to begin there instead of the end. If I'd wanted you to begin at the end, I'd of said so. Where'd you meet up with Sanborn first?"

"I met him about four or five years ago in New York. I was working for the Rayman Publishing House at the time. He had some ideas about a new novel that he wanted us to handle. I brought him home for dinner. That was where Maida met him first. We both liked him. He was amusing, witty, interesting and a good talker. We developed a friendship with him. Maida had a friend, Alice Harding, and the four of us ran around together a lot."

"Alice Harding?" Dot interrupted. "I used to know her. Didn't she kill herself or something?"

"Yes." Kurth's tone was bitter. "I'll tell you all about that later. We were all very intimate. You know how it is when four people are together a great deal. Well, the long and short of it is—do you remember the book Sanborn wrote that was called the greatest expose of married life in America?"

It was the book I had tried to read and given up, as I had told Bill. "About the girl who loved a man who was married to a woman who loved a man who cared for the first girl?" I asked.

"Yes. That's the one. If you think it out you can see how it applied to the four of us, Alice, myself, Maida and Sanborn.

I gasped. "Do you mean——?"

"Exactly. That was the way Sanborn repaid our friendship. We read the book when it came out, expecting it to be the one he had told us about, the life of an opera singer. But we found the story of the four of us. It was the reason for our divorce."

"But I never dreamed of such a thing," Betsey said.

"You didn't know we were the characters? Probably you wouldn't. Sanborn stuck very much to the truth, but the whole thing was colored and touched up and distorted so that the whole affair was ugly and sordid. Alice read it and came over to see us about it. We called Sanborn in and asked him to explain."

"Did he?" Asey asked.

"He laughed at us as though we were so many puppets on a string. He admitted that he had taken us for his characters. He thought he had been exceedingly clever."

"Did every one know it was you?"

"No one knew for sure. There were a good many whispers, though. You know how it is in New York. You have different groups of friends but most of them don't know that the others exist. And the book wasn't exactly the type that friends would care to connect you with, to your face, at least. But we knew. The hellish part of it was that I didn't know how much of it was true, about Maida and Sanborn, of course. Nor could she tell about Alice and myself. As a debunking of married life it certainly dug deeper into the muck than any other forty books you could name. But can't you see how it was? We didn't know how much was true and how much was Sanborn's imagination. We couldn't tell how much of us people recognized. There is always a certain amount of petty deception between two people, but we couldn't tell from what he'd written how much each of us had been deceiving the other. Things went from bad to worse. I let Maida divorce me, though we did the thing as quietly as we could and neither Sanborn nor Alice was mentioned. We couldn't bring him in without dragging her through the mire, and we didn't want to do that. We were in an uncomfortable position. If we sued him or made any fuss about the book we would be overwhelmed by the publicity, and at the time it simply would have meant that I'd have lost my job and all the chances of getting another one."

"So you went an' divorced yourselves without gettin' at the root of things?" Asey asked disgustedly.

"You can't imagine how terrible it was, Asey," Maida told him. "You see, it was true that I'd been indiscreet with Sanborn, though not nearly to such an extent as he portrayed it in the book. It was really a very mild flirtation. I couldn't make Johnny see it and of course I had been a little jealous of Alice. None of the three of us really trusted the other at all. It just got more and more involved all the time."

"What about the other girl?"

"We thought, and so did she, that Sanborn really cared for her," Kurth answered. "I think she played about with me more to pique him than anything else. But after the book episode, he left her absolutely alone. Didn't go near her or write her or anything. One night as she was waiting outside a theater for a cab with another man, he casually asked her if she'd seen Sanborn lately. She was abnormally sensitive about the affair. We all had been upset over it, but she had taken it even harder than we, I think. She made some answer, turned away from him, then slid and fell in front of a taxi that was drawing up to the curb. The police called it an accident but we knew better. The man she was with was certain it was done on purpose, too. The girl she lived with told Maida that the night before she'd come home unexpectedly early and found Alice all but unconscious. She'd shut herself in the kitchenette and turned on the gas."

Schonbrun nodded his head vigorously. "That makes two girls, his mother an' two others I know of that's got Dave to thank for gettin' themselves killed, one way an' another. An' a divorce. They was probably more, too. I told you so."

"What's that got to do with this here libel suit?"

"Coming back from China," Kurth answered, "I met a chap on the boat who told me about Sanborn and his habit of debunking people. Debunking humanity is his term. He was a doctor who had known Sanborn and if you remember, there was a book not so long ago about doctors and the medical profession. Only Sanborn had made his character too much like the original and this fellow had been forced to leave his practice. He told me his own story and then described what Sanborn had done to it. Suddenly I realized what an ass I'd been. When I got back I dashed to a lawyer and started that libel suit in both our names. I don't know why I did, except that I was more furious than I'd been before about the whole matter. I didn't know where Maida was or anything about her, but I went right ahead."

"N'en what?" Asey asked.

"Then my lawyer made me see light. Such a suit was bound to cause a lot of talk, bring the matter up again and drag out all sorts of unpleasant details. In all probability it wouldn't do any good and a lot of harm. So he dropped it. I saw Sanborn once. He tried to duck me, and it made me so mad I knocked him down. After that he kept out of my way. Then last week I was in Boston and read of his being down here. I thought I might be able to collar him and drag the truth out of him, that is, find out how much of that story had been his imagination. I sent you that telegram. Then when I had no reply I came down on my own hook."

"What'd you use another name for?"

"Because I didn't think any one would recognize me and I scarcely wanted any one to know how anxious I was to get at Sanborn. After all, it was a ten-to-one chance that I'd never see the Whitsbys. I didn't know that he'd moved up next door to them. I had every intention of getting a written statement from him and then beating him within an inch of his life. Then I was going to find Maida and get things settled again. You can imagine how I felt when I saw him lying there."

"What about you?" Asey turned to Maida. "How do you come into this at this point?"

"I'd always felt that John and I had acted like two idiots to have gone and separated like that without finding out about things. But at the time I was as wrathful as he was. Last week I landed in Boston and saw Sanborn's name in that paper as staying down here; and I thought I would come down and see him and try to find out about things. I don't know why I was reading the Cape news so assiduously except that we had a lot of friends down here and I had been out of touch with them so long. I telegraphed Miss Prudence thinking that the hot weather would be a good excuse to ask to come down. Then I met a man I knew in Boston who said he'd seen Johnny and that he was coming down to see some one here. It was Carl Thorndike, John, and he said that you must have some deep-seated reason for coming because you'd refused to go to Maine with him. I put two and two together and decided that you were after Sanborn too, and I had some notion of stopping you before you did anything rash."

"That's all?"

"Absolutely all, Asey. I came here Friday night. I went into the cabin,—I found out where it was from a man at a gasoline station,—intending to wait till he got home. I thought of course when I saw no light that he was out somewhere. You know the rest. Except that I should be only too glad to get the person who killed him off, even though I'd like to help Bill."

"Speaking of doctors and things," Kurth remarked, "I wonder about that doctor who's popping about here. That physician I met on the boat said that there'd been another involved in that. He didn't mention his name, and it's a very remote chance, of course, but do you suppose this Reynolds has anything to do with this? He seems almost too anxious to get the murderer. Is there any reason for him to involve himself in this?"

"He's the medical examiner," I said, "and I suppose he thinks it's a part of his duty since Sullivan is so dead set on convicting Bill. What do you think, Asey?"

He shook his head. "Beyond me. He sure knew a lot about what killed Sanborn. And I saw his car comin' up the beach road Friday afternoon myself. I don't know. Miss Prue, I'm still sure what I told you is right, and this suggestion of Mr. Kurth's here might be an explanation of it. Abe, are you dead sure you saw that flash of white before you went to the cottage?"

"I'm pretty sure, boss."

"If that's true, it ought to of been a woman. I don't think it was Dot, though all we got to go on is that fact about the time, an' that's kind of slim. Dot, it 'pears to me that the sword hangin' over your head is danglin' from an awful thin thread."

"I know it is," said Dot resignedly. "But on my word, I didn't kill Sanborn. He was alive when I left that cabin. That's the truth, though I can't prove a single word of it."

"The doctor wears white knickers most of the time," Betsey suggested. "That could have been the flash of white, couldn't it?"

"It could of. Abe, you take the floor. You picked up that tin of sardines, didn't you?"

"Yes. An' how you know beats me."

"You shouldn't of left the key lyin' around in your pocket, even if lyin' is a habit of yours. I picked it off you when you was bangin' my head in. Why didn't you want to tell us about them sardines?"

"Well," Schonbrun began, but Asey interrupted him.

"Don't go beginnin' by sayin' well an' hedgin' an thinkin' up more things. Tell us right out."

"Those folks will tell you why." He motioned to Kurth and Maida.

Asey looked questioningly at Kurth.

"Sanborn was a perfectly normal person in most ways," Kurth explained, "but he had a horror of sardines that was definitely abnormal. There are plenty of people who don't like certain things to eat. Almost every one has something that they'd just as soon pass by. But Sanborn went absolutely off his head when he saw a sardine or even heard them mentioned. It resembled an epileptic fit more than anything else. He simply wasn't right in his head or something. One night at the apartment I opened a tin of sardines. Alice started to caution me, but before I'd caught on Sanborn had seen them. He all but frothed at the

mouth with rage and left the house. We never mentioned sardines after."

"I wonder why he did," I said.

"I don't know. But I've heard of stories of shell-shocked men
who became unconscious when a car back-fired and all that. I
suppose it's a complex or a phobia of some sort."

"I still don't see why you wouldn't tell us about the tin," I
said to Schonbrun. "And do you know why he acted that way
about them?"

"I didn't tell you, an' I wasn't goin' to. I'll have to go back to
the beginnin' again. You know I told you he worked in a factory
afternoons when he was in school?"

"Yup." I noticed that Asey had pocketed his jack-knife.

"It was a sardine factory. We didn't have much money an'
Dave used to bring home sardines when we didn't have anything
else to eat. He hated sardines, always, because he got sick from
eatin' too many of 'em when he was a kid. I guess workin' over
'em all day didn't help him to like 'em any better. Once when ma
wasn't workin' an' they'd laid off hands at the factory we lived
on 'em for a whole week. I got tired from eatin' them myself.
But Dave, he used to get just like these people said, whenever
he saw them. An' there wasn't nothing else for him to eat, that
time. Soon after he went back to the factory again he got fired
and got another job. It wasn't much later he beat it for good."

"But why——" Asey persisted.

"I'm comin' to that. Friday I found the tin at the foot of the
hill. I was kind of hungry so I put it in my pocket an' when I
got to the cabin an' Dave wasn't there I sat down an' ate 'em. I
busted the end an' couldn't use a key so I found a can opener an'
used that. If that cop had been any good he'd have noticed that

an' looked at the opener. Only I pulled a fast one, see? I wiped it off, handle an' all, when I got through with it. I'd just thought about Dave an' the sardines then, that's why I did it. An' just as I was finishin' I heard him comin', so I tossed the tin way under the table so's he wouldn't notice it, see? That's all there was to that. But you know I said that there was others that would kill that guy in a minute? Well, one day Dave made a mistake at the factory, just after he went back that time I told you about when he was laid off, an' he put something in some oil or something that he shouldn't an' some people got poisoned. The boss found out who done it an' that was why he got fired, see? An' one of the men who worked at the factory with him had swiped some of the bad tins an' his two kids took sick after eatin' them. One died. He swore he'd get Dave an' he nearly did. A week before Dave left home he got hold of him an' beat him up plenty. That's why when I went back the second time an' found him dead I thought I wouldn't say anything about the tin if I got pulled into this, which I thought I wouldn't. I didn't know as the Porter guy was mixed up in it, an' I thought the tin would confuse people. An' it would lead people off the track if detectives got on the job an' started things. See?"

"You ain't so dumb as I thought," Asey informed him. "I get what you're aimin' at. You thought they'd go on the track of the sardines an' find out about the guy that threatened him or one of 'em out of that there sardine episode?"

"Sure, why not? I knew it wasn't. An' how was I to know that even this bum sheriff could track 'em down? I thought when you got me that you suspected me, so I didn't tell you. I wanted you to get off the track on the things too. That's mostly why I didn't tell you. The rest was that they were blamin' Porter an' why should I stick my feet into any puddle?"

"Is that all, Abe? It ain't any too convincin'."

"Every bit is true. I didn't want to get myself into this, an' I told you that whoever done this was a friend of mine. It's all the same to me if you never find out who done it. That's all there is, there ain't no more. An' that's straight."

"Hm." Asey sighed. "It looks to me like we'd reached a dead end. Ain't nothin' like pullin' in forty fathom of cod line an' findin' you got a lot of sea-weed on the end of it. It ain't no more than I expected, but I did kind of hope for a little more than this."

"But the doctor," Betsey suggested. "What about him?"

"For one thing, they's about twenty million doctors in the United States, if you believe the cigarette ads they endorse. For another, a flash of white might be a pair of knickers or anything else in Christendom. I s'pose we can look into the thing, but I got to admit I'm pretty dubious about it."

"Speaking of angels," Emma muttered, "here comes the gentleman in person. The worthy Sullivan is with him and both look very determined. Which of us d'you suppose they're after?"

"Me, of course," said Kurth. "The doctor never forgot that grand slam of mine. He pretends to admire it but actually it cost him money."

"More likely," I said, "they're after me. The doctor has been getting very irate because I've not told him things he thinks he ought to know."

I spoke flippantly. That they actually were after me did not enter my mind as being humanly possible. But I was mistaken. To my horror, they ranged themselves before me threateningly.

"Miss Whitsby," said the sheriff, "I'm arresting you as an accomplice in this murder of Dale Sanborn."

I had done a lot of gasping in the past two days, but this was the last straw. If Sullivan had hit me on the head with his billy I think I should have been less stunned. But I managed to answer him calmly enough.

"I do hope you're not intending to put me into a boxcar or the bilboes? For a woman of my age and position I consider them scarcely dignified."

"Are you stark ravin' crazy?" Asey demanded.

"No, Asey Mayo, I ain't. I've stood your goings-on long enough. You can make a monkey out of some folks, but you can't make a monkey out of me. An' if you make any more fuss I'll arrest you along of her."

Asey shrugged his shoulders. "Why not arrest the whole ca-boodle of us an' be done with it? Slough, you come on an' 'rest me. I dare you to. Come on. I double dare you."

Sullivan's red face grew still redder. "You better keep quiet or I will."

"See here," said Kurth sharply, "is this a part of your work, Doctor Reynolds? Because if it is, I shall personally make sure that you rue the day you ever had any such brilliant little thought. Just what mental process was it that brought you to this clever conclusion?"

"It's not so absurd as you may think," the doctor replied tart-ly. "Tell them, Sullivan."

"That's right," said Asey contemptuously. "Pass the buck. Let George do it."

"All right," said Sullivan heavily. "Well, the doc here was sure that there was more to this than I thought at first. So we moseyed around and found out a lot. I got hold of Ramon Bar-radio an' he told me something that looks important."

"That's the way to get inf'mation," said Asey admiringly. "How many times he been in jail? Six or eight, Slough? An' didn't you never read in the Bible about lookin' a gift hoss in the mouth? Or the Portygees offerin' information? Huh?"

Sullivan glared at him. "You're real funny, ain't you? Well, Ramon told me about something that happened up to Pete's dance hall on Wednesday night. Seems like Miss Betsey here an' Sanborn, they was up there an' they had a little difficulty."

"You didn't tell me——" I began.

But Betsey, white as a sheet, interrupted me.

"I know I didn't tell you we were there. Let him go on, Snoodles. If he's got to."

"Well, Miss Whitsby, your niece an' Sanborn had a little altercation. Ramon said he didn't know how it all started, but he happened to hear what went on."

"Funny how things happen like that," Asey murmured softly. "Real funny. All the in'cent bystanders ain't got killed off in Chicago, I cal'late."

"Will you keep your gab quiet, Asey Mayo? Anyway, Miss Whitsby, Ramon heard your niece say, 'If Bill Porter or my aunt heard you say any such thing, they'd kill you on the spot.' And then Sanborn laughed and said why didn't she tell if she was such a fool as to do it. And then Miss Betsey said she'd like to kill him herself."

"What was it all about, Betsey?" I pleaded.

"He was annoying me, that was all." Her voice was toneless. "I did hope we could get through this without unearthing all the combined scandal of the family and our friends."

"Anyway," Sullivan continued, "Sanborn says why didn't she tell them and see what happens? He said he bet that nothing would because other people had offered to kill him but nothing ever came of it. What do you think of that?" He concluded triumphantly.

"Not much," said Asey. "What's the good of all that if Betsey didn't tell Miss Prue or Bill about it? I can't see it."

"How do you know she didn't? Answer me that? How do you know?"

"He doesn't know," I retorted. "But he's perfectly right about it. I didn't know and I'm sure Bill Porter didn't. And will you please tell me in the name of all that's sensible how you can arrest me for being an accomplice of Bill?"

"I got that all figured out. You say you was out in the kitchen all that time. What was to keep you from standin' around an' seein' that no one interfered when Bill come an' done the murder? Or maybe you even held his attention while Bill killed him. No one can prove that you was where you said you was all that time."

"Not only that," the doctor continued, "but hadn't you sent Betsey up to town to get her out of the way?"

"Sure," said Asey. With great deliberation he relieved himself of an outworn quid of tobacco and cut himself another. "Sure. An' she left Mrs. Manton an' Dot around to see what was goin' on, an' they did it in broad daylight, just so's no one else would know. You two are real deep thinkers, that's what you are. That two small brains could carry all you know is a growin' wonder, as the feller said."

"I don't care what you say!" Sullivan shook his fist in Asey's face. "Captain Kinney of the old second precinct——"

"To hell with Captain Kinney of his ole second do-funny!" Asey roared. "An' keep your dirty hands where they belong. If you had the brains of an ox, Slough Sullivan, you'd know your boy friend the doctor was mixed up in this more than Miss Prue here ever was."

"Whaaat?" Sullivan looked startled.

"Sure. What do you think he's so int'rested in gettin' the murderer all done up in nice steel bracelets for? What else but 'cause he's got a guilty conscience himself? Don't you know it's the folks that give the biggest checks to charity as own the sweat shops? Ain't it the helpful one that burns the soup? Look at him. If he ain't guilty I never seen a guilty man."

Sullivan scratched his head. "By golly, I never thought of that." He was completely crestfallen.

"Sure," said Asey nonchalantly. "Look at him. Purple to the gills an' he can't speak a word. For why? 'Cause he done it himself. See his hands tremble? Hear him breathe? What more evidence does a man like you want, Slough? Go on an' arrest him. He's the one that came after Bill Porter left. He bashed Sanborn on the head himself. How'd he know so much about it an' about what did the killin' if he didn't do it himself?"

"I never did any such thing," the doctor spluttered. "It's a lie. An infamous lie."

"Didn't, did you?" Sullivan turned to him. "I don't know but what Asey's right. You look guilty as sin. I ought to of known when you come botherin' around with all your talk about blunt instruments an' all your clues. Gettin' me up here to arrest a nice woman like Miss Whitsby an' makin' a fool out of myself. Huh. You probably wrote them notes yourself."

"That's the boy, Slough. You're right," said Asey approvingly. "You go right on an' arrest him. I would if I was you."

"I'll do just that," said Sullivan delightedly. "I'll put him in the box-car longside of Bill."

"Ain't you goin' to let Bill go free?"

"Nun-no." Sullivan shook his head. "I might as well take the both of them. I want to make sure before I let Bill go."

"Look here," protested the doctor hotly, "you can't do a thing like that. What motive would I have for killing a man I'd never even met? This is fantastic. I'll have you prosecuted."

"I don't care. I don't care about motives either," said Sullivan cheerily. "If I got two people who might of done it, it's all the better for me to-morrow mornin'. Bill's got plenty of motives and you got plenty of suspicion tacked on to you. Come along. I'll take you right along now."

"But," the doctor began.

"But nothin'. Come along. It won't do you no harm to sit an' think for a while. You do enough talkin' as a rule. Now you can get yourself talked about. Say, did any of you see him up this way?"

"I saw him comin' yonder along the beach road at four-thirty on Friday," Asey informed him. "I've thought of it plenty before. He parked his car at the bend in the road and got out an' come in this direction. I was watchin' through the glasses. But you got enough to go on, Slough. You don't need no more."

"Guess I have, at that."

"When you goin' to start up to court to-morrer?"

"At eight. That'll give me time enough."

"Fair enough."

They left, with Sullivan's great ham-like paw firmly gripping the doctor's shoulder.

"Asey Mayo," I demanded, "did he really do it?"

"Not a chance in the world," that gentleman retorted comfortably. "Only he had a hankerin' to 'rest some one an' it might as well been the doc as you."

He warbled a bar from the Floradora sextette.

"An' why not him?" He paraphrased. "An' why not him?"

Chapter Eighteen
THE FUTILE SUMMING UP

"HAVE YOU," I demanded, "had———"

"Had that poor in'cent doc all incarc'rated for nothin'? Yup. I have. Wouldn't you rather it was him sittin' wastin' away in a box-car 'stead of you?"

"Of course," I said with entire sincerity.

"Well, he was the only one I could think of off-hand like who could take your place. I might of suggested Abe here or Mr. Kurth, but I kind of thought it would do the doc good. Teach him a lesson. It won't hurt him none and like as not he'll get himself off before he ever gets to court. But I didn't think the Whitsby name ought to get smudged none an' Slough's kind of an easy soul to make believe things."

Kurth wiped the tears of laughter from his cheeks. "And I believe he said you couldn't make a monkey out of him. Asey, I wouldn't have missed this for years of my life. But if I were you and I ever felt sick I shouldn't go to Reynolds with my aches and pains."

"I know," said Asey feelingly, "it's goin' to be real unhandy when I get sciaticky to go trottin' all over creation for another salve 'plier but I cal'late I'll have to."

"What about us, Asey? What do you want us to do now? Shall we stay here?"

"I guess Miss Prue ain't got room to put you up. You an' your wife had better go up to the hotel an' stay an' if you can't get in there, take one o' Bangs' cottages. Only thing is, I want you back here at six to-morrer mornin'."

"Very well." Kurth rose. "Will you leave your car here and come along with me, Maida? I think we have a great deal to talk over."

Maida smiled at him. "I think we have."

"As for Abe," Asey thought out loud, "I'm kind of tired watchin' him. Will you take him along with you an' see he don't do no runnin' away? Will you promise not to run away if I give you expense money, Abe?"

"I won't do no runnin'," Schonbrun assured him. "I ain't got anything to run with or for. I'll go with 'em."

"That's straight?"

"Yeah. I guess I ain't got no reason to go."

"All right. Trot along with them, then."

"Do you think," I asked him as the three drove off, "that it's quite safe to let them go that way?"

"Why not? We found out all we can find from them, ain't we? We know too much for any of 'em to try an' beat it. I guess it's safe enough."

"I still don't feel sure about that brother," I remarked.

"I do." Asey got up from his chair.

"Where are you going now? Do you want me to come with you?"

Asey smiled. "Well, I'm goin' home to go to bed."

"But aren't you going to do anything more?"

"Miss Prue, I spent Friday night out in a mahog'ny boat in the bay an' I ran around till past midnight yesterday. An' I didn't get much sleep last night, what with lookin' after Schonbrun an' this bunged-up head of mine. I'm goin' to get a little sleep before I do one more thing. Like the feller in the poem, 'I'm weary an' overwrought with too much toil an' too much care distraught.' Yup, I'm goin' to go to bed."

"But Asey!"

"Can't help it none. I ain't no six-day bicycle racer. I got to sleep once in a while."

I followed him out to the roadster. "What are you going to do about the bath house and your mystery there?"

"Oh, yes. Well, I got to go there, an' you better cajole your people inside somewheres where they won't see me till I got what I'm after. Ain't no sense in givin' everything away now."

"I think you're inconsiderate and heartless," I said, "to go off in this manner. We haven't got anywhere and you were so sure you'd find out everything by to-morrow. And what are you after at the bath house?"

"Forget all about it, Miss Prue. I said I'd get this fixed up by to-morrer, an' to-morrer ain't here yet. Sufficient unto the day is the deed thereof. You put everything right out of your mind an' go get some sleep too. Your eyes is got as many hollers around them as mine has. You an' me ain't so young we can afford to run like a top all the time. You just run along an' c'mpose your mind. We'll get there. But even Napoleon had to sleep."

I stalked back into the house without replying. My suggestion of bridge was sufficient to bring Emma and Betsey and Dot off the porch into the living-room.

"It's funny," Betsey remarked as she set up the table, "the way that key disappeared, I mean. I don't see where it could have gone to."

"Doubtless Asey will find it," Emma suggested.

I looked at her curiously. "What makes you think so?" I asked.

"I don't know, except that he is the logical one to find it if it's lost. I don't see, Prudence, how you're going to get along without him after all this is finished."

"Maybe he'll get to be a permanent fixture," Betsey suggested, rolling her eyes at me.

I sniffed. "We have one semi-permanent fixture," I retorted, "now ensconced in a freight car, who seems quite sufficient for the needs of all concerned."

My niece had the grace to keep silent.

"It's too bad that the poor boy's suffering," Emma remarked. "But I do think it's lovely about the doctor. Fancy his temper after being boxed up for the night. He'll undoubtedly write it up for a medical journal under the heading of *The Relationship of Heat and Criminology*. I'll wager it's warmish up there. It'll be conversational material for months to come."

"Don't talk about it," said Betsey. "It's hard enough for me to try to play this hand with you two anyway, without your bringing up this awful business."

"I'm sorry." Emma gathered in the trick that set Betsey down. "But it's really rather blotting other subjects out, you know."

"Down three." Betsey tossed her hand on to the table. "Hereafter you play in silence."

Emma's run of luck continued, and she and I all but whitewashed the two girls. At ten o'clock Betsey announced that she had had enough.

"You confirmed gamblers are impossible. You use rules that were discarded before I was born and you never do the same thing twice running. I can't understand it."

"Don't try to," said Emma consolingly. "Your aunt and I have played together too long to have your newfangled rules and regulations upset the even tenor of our way in the least. We'll waive your losses if you'll get us some food."

"Come along," said Dot. "If we don't I'll have to foot it back to New York, absolutely on my two feet."

We went out on the porch to wait for them.

"Tell me," Emma asked, "this is more serious for Bill than we have thought, isn't it?"

"Asey seems to think so," I answered. "I suppose it is. Have you seen the papers? They're calling Bill a millionaire roisterer and demanding action. It's really remarkable how the American people love to drag a rich man through the courts and I think they revel particularly when he's indicted for murder. They've brought out all the details of Jimmy's yacht and that party he and Bill gave to the English manufacturers two years ago, and all about their uncle Phineas' divorces and everything else. I'm waiting with bated breath for them to start in on Betsey and me. I can't see how we've managed to escape so far unless it's because Cousin John Whitsby is putting his veto on the subject."

"If Bill is taken up to-morrow he'll be put in jail, won't he?"

"Yes. I hope Jimmy has attended to lawyers as Asey told him. This is rather a mess, Emma."

"Grim. Very grim. Were you ever in jail, Prudence?"

"Certainly not," I said in a horrified tone.

"I didn't mean it that way. Were you ever in one? That is, did you ever go through one?"

"Once when I was a child with my father. I don't remember much about it except that I cried and it was smelly. Why?"

"I went through one once with Henry Edward. It was grim, Prudence, very grim indeed. Bars and bare concrete and an odor of carbolic acid and disinfectant and too much humanity in one place. I don't wonder that there are prison riots."

"Possibly Bill won't have to go at all. Asey still seems to think that he can get him off."

"I hope so. Prudence, that harbor is beautiful. You don't know how I've loved being here these last few days in spite of all that's happened. I've been very lonely up there in Boston."

"You miss him, don't you?"

She nodded without turning around. "Yes. You know, Prudence, people called Henry Edward eccentric and I suppose he was. Most ministers know more about the next world than they do of this, but he was different. He believed firmly and thoroughly that religion had more to do with the present than with any possible future. He tried to help people and he gave as much attention to a common bum from the gutter as he did to the soul needs of his richest parishioner. His methods of aiding people were what startled every one so. But he did what he set out to do."

I realized suddenly that I had never heard Emma talk like this in all the years I had known her. She rather prided herself on not being serious if she could help it.

"I didn't think it was possible," she continued, "to miss any one as much as I miss him. I can't understand how people say that time dulls memory and all that sort of thing. Time only makes it worse. In some ways, Prudence, you're very lucky. You have Betsey to look after and worry about and suggest wearing rubbers to and I haven't even a cat. But then, I don't suppose that there's any use in running on about it."

Dot and Betsey came back with a heaped-up tray. We left it an unsightly mess of paper napkins and empty plates in no time at all.

"I'm going to bed," Emma announced. "If we are to have the final analysis at six to-morrow, I think it's high time we all got some sleep."

Betsey agreed and the two of them went up-stairs. Dot announced that she wasn't the least bit sleepy. "Besides," she added, "I can't see that a few hours one way or another will make much difference when one has to get up at that ungodly hour. I shall be half-asleep anyhow and it won't make me any less yawny if I go to bed now or at five-thirty."

She lighted a cigarette. "Miss Prudence, what do you think that man has up his sleeve?"

"Asey? I haven't the faintest notion. You know, Dot, this thing isn't going the way it ought to go. We've followed up everything that can be followed and it's been just so much time wasted. The more that is explained, the less involved people become. Just the same, I can't imagine why that man has gone home to bed at this crucial moment. Either he knows a lot more than he has condescended to tell me, or else he's putting up a tremendous bluff."

"It is peculiar. You don't think, do you, that he's going to land on me?"

"My dear child!"

"I know, but you've got to admit that if any one really is in deep it's me. After all, I was the last person to see him alive."

"You couldn't have been," I told her. "If that was the case you'd be the murderer. You say you left him alive and Schonbrun says he was dead when he came back the second time. I'll admit it doesn't look any too good for you, but there must have been some one who came after you and before the brother."

"Asey seems so sure that the brother didn't do it."

"I know he does. Though I feel he's scarcely the person whose word I should take about anything."

"This business of Betsey," Dot said. "I mean Betsey and Sanborn and the man who overheard them. That's going to get you all mixed up in this. That doctor is going to make trouble for you. It may have been a frightfully brainy notion of Asey's to trick Sullivan into arresting him, but it's not going to help you any. When that dull sheriff comes to his senses and realizes what an ass he's been, I'm afraid he's going to land on you and Bets."

"I've been thinking of that. Ramon Barradio is not what you might call a trustworthy person and I don't think that his word would stand in court, but the fact is there. Dot, I give you my word that I am so confused that I feel you or Betsey or I might have done this in an absent-minded moment. I'm beginning to see why John and Maida got divorced over a matter like that book. In an affair like this you lose all sense of values. You don't want to suspect the ones you know and like, but after everything else has failed, you come back and wonder."

"I know. I found myself feeling you were the guilty one this afternoon when the doctor and Sullivan were powwowing. I knew you weren't, but I just did."

"The more I think of it," I said, "the more it seems that Schonbrun was right. His brother ought to have been done away with long ago. I wonder if it wouldn't be best to let Bill take the consequences and see if he couldn't get off all right."

"It would if the doctor hadn't got this fixed idea about you.

Think if I'd ever married that man and then found out about all this. I suppose I was an utter idiot not to have known that there was something wrong somewhere but you really don't expect to find such men around."

"Particularly when they wear such elegant clothes. I know what you mean."

Emma clumped down the stairs. "Are you still worrying about this business? Your chum Mr. Mayo, Prudence, has promised to get the guilty one, and I should think that was enough for you. I have some letters to go. Where can I put 'em?"

"On the desk," I told her. "There's a collection there already. And I do wish you'd stop twitting me about Asey Mayo."

"I'm sorry," she said in a tone that had no sorrow in it. "But you must admit that you've laid yourself open to being twitted, haven't you, now?"

"Not at all," I answered with some dignity. "Just because I seem to have been thrown into his company through sheer force of circumstance is no reason why you should——"

"Should twit you. I see, Prudence, I see. Rest assured that I shall say no more about the situation. But it would make a lovely romance, wouldn't it?"

She laughed and clumped up to her room.

Dot snickered.

"And as for you and your noises," I said to her firmly, "you can go to bed."

Dot crushed out her cigarette and kissed me. "We're all horrid and nasty and batty as hedgehogs. All right. I'll go up and annoy Bets. You'd better come to bed yourself soon. You need sleep as much as the rest of us."

And she dashed up-stairs.

I picked up Ginger and held him in my lap. It is a habit of

mine whenever I have any particularly serious thinking to do. Some women, like Emma, prefer to knit and others do fancy work or puzzles; still others, more modern possibly, like Betsey and Dot, prefer a cigarette. But there is something very comforting about holding a warm purring cat.

I tried for the millionth time to get things settled in my mind. We had found out that the people with motives for killing Sanborn were legion. Kurth, Maida, Dot, Betsey, Bill, Schonbrun, all had reasons. Then there was Maida's friend Alice, the girl who had committed suicide. Perhaps she had friends or a family or some one who had found out about her and attempted revenge. There was the man of the sardine factory. There was the doctor Kurth had told us about and the other unknown doctor whom he had suggested. All of the motives were varied and none of them was weak.

I myself was not exempt from the list of suspects. Olga had an alibi if her friend Inga had not been primed beforehand, which Asey and I both doubted. As Dot had insinuated, even Asey himself might have done it. I recalled his suggestion that Sullivan's billy might have been used to kill Sanborn.

There was the problem of the weapon. We were not even certain exactly what blunt instrument had been used. A blunt instrument: I looked around the room. A lamp, a smoking stand, a golf club, the footstool,—there was no end to the blunt instruments in sight.

We didn't know whether a man or a woman had done the murder. As Asey said, not many of the latter knew about rabbit punches and jiu-jitsu or the vulnerability of the part of the head where Sanborn had been killed. On the other hand, had Schonbrun seen that flash of white, and had it been a woman? Or was it, as Betsey suggested, a man with white trousers?

We had no finger-prints, no foot-prints, no clues of strands of red hair, like my friend Wyncheon Woodruff in the now discarded *Lipstick Murderer.* There were no cigarette stubs strewn around, no cigar ashes of a peculiar type; though I doubted very much if they would have told us anything had we found them. There were no buttons clutched in dead fingers, no strange initials, no anonymous letters to wonder about. What we had found we had followed through. But, I thought despairingly, we might as well have left the entire matter to chance.

We knew that Sanborn had been killed between four-thirty or a little after, and a quarter past five. We knew of six visits that had been paid him by five different people who had come there from the time he left us at the cottage till I found him at night. But was Asey right? Was there a mysterious sixth person who had swooped out of the blue close on Dot's heels and fled as quickly as he or she had come? Who was it? Could it possibly have been the doctor? Had Asey really been tricking Sullivan into thinking the doctor was guilty?

I picked up the bridge score and the stubby pencil and tried to diagram the matter. Bill, Betsey, Dot, Kurth, Maida, Schonbrun, Olga, Emma and myself were the ones most intimately connected with the affair. Much as I wanted to think otherwise it seemed to me that one of us must have committed the murder. That was the first circle about Sanborn. Then there were the more remote possibilities, unknowns whose motive must have been revenge for the deaths or the havoc that Sanborn had caused. Then there was still a third and limitless circle from which the murderer might have come.

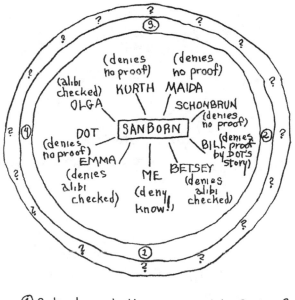

① Girls whose death is caused by Sanborn?
② Maida's friend Alice?
③ Other doctor — Reynolds?
④ Doctor — the one Kurth mentions?

I checked all the names in the first circle save Dot, Schonbrun, Maida and Kurth. It seemed clear to me that the others were exempt. Had one of these whose alibis had not been proved done it? Was it one from the second circle, out for revenge, or was it some one whose existence we had not known of, some one still farther afield?

Ginger uncurled himself from my lap. He yawned majestically as though to say that he for one had had quite enough pondering for a time. I let him jump down, crumpled my diagram into a ball and tossed it into the fireplace.

The next time any one was murdered in my vicinity, I thought sleepily, there was one spinster lady who was not going to concern herself with amateur detecting.

Chapter Nineteen
ASEY AND THE BLESSED HOPE

THE GLARING sunrise woke me early Monday morning. I could hear the faint chugging of the fisher boats as they started out to the grounds. Outside the cottage the beach grass was heavy with dew and the meadows beyond were still thick with mist.

I watched the purples and the oranges of the horizon change and melt as the sun came creeping up. The twinkling morning star faded away with the garish color. The curtain of the window next mine rattled and Emma's head was thrust out.

"Gorgeous, isn't it?" she remarked. "But a little thundery, like Mr. Kipling."

I agreed that it was. "It's a source of constant wonder to me," I added, "that Cape Codders can be quite so bleak with all the glorious sunrises and sunsets put on for their special benefit."

She laughed. "I never thought of that. Maybe we should start an 'up for sunrise' movement. Ugh. I'm withdrawing. It's a beautiful sight but the air is chilly." She closed the window.

I drew my kimono more closely around my shoulders and perched precariously on the sill. Out by the wharf a school of small fish were churning the water and above them circled a flock of gulls. I thought of the diagram I had made the night before and watched them closely to see if I might glean some omen from them. I didn't.

The milk truck jounced along the beach road and I heard the empty bottles clinking. Ginger clamored to be let out. I opened the door and in two seconds he was galloping away to the meadows. Olga banged a dish in the kitchen. I dressed and went down-stairs. The others followed me.

Breakfast was a silent meal. All of us were tired and nervous and expectant. No soldier ever waited for a signal to go over the top with more impatience and more misgivings than we awaited the coming of six o'clock.

Ten minutes before the hour Kurth and Maida arrived with Schonbrun in tow. Promptly at six Bill's roadster drew up in front of the door with Asey at the wheel.

He greeted us with a yawn and requested a cup of coffee.

"I thought you told me that you were going home to get some sleep," I remarked severely. "From your looks I'd say you hadn't had forty winks. And you slept in your clothes while you had those, didn't you?"

He nodded and poured out another cup of coffee.

"And the hollows under your eyes," I went on. "They're disgraceful."

"I know. Look's if I'd spent ten nights in a barroom, shouldn't wonder. I'm real sorry. But this here compulsory in-somnia has been an' got itself into a habit."

He set down his cup and looked around the room. "All of you present an' 'counted for?"

"All of us. Have you seen Bill?" Betsey asked.

"Yup. I drove around that way this mornin'. Bill he was fine's silk, but he says he'll be glad to see the insides of a nice warm jail where he can sit on somethin' soft for a change."

"And the doctor?" I asked.

Asey snickered. "He's madder'n hops. Wanted to get a lawyer but no one'd get one for him. Got neuritis in both of his arms though; an' he didn't get much sleep, I cal'late, an' I guess he got kind of bothered by moskeeters. You know they don't seem to bother Bill much. I kind of guess the doc ain't goin' to bear much love to any of us for a long time to come."

"I don't like to hurry you," said Kurth nervously, "but the fact is, have you found out anything? What's the verdict?"

"I'll get to that. Keep your shirt on. We got near two hours before Sullivan an' his desert caravan starts out. A lot can happen in two hours. Besides, I want to tell you a story."

"Do you think that this is any time to play Scheherezade?" I asked impatiently.

"Play who? I'm goin' to tell you a story. You may not want to listen, an' you don't have to if you don't want to. But I'm goin' to tell it anyways, so you might as well. It's a simple sort of story an' maybe you'll get what I'm drivin' at toward the end or even before. But I'm goin' to give it to you from *A* to *Z* an' you can take it for what it's worth."

"A parable?" Emma suggested.

"Nothin' so high-toned as all that. It's just simply a story of something as happened a long time ago. But if you want to call it a par'ble you got a perfect right to."

He stretched his long legs out before the fire.

"Here goes. I told Miss Prue the other day that all folks was like other folks in one little thing or 'nother, an' usually if they was alike in that one little thing they was like them in other ways too. That's one of the reasons why I believed them stories of all you people who had to do with Sanborn over to the cabin on Friday. But you'll see what I mean.

"When I was a boy about fifteen years old I shipped as a cook on a schooner called the *Blessed Hope* out of Boston for Littleton, New Zealand. That was what they named her, the *Blessed Hope*, but I don't think any ship ever had a less suit'ble name less'n it was a tradin' schooner out Samoa way called the *Ice Maid.*

"It wasn't a big boat. Only about ninety ton if it was that an' there was twelve of us on it. Me, as cook, an' a crew as had an Irishman we used to call Paddy, an Englishman,—not a real one but a Limey,—an' a dumb Swede. They was three mates. One was a real nice feller as come from Halifax, one come from Boston an' the first mate was a man from Cape Cod name of Lysander Trask. Then there was the Cap'n, he was a state of Maine man, but there wasn't any one much more against his native state pro'bition than him. He was a livin' example for the W. C. T. U. to use for wantin' people to sign the pledge. The Boston mate he had his wife an' sister along with him, an' then at the last minute some one persuaded the Cap'n to take two passengers, a school-teacher from Salem, Massachusetts, an' his wife. He had a brother that was sheep-farmin' out in New Zealand an' so they was goin' out to pay him a visit.

"Well, we crossed the 'quator in about twenty-five days which wasn't bad goin' for a schooner the size of the *Blessed Hope.* Everything went along nice an' easy. The mate's wife stuck to her cabin an' read books an' the sister was sick most of the way, but Mrs. Binney, that was the school-teacher's wife, she was a great cook an' so to take up her time she used to come into the galley an' help me out. It didn't bother me any an' in fact it helped me considerable as most of the time I had to do an able seaman's job too. She was a real capable homey woman, sharp as a whip, an' real 'complishin'. She made curtains for the Cap'n's cabin an' darned up all our socks an' we liked her. Her husband was all right but kind of weak-jointed an' more int'rested in lookin' at fishes than anything else.

"Then we begun to run into nasty weather. Down around the South Seas there's gales run most all year 'round. More sou'west to nor'west storms'n you could shake a stick at. You don't, or at least you didn't in them days, see a boat from one week's end to another. It got kind of tiresome an' we all began to hate each other. Bein' all cooped up the way we was wasn't no fun attall. The Cap'n he just took to his bottle an' let the mates run the ship, only comin' out once in a while to blow some one up about somethin'. He fussed with the Boston mate about a chart an' he run after the wife an' the sister. He give the Limey blazes for the cargo not balanced right. He come to blows with the Irishman an' he even picked a fight with Lysander. An' Mrs. Binney an' the other women folks all was cross an' fightin' about the boat an' the weather an' the smells an' not bein' able to take a bath an' things like that. Gettin' bored?" He asked us suddenly.

"We're hanging on every word," Betsey told him sleepily. "Get on."

"Well, one day we got out of our bad spell of weather an' everything was all right again. The Cap'n stopped his boozin' an' everything was peaceful an' happy. Then we got more storms."

"You and Noah," Kurth murmured.

"An' one night," Asey ignored the interruption, "while I was dishin' up the stew for supper I heard a c'motion in the Cap'n's cabin. I went in an' found him dead's a door nail, all bashed over the head with a belayin'-pin. When I say bashed I mean bashed. It wasn't any gentle tap like Sanborn got. I ran an' got Lysander, bein' as how he was first mate, an' the two of us got things straightened out an' then we started t' investigate.

"The Limey was a yellow sort an' he'd of used his knife if he'd 'a' done it."

Suddenly I remembered that this had been his comment about Schonbrun.

"An' the Irishman, well, he got into tempers an' he loved to pick a fight, but he wouldn't go around bashin' peoples' heads in when he could use his fists. Likewise the mate from Boston."

"Bill," I thought to myself, "and Kurth. They're out of this."

"The Swede was a peaceful sort an' feller an' he kept a pair of white mice. Besides that, he didn't have no quarrel with the Cap'n. He was the only one who didn't."

All eyes turned toward the kitchen. We were paying more attention to Asey than we had previously favored him with.

"The mate from Halifax might of done it, but he was down in the hold. I seen him go an' I seen him come back after I'd found out about it. I didn't do it myself an' I knew Lysander Trask hadn't."

Mentally I checked up. He was eliminating himself, Betsey and me.

"We'd reckoned suicide as out of the question, so it wasn't that he'd done it himself. The mate's wife an' sister was both sick in their bunks an' had been for two days before the thing happened. That sister had yellow hair, too, an' the wife was dark an' pretty, if you want me to go right into details." He grinned.

I exonerated Dot and Maida.

"The school-teacher he'd been aft talkin' to Lysander at the wheel. That let him out of it. An' the wife had been in her cabin the whole time."

"Who did it?" I couldn't contain myself another second.

"All in good time, Miss Prue. All in good time. When we reached Littleton after stragglin' through one storm after another, we stuck the whole jim-bang business into the hands of the American Consul there." He stopped. "I'd like another cup of coffee if you don't mind."

He drank it slowly and deliberately.

"Get on, man!" Kurth urged. "What happened?"

"Well, the Limey said he'd heard the Cap'n an' the Irishman quarrelin' an' the Consul believed him. He'd never had a crew, that Cap'n, that he hadn't drove like a bunch of pack-hosses when he was sober an' bullied an' fussed at when he was drunk. But bein' a cousin of the owner like he was, nothin' ever happened. I heard of crews he fed on maggoty meat an' rotten hard tack an' I know of others he just worked to death. Anyway, the Irishman couldn't prove he hadn't killed the Cap'n an' so just to make an example of him,—they'd been havin' a lot of trouble with crews about that time,—they took him back to the States an' hung him by the neck till he was dead. I don't know how or where or why, but that's what happened."

"But what does all that prove?" Kurth demanded.

"Nothin'," said Asey slowly, "'cept that about five years later I run across Lysander Trask out in Hong Kong. He had his own boat then an' he'd just come 'round from New York. It seems that Mrs. Binney had died out in New Zealand but they'd got word in New York that before she departed this world she confessed to killin' the Cap'n."

"But how? And why?"

"Well, it seems like we didn't ever really suspect her, what with her makin' curtains an' darnin' our socks an' all. An' she was such a pleasant spoken woman, too. But once when the

Cap'n was drunk he'd hit her husband an' called him names. He wasn't any coward, that school-teacher, but he was smaller'n the Cap'n an' couldn't hit back an' he didn't know quite what to do about it. He couldn't fend for himself, so she showed him how. Course, it didn't do much good for by that time Paddy had already been all hanged an' punished for it, but there you are."

The fear in my heart which had steadily been growing was now established. Suddenly I knew why Asey had refused to tell me so little of his plans and decisions of the previous day.

"Where's that new book of Mr. Sanborn's?" Asey asked quietly.

I had completely forgotten about the purple-backed book I had lent Emma on Friday.

"Mrs. Manton has it," I said.

"Have you got it?" Asey asked.

She smiled at him and shook her head.

"Where is it?"

"In the bath house." Her tone was composed and even.

"In the bath house?" Betsey repeated wonderingly, "but it can't be there. You had it up here Friday afternoon and we haven't been into the place since that morning."

"That's where it is," Emma stated.

"Will you get it for us?" Asey asked slowly.

She looked at him for a long minute, then rose from the wicker chair.

"Of course I'll get it, Asey."

"Don't be a goose," Betsey said. "I'll take the bug and run down for it. I left the car out and it's right by the door."

"No matter." Emma folded her afghan and carefully put it into her knitting bag. "I'll run down myself."

I laid my hand on Betsey's arm as she was about to remonstrate, and fiercely whispered for her to keep quiet. Betsey looked at me questioningly and turned a little white.

"John will go for you," Maida said. "I can't see any sense in making her go all the way down there just for a silly book."

But Asey shook his head. I watched Emma as she clumped casually to the door. At the threshold she turned and smiled, then clumped down the porch steps.

"Asey!" Betsey ran to him and shook his shoulders. "Asey, what do you mean? What are you like this for? Why are you sending her for that book? What's the matter with you all, anyway? You're like a pack of waxworks!"

Gently Asey withdrew her hands and put his arm around her shoulder.

"I can't help it, Betsey girl. God knows I don't want to. But I thought I'd give her a sporting chance to get away from this place while she could."

"You mean, Asey,—you can't mean that it was Emma?"

He nodded. "Only I meant for her to take Bill's roadster an' she's taken yours. I wanted her to get away."

We crowded to the window as we heard the hum of Betsey's tiny car. Straight down the oyster-shell lane it shot like an arrow. Then at the beach road it turned, but it turned too quickly. The car jumped off the ground, rocked in the air a second, then fell. There was a crash. The car rolled over and over, landed on the beach.

We were so quiet that we could hear the soft splash of the bright waves rolling in. Somewhere in the sky a seagull screamed.

A flame shot up from the car and Asey and Kurth ran for the roadster.

Chapter Twenty
MERE BAGGY-TELL

ACCORDING TO the doctor who was hastily removed from his prison, Emma had died immediately.

"I wonder if she meant to do it?" I asked Asey when he came back with the news.

He shook his head. "I don't know. I don't guess we ever will. I'm inclined to think she did, but she might not have. But perhaps it's better all around."

"How did you know?" Betsey asked.

"That book. I knew from that telegram from the feller in New York that it was a libel suit that Kurth had brought, like I told you. The only reason I could think of was from his books. You'd said Emma had been readin' his latest, an' I remembered that. I kind of thought that if Kurth had got mad at one book, maybe she had at another."

"But this business of it's being in the bath house? How did you know that?"

"You said you heard a noise on Saturday night. You thought it was Dot, but when you said that cat of yours was still riled up, I begun to piece the thing together. Suppose she had read the book an' found something in it, an' suppose that was the reason why she killed Dale. She didn't have no chance to get rid of the book, an' she knew better than to leave it lyin' around where one of you might see it. This was all sup'sition, you see. I'd remembered that story I told you, too. It was gospel truth. I'd been fooled once by a woman a lot like her, smart an' cheerful an' nice, an' I begun to suspect her. She was the one movin' around, I figgered, gettin' rid of that book. All day Saturday she set here, knittin', but she didn't have no chance to do nothin' about it. She was only alone when Dot an' Betsey went to see them folks that had been playin' tennis. But that wouldn't of done her any good; Olga was still here an' all them folks was around the rope. The cottage wasn't no fit place to hide it. I thought she might of, though, an' that was why I sent Olga around yesterday afternoon, to see if she could find it."

"But how——"

"Wait up. I'm gittin' there. She didn't have no chance to do anything about it Friday night because Slough an' all was around. Only Saturday night when all of you was to bed and asleep. Then she went out most likely intendin' to throw it in the water. She was too sensible to think of just lyin' it around. That purloined letter business ain't so good as a rule. I don't know's you notice such things, but the tide was comin' in that night an' so she couldn't do anything of the sort attall. Probably, she, bein' intel'gent, thought of that as a possibility an' took the bathhouse key along with her. Where else was there a better place than to hide it in her bathin' things? So that's what she done, intendin' to get rid of it when she could, I shouldn't wonder. It was wrapped in her bathin' suit."

"How were you so sure about the book?"

"It was just the way I thought of it an' it's proved all right.

When Kurth told us all, then I was a lot surer. She was the only one that had the new book, she was a lot like Mrs. Binney an' after all, didn't you notice she didn't deny she'd been there? She just said wouldn't you all of heard her."

"But when did she go to the cabin? What was there in the book? Whom was it about? And how in the world could she have acted the way she did afterward?"

"I shouldn't wonder if she'd left you a better explanation than I could give. Didn't she leave a note?"

"Those letters she brought down last night," Dot said excitedly. "Don't you suppose there would be something in them?"

Betsey ran to the desk. "There's one addressed to you, Snoodles. Read it!"

I tore it open. Pages and pages in Emma's neat handwriting fell out.

"Why, it's dated Friday night," I said.

Asey nodded. "I guessed as much."

I read the letter aloud.

"My dear Prudence:

"By the time you will have read this,—I believe that is the classic way to begin such letters,—I will probably not be around. But you might as well know, in case that Bill or anyone else is incriminated badly, the truth of the whole matter.

"I killed Dale Sanborn. That sounds horrible, possibly, but I am not so sure that it is. You didn't know when you gave me that book what it really contained. I didn't know myself till I was well into it. *Reverence.* You ask yourself what a book named *Reverence* has to do with me? It is all so simple. *Reverence* was taken from the life of my husband Henry Edward Manton.

"You know that Henry Edward was famous for his eccentricities. He did many things which most clergymen would not think of doing, many things which his confreres held up their hands in holy horror at.

"In 1918, shortly after the war, Henry Edward was coming back from a meeting in Boston one night and found wandering around in the streets a young girl whom he brought home with him. I don't know who she was or where she came from. We called her Rose. It was the usual sordid story of the war, some soldier who had led her astray and then gone off and forgotten all about her. Of course Henry Edward wanted to help her. I don't know whether you knew about her, for few did, but she stayed at the house with us until she died with her baby. That in itself is a simple enough story, isn't it? But in *Reverence* you will find Dale Sanborn's interpretation and that is not so simple. The girl Rose in his book is Henry Edward's mistress, I am the wife who allows her to stay in the house with me. You can read the rest of it yourself.

"How did Sanborn know? Simply because Henry Edward found him when he was a student at college, working his way through, and helped him along. I knew him the minute I set eyes on him down on the beach to-day though he pretended not to recognize me. Prudence, my husband and I had nursed that boy through typhoid. We had paid his bills, given him clothes and kept him alive. He knew about Rose, had been there while she was at the house. Henry Edward and I have long since ceased to expect any gratitude from the people whom we tried to help. I did not expect gratitude from David Schonbrun, but neither did I expect *Reverence*. I read it through, then skipped through it again, trying to assure myself that it was not my husband or myself who were pictured in its pages. But I couldn't do it. We were the characters, but so colored with red pencil as to achieve Marlovian proportions.

"It was possibly four-thirty when I finished that book the second time. I decided to go and see Schonbrun, to see if it really was the truth, for I didn't want to believe it. There were too many people who would know, and I didn't want the story public in that version.

"I went down-stairs as I always do, clumping a little, and intending to make some explanation to you. But you weren't there; I heard you moving about in the kitchen, banging pans. Then as I came out on the porch, I saw Dot hot-footing it over to the cabin. I followed closely behind her, waiting outside the cabin and heard her conversation with Schonbrun. It strengthened my conviction that he was a knave, even a greater one than I could have imagined. After she left I went in, still gripping the book.

"He greeted me cheerfully and asked if all the indignant females in the world were paying him visits that afternoon.

"For answer I held out the book. 'Did you take this from the story of Rose and my husband?' I asked.

"He laughed. 'Why not? It's a part of my debunking humanity series. The ministry hasn't had a jolt for a long time.'

"I controlled myself as well as I could. 'Do you mean to tell me that this is the way you reward us for all we did for you?'

"He waved his hand airily and said it was a minor matter. 'Manton's dead and who cares? Who'll ever know?'

"I tried to explain that that was just the point. It was because Henry Edward was dead that I cared about it. If he were alive and could fight back, that would be a different matter. The truth could be told. But even if I could give my version publicly now, no one would believe me and I would only be ridiculed.

"He looked at me scornfully and said that there was nothing he could do about it. That after all, he had to live. 'Is there any reason in the world why your husband should not prove a source of income to me after he is dead as well as when he was alive?'

"Suddenly he stopped and looked under the table. He saw that sardine tin which the sheriff ascribes to Bill Porter. Paying no attention to me and to my questions, he bent over and looked at it more closely. I have never seen a man in such an infuriated mood. 'Who left this here?' He demanded. 'Who brought it?'

"To have my pleas thus disregarded while he fumed about an empty sardine tin was more than I could stand. As he leaned over I brought his own book down on his head with all the force I could muster. He dropped like a log.

"I knelt beside him and I knew he was dead. I had heard Henry Edward tell of that blow on the base of the skull even though I had no intention of using it. I did not mean to kill Sanborn, but if I had, I was not afraid nor was I sorry. He needed to be killed. His conversation with Dot alone bore that out.

"I did not stop to think particularly. I left him lying there and hastened back to the house. I expected instant discovery and I was prepared to face the music. But when you chose to think I was coming down-stairs when I was actually coming up the porch steps, it seemed to me that I might as well take a chance and await discovery before coming forward and giving myself up. I stuck the book in my knitting bag and went out into the kitchen as you called me.

"Possibly I should have told you everything then, or tonight when the sheriff was here. But it is hard to relinquish your freedom when you have killed some one who deserved it. I do not think from what I have seen of your sheriff that he will succeed in convincing people that Bill Porter was the murderer. That there would be others involved did not occur to me at the time. I will wait and see what happens and then when the time is ripe, I shall see what I can do in the way of cheating the gallows. Once I went through a jail and I did not like it; I am sure that I could not endure that. And besides, dear Prudence, life without Henry Edward is not the life I care to lead. I have nothing now to live for and life has lost its zest as far as I am concerned. This world hangs on a very fine thread. Some day something is bound to make it snap, and a little sooner or later makes no difference. So if anything should happen and there should be an accident, please try to think as kindly of me as you can.

"You will remember, too, that I have told, or will tell, no lies about this. I may slide over the truth,—that is only human,—but the whole thing is in black and white for whoever wants to find it out.

"I have enjoyed my visit, strange though it may seem. And if you will send my other letter to Norton and West they will arrange all the details that have to be arranged.

"I have written this Friday night while everything is still in confusion but these are the true facts and this is the whole truth."

"Then she meant to kill herself," I said, "meant it from the very first. And to think of how she acted, as cheerful and as unmoved as though nothing were going to happen."

"I know," said Asey. "I don't think I ever felt much worse in my life than I did this mornin'. You see, I went to the bath house an' got that book an' spent most of last night readin' it. I knew then. I guess she knew I did, too."

"But how did you know it was Emma and Henry Edward?"

"I called up Boston long distance last night when I got half-way through an' got hold of a preacher I used to know an' he told me. He was one of them who knew about the girl."

"There's a post-script you haven't looked at," Betsey said, passing me another page.

"This is dated last night," I said.

"I don't like to add post-scripts, but it is increasingly apparent that that lean Asey Mayo knows about the book and about my hiding it in the bath house. After Maida and John and their story, it's plain as the nose on your face who did it anyway. And Asey has wit enough to bring out the truth before they take Bill away. So, as these moderns say, that is that. In case I should have forgotten, there is some catnip for Ginger in my bureau drawer which in the press of excitement I have neglected to present you with."

I think it was the last sentence which made me break down and cry. Even the imperturbable Asey blinked self-consciously.

"I know it's terrible, Miss Prue, but maybe she's happier an' surely it's better than what would have happened if she hadn't done it. By gum!" He struck his thigh. "If I haven't forgotten all about Bill!"

He dashed for the car and in a few minutes Bill was back at the cottage, apparently none the worse for his sojourn.

"Asey's told me everything," he announced, "and I know one thing that the Porter money will be good for. I just telegraphed and that part of it is going to come out all right if Jimmy has to sell the darned old business."

"And that is?"

"I telegraphed the publishers, Snoodles, and if one copy of that beastly book ever gets given to the public, it'll be because the Porter family has gone broke. After all that's happened, it seems to me that we can have the decency to keep that book away from scandal-mongers. I'm going to buy up everything connected with it if it's the last thing I ever do. I'm going to burn every leaf and destroy every linotype or whatever they are myself. You can tell the police the truth but I'm going to keep it away from the newspapers and everything else. No one is going to know about the last victim of Mr. Dale Sanborn if I have anything to do with it."

Schonbrun spoke up. "Far's I can see, Mr. Porter, I guess I got the right to make the publishers do what I want 'em to do about Dave's things, an' Jeese, I'll go with you an' see you do what you say. That brother of mine has done enough damage without doin' any more to that lady. But I didn't tell on her, did I, even if Asey called me names?"

Asey turned on him. "Do you mean to tell me she was that flash of white you saw?"

"Yeah."

"Can the leopard change his spots?" Asey said sorrowfully. "An' you didn't tell?"

"Naw. She knew I knew, too. But she done something I never had the courage to do an' I wasn't goin' to tell on her. I didn't think you'd spot her. I didn't know you suspected her till you told that story. But I wouldn't of told on her unless my life depended on it. She," he added feelingly, "she was a lady, she was. I ain't never seen no one like her. Yes, sir, Mr. Porter, you burn the books an' I'll help you while you do it, I will."

"I will too," Dot announced. She had suddenly regained her old manner. "I mean, I shall positively revel while I do it. Actually I never heard of a brighter thought."

"We'll be there too," Kurth announced. "I only wish we could have done the same with the other book."

"And I am going to be first assistant," Betsey announced.

"Just this once," Bill wanted to know, "or does that stand?"

Betsey blushed, to my surprise and joy. "Well," she said defensively, "if you're going to go around and get yourself all tangled up with murders, some one's got to look after you, haven't they? And as Asey sings, why not me?"

Asey sighed. "It's almost worth all this to get them two settled for keeps. Look at the fools in their movie clinch. It's disgraceful, that's what it is. But I sure am glad to get that boy off my hands. He's been a ter'ble worry for years." He stretched his arms high as though invoking a spirit, then let them fall. Abruptly he yawned and started for the door.

"Hey!" Bill disentangled himself. "Hey! Where are you bound?"

Asey pulled out a large old-fashioned silver watch, held it carefully to his ear, then wound it with great deliberation. "Where'm I goin'? I'm goin' home to get a little sleep, 'n then I'm goin' to take m' rowboat an' go out 'n' get some flounders 'n rock cod n' bait m' lobster pots. That's where I'm bound. D'you realize them pots ain't been baited since Friday, young feller, with all your goin's-on to look after? Well, they ain't."

"But, wait up a moment, Asey! Hey! Wait up! I haven't told you yet what a swell you were to ferret all this out——"

Asey looked at him sternly, then turned and grinned at the rest of us.

"Mere baggy-tell," he announced. He waved his hand nonchalantly and stepped out on the porch. We heard him murmur as he went down the steps. "Mere baggy-tell, mere baggy-tell!"

THE END

DISCUSSION QUESTIONS

- Were you able to predict any part of the solution to the case?

- Aside from the solution, did anything about the book surprise you? If so, what?

- Did any aspects of the plot date the story? If so, which ones?

- Would the story be different if it were set in the present day? If so, how?

- Were there any historical details that the author included that surprised you?

- What role did the setting play in the narrative?

- What sort of detective is Asey Mayo? What characteristics make him a successful sleuth?

- If you were in Asey Mayo's place, is there anything you would have done differently?

- Can you think of any contemporary mystery authors that seem to be influenced or inspired by Phoebe Atwood Taylor's writing?

SIMILAR TITLES FROM
═══ AMERICAN MYSTERY CLASSICS ═══

If you love Phoebe Atwood Taylor's
The Cape Cod Mystery, try one of these other delightful
vintage mysteries in our series

OTTO PENZLER PRESENTS
═AMERICAN MYSTERY CLASSICS═

The Cat
Saw Murder
—
DOLORES
HITCHENS

Introduction by Joyce Carol Oates

OTTO PENZLER PRESENTS
═AMERICAN MYSTERY CLASSICS═

The Wall
—
MARY ROBERTS
RINEHART

"[Rinehart] at her best."
—*New York Times*

OTTO PENZLER PRESENTS
═AMERICAN MYSTERY CLASSICS═

The Case of
the Borrowed
Brunette
—
ERLE STANLEY
GARDNER

The character that inspired the
Perry Mason television series

OTTO PENZLER PRESENTS
═AMERICAN MYSTERY CLASSICS═

The American
Gun Mystery
—
ELLERY
QUEEN

"A genre giant." —*Publishers Weekly*

OTTO PENZLER PRESENTS
═AMERICAN MYSTERY CLASSICS═

Eight Faces
at Three
—
CRAIG
RICE

Introduction by Lisa Lutz

OTTO PENZLER PRESENTS
═AMERICAN MYSTERY CLASSICS═

Cat's Paw
—
ROGER
SCARLETT

Murder strikes
in a Boston mansion

H.F. Heard, *A Taste for Honey*

Dolores Hitchens, *The Cat Saw Murder*
Introduced by Joyce Carol Oates

Dorothy B. Hughes, *Dread Journey*
Introduced by Sarah Weinman
Dorothy B. Hughes, *Ride the Pink Horse*
Introduced by Sara Paretsky
Dorothy B. Hughes, *The So Blue Marble*

W. Bolingbroke Johnson, *The Widening Stain*
Introduced by Nicholas A. Basbanes

Baynard Kendrick, *The Odor of Violets*

Jonathan Latimer, *Headed for a Hearse*
Introduced by Max Allan Collins

Frances and Richard Lockridge, *Death on the Aisle*

John P. Marquand, *Your Turn, Mr. Moto*
Introduced by Lawrence Block

Stuart Palmer, *The Puzzle of the Happy Hooligan*

Otto Penzler, ed., *Golden Age Detective Stories*

Ellery Queen, *The American Gun Mystery*
Ellery Queen, *The Chinese Orange Mystery*
Ellery Queen, *The Dutch Shoe Mystery*
Ellery Queen, *The Egyptian Cross Mystery*
Ellery Queen, *The Siamese Twin Mystery*

Patrick Quentin, *A Puzzle for Fools*